SATELLITES

nine stories by *TOM PAPPALARDO*

OBJECT

- A clingy new friend from the landfill

- Half-hit wonder and the Night Man

- Rebuilding friendships on post-exodus Earth

- Job-hopping at the coffee shop

- Catsitting at the dollar store, 1991

- A vengeful force descends upon the landscape

- Time travel, except vertically

- Never order an illegal soda

- Small town, big dog

BY TOM PAPPALARDO

Broken Lines

One More Cup Of Coffee

Everything You Didn't Ask For

Through The Wood, Beneath The Moon
(with Matt Smith)

OBJECT PUBLISHING
PO BOX 880, Northampton, Massachusetts 01061 U.S.A.

"Chosen" appeared in *Infinite Lives: Short Tales of Longevity,* ed. Juliana Rew (2019) and *Third Flatiron Best of 2019*, ed. Juliana Rew (2020).

"Gigantic" first appeared in *Juked*, ed. Ryan Ridge (2018).

The first chapter of "Bygone" appeared in *Andromeda Spaceways #65*, ed. Terry Morris (2016).

"This Town" first appeared in *Fark in the Time of Covid: The 2020 Fark Fiction Anthology*, ed. Toraque (2020).

Both "Bygone" and "Mind the Gap" were previously self-published as limited edition chapbooks, Object Publishing.

This is a work of fiction. Names, characters, places, and incidents are products of the author's imagination or are used fictitiously and are not to be construed as real. Any resemblance to actual events, locales, organizations, or persons, living or dead, is entirely coincidental.

FIRST EDITION

LAYOUT & ILLUSTRATIONS BY STANDARD DESIGN
SET IN CASLON

ISBN 978-0-9983278-3-9

TOMPAPPALARDO.COM

For Charlie, my buddy,
and Buddy, who can't read.

Thank you:
Josh, Mark, Matt, and Amara.

CONTENTS

Chosen —————————————————— 1

Landscape —————————————————— 11

Bygone —————————————————— 35

This Town —————————————————— 87

Pop Override —————————————————— 113

The Bottle Man —————————————————— 133

Dead Mall —————————————————— 149

Mind The Gap —————————————————— 173

Gigantic —————————————————— 229

choSen

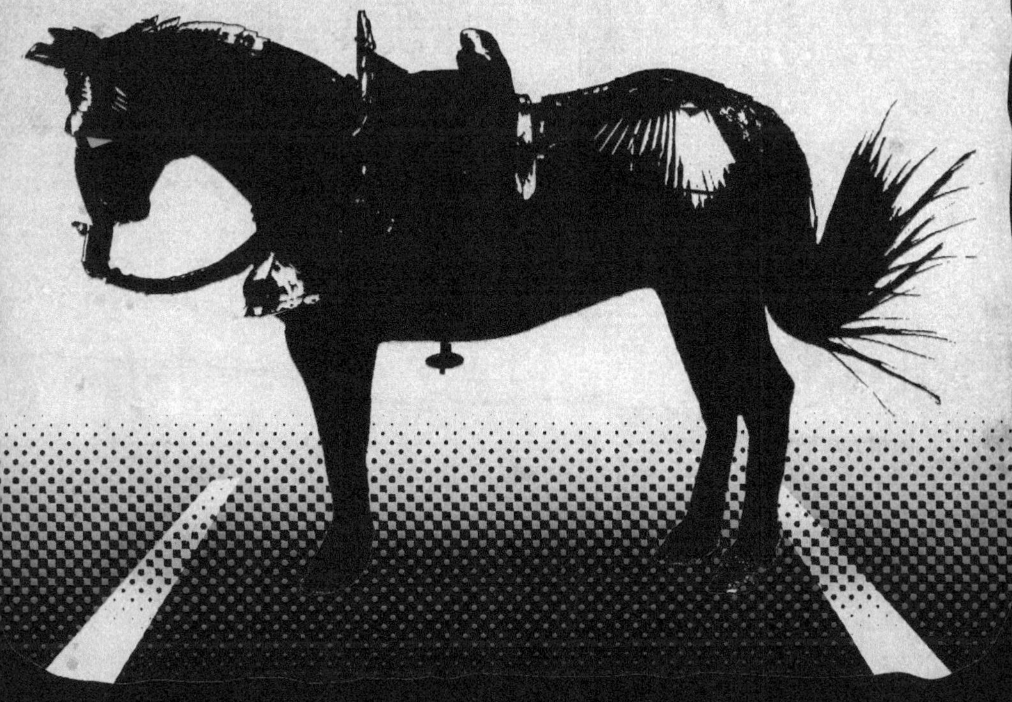

CHOSEN

Beyond the irate customers, outside the cafe's front window, Maddy saw the black horse. *You can barely even call it a horse,* she thought, her finger hovering above the cash register touchscreen. A customer tapped her ring on the glass case and asked a question about gluten. *Thing's a goddamned MAJESTIC STEED, is what it is.* How was no one else noticing? Pointing? Taking pictures? Maddy stood behind the counter transfixed, searching for any detail within the light-sucking silhouette in the Cup 'N' Bean parking lot. It was all blackness, a steed-shaped hole you could jump into. Escape through.

The black rider slipped between the cafe's doors, a twist of undulating black fabric. Maddy's backlog of customers chose that moment to point their eyes elsewhere—phones, watches, paperbacks—making way for the imposing figure. His face shrouded in a deep hood, he approached like smoke. When the specter struck his scythe handle against the tile floor, the sound reverberated through Maddy's bones and settled heavily in her chest.

Maddy had never faced death—definitely not capital D Death. She'd been a passenger in a minor car accident when she was twelve. She'd struggled against an undertow off Block Island. Nothing serious. Nothing *grave*. So what now? Was she about to choke on her gum? Was a gun nut about to shoot the place up? The grim reaper stood motionless before her. *What did I do to deserve this?*

The cafe had gone dim somehow, the customers' movements sluggish as they avoided the figure at the cash register. For them, time had slowed to a crawl. **I am early,** Death announced, his voice a distant bass thrum. **My steed moves swiftly, Madeline.**

He knows my name he knows my name Jesus Fucking Christ he knows my name. Maddy nodded, biting her inner cheeks to hold herself together. Inside his cloak, Maddy caught a glimpse of pale skin, paper-thin and stretched across ancient ribs. She thought of Time. Decay. Doom. Her eyes glossed with tears. "Who are you."

You know.

Death, she thought. *Fate. Time. Judgment.*

Not a judge. A steward.

He was in her head. This did not put her at ease. "What—"

"Sorry I'm late, Mads," Allison said, dropping her bag behind the counter. Maddy's co-worker arrived for her shift as she did every day: sleepy eyes hidden behind '50s-retro sunglasses, an iced latte from Starbucks, and an apology. "There's a guy sitting in front of CVS with a typewriter writing free poems for people and I totally had t—" She peered over her sunglasses at her trembling friend and followed Maddy's gaze to the customer. "Cannnn we help you?"

Death opened his hand, the finger joints creaking, and beckoned Allison to join the conversation.

She eyerolled hard. "Don't let me intrude on your guys's mome." She shrugged off her jeans jacket. "You from Trivia Night? Maddy won't shut up about her Trivia Night nerd buds."

I am not from Trivia Night, Death said.

Maddy gripped Allison's hand. "He's not," she whispered hoarsely. "He's not from Trivia Night."

"Ow, bitch, ya trying to disfigure me?" Allison yanked free. "You *know* I'm going to be a hand model." She parked her iced latte cup on the counter, ice cubes clattering. *You're not supposed to leave that where customers can see,* Maddy thought distractedly. *Doug will be pissed.*

"Aaaanyway," Allison said, peeking at the line over Death's shoulder. "Busy for a Tuesday. What are you guys yapping about?"

My business is death, Death declared. **The time of passing is at hand.**

"Cool," Allison said, nodding. "Cool cool."

Maddy's gaze darted around the room. *Who is seeing this? Where's an impatient commuter when I need one? Why isn't there a douchebag shoving his travel mug in my face and shattering this DOOM?* She dug her fingernails into her palms to stop her hands from shaking. Attention from this being was too much to bear. It was the terror and exaltation of a god glancing in your direction. She stood naked before an unblinking eye, the map of her life unfolded and pressed flat on the counter. "I don't want to die," she heard herself say, but wasn't sure if she believed it. She felt *seen* by the universe, exposed, singled out. What better time to leave?

Want is not my domain.

Allison folded her arms. "Cool scythe," she monotoned.

The C is silent, Death said. *Scythe.* **Like** *seethe* **with an** *I.* **Scythe.**

"What? No," Allison said with a frown. "It's *scythe* like if you said *skies* but had a lisp." She laughed and leaned into Maddy. "I just thought of that."

Maddy ignored her. "What are you going to do with it?" Maddy asked Death, raising her chin towards the blade.

Death sighed. It was a raspy and distant exhale, an echo in

a cave. **Do you know what I do, Madeline?**

"Haunted hayrides?" Allison asked. "Halloween store at the mall?" She doubled over in laughter, holding her hand up for a high five.

Maddy shot Allison her Shut The Fuck Up look. They'd been friends since sixth grade, and in all that time it had never once worked. Maddy never stopped trying. "Couldyounotrightnow?" she hissed.

With the heel of my scythe, I usher my ward on to the next world. At 'usher' he struck his palm out towards Maddy. She flinched.

"What, you push 'em?" Allison asked.

Death outlined a circle over the counter. **The pit of despair is wide and deep. One requires assistance to make it over to the fairer land beyond.**

Maddy could almost see flames swirling in the circle. "H-heaven?" she asked. "You're talking about Heaven and Hell?"

Names do not concern me.

"But you… *help* people?"

I fulfill my duties as those who came before me fulfilled theirs. Each time I act, I surrender a bit of myself so a soul may pass. Each time, it is my honor.

"Fuckin' A," Allison said, tipping her latte towards him. "Respect."

Death stood straighter. **Time grows short. What binds this frame is untenable. The time of passing is nigh.**

"I don't want to pass," Maddy said, tears rising again. "I haven't even—"

The black rider massaged his boney temple. **I speak of the stewardship of the scythe.**

"Huh?" Maddy said.

"I think he's offering you a job," Allison said, elbowing her friend. "You could be the Grim She-per. BA-HA-HA-HA!" Leaning against the counter for support, she literally slapped her knee.

Maddy stepped back. *This is crazy,* she thought. It felt like a pretty fair assessment of the situation so she said it out loud. "This is crazy." Her eyebrows furrowed. "So you're not here to scythe me into a thousand pieces?"

I am not.

Maddy forced her fists to loosen and put her hands on her hips. "Well, I'm not going to become *you*. No offense." The black rider said nothing. "No, sorry. I can't do that," she continued. "I can't be Death. Pick someone else."

Death laughed, a tongueless bark that caused the steed outside to stir. **I do not pick. I arrive. I do not seek. I follow the light that shines upon my successor, the same light that once shone upon me.**

Maddy looked up. No light, just a menu board hanging from the tin ceiling. She pointed at it and gave him her best *duh* face.

I recollect when the black rider came to me and beckoned from the saddle. He called me Chosen and held this blade aloft. Death swung the scythe over the counter and held the scythe dead-still, his knucklebones almost touching Allison's forehead. **These words he said unto me:**

"Wait, what?" Maddy asked, her eyes darting between the black rider and her friend.

Allison grinned and clapped. "Oh, *daaamn,* this is like a *proposal!*" She grabbed her phone out of her bag. "Missus Grim REEP!" she hooted to the indifferent cafe.

Death bowed his head. *This scythe shall endure, both snath and chine.*

"Her? You want *her?*" Maddy couldn't believe this shit. "To be Death. Seriously."

"What? I can do it!" Allison punched Maddy in the shoulder with one hand while steadying her Instagram with the other. "Get to go around slapping people across the pit of Hell like a hockey puck? That sounds tight as fuck."

"Allison!"

She shrugged. "Whaddaya want me to do? Be all 'Uh, no thanks!'?"

"YES!"

She pointed at the ceiling. "The friggin' light chose me!"

Maddy tilted her head back, tears in her eyelashes. "I don't see it," she whispered.

This mantle shall shroud thy journey, Death intoned.

"Oh, I'm not wearing that," Allison said. "Fat freaking chance."

"There!" Maddy shouted at Death. "She's not gonna wear the cloak! She's a crazy choice. This is insane." She spun towards the seating area, looking for someone to back her on this. Lowered heads and laptop screens and earbuds. No different than usual, really. "THIS IS ALL INSANE."

This steed shall ferry from hither to yonder, Death said.

Outside, the mighty horse turned and looked through the front window, its eyes fire. "No shit?" Allison wondered. She flipped her camera around and gave it a *not too shabby* nod.

Maddy's jaw dropped open. "She gets the *steed?*"

"Why can't I get a steed? Don't I deserve a steed? What's your problem, Mads?" Allison said. "You were all cryin' when you thought he was here for you."

"I THOUGHT HE WAS GOING TO CHOP ME UP."

Allison folded her arms and shook her head in disappointment. In the lenses of her friend's sunglasses, Maddy glimpsed the reflection of an unearthly light. "That scythe is for pushing," Allison said.

"THE C IS SILENT!"

This servant shall give, so others may pass, Death said. He leaned over the counter, twisted his fleshless wrist, and planted the scythe handle between Allison's All-Stars. **You are Chosen.**

"Allison, everything about this is totally one hundred

percent wrong!" Maddy cried.

"You're fucking this moment up for me, Madeline," Allison said, wagging her phone at her friend. "I'm gonna have to mute the sound when I post this and that really sucks." She slung her bag over her shoulder. "I'm out."

Allison grasped the ancient hardwood, the scythe passing from Death to Death. Outside, the steed struck a hoof against the parking lot, leaving a mark in the asphalt Maddy would study every time she worked a shift for the next three years, whenever she visited the dry cleaner that took over the storefront after the cafe closed, and when she visited in her final years, carefully bending low to touch the spot with arthritic fingers.

Cup 'N' Bean customers parted for Allison as she swung around the counter, scythe in hand, the reaper following closely at her heels. The Deaths joined into a single silhouette and slipped between the doors. The line reformed in their wake as the cafe undimmed. Maddy's jaw moved but no sound came out. Tears streamed down her cheeks, the clamor of impatient consumerism refilling the room. The black rider mounted her steed.

She doesn't even pronounce it right.

Allison's Instagram got a ton of likes.

●

LANDSCAPE

LANDSCAPE

"A smooth, closely shaven surface of grass is by far the most essential element of beauty on the grounds of a suburban house."
— Frank J. Scott, *The Art of Beautifying Suburban Home Grounds* (1870)

The man descended a mountain road, walking the narrow shoulder separating morning commuters from a steep drop. I floated above him, peering over the edge at honeysuckle and poison ivy and shattered granite. Beyond that a town stood silent, save for the faint buzz and whine of early bird scapers. He tilted his ear towards the valley and I tilted mine, or what I thought to be mine. Wrights and Husqvarnas. Stihls and Kubotas. Cub Cadets and Graingers. The sounds delighted me and gave me pangs, too. The scent of freshly shorn grass hung above the town in a cloud of murder. I did not hang. I bounced, tugged along by an unseen tether connecting me to this man, this keeper of souls, this devil. I listened to the scapers below us do business and I worried on them.

How many towns back I can't say, when he'd come for us.

We didn't understand. I understand now as we are connected. His boundless rage. His righteous vengeance. He had at us, picking us off one by one. We rallied and got the upper hand, though not before he gave me a Fiskars 28-Inch Bypass Lopper blade through my gut. My crew cornered him then. They thrown a loop of double-braided nylon rope over an oak bough and noosed him up. I settled into the grass under the hanging tree, bleeding while the man tiptoe-balanced on the roll bar of our John Deere Z997R Diesel ZTrak™ Zero-Turn Mower (oh that machine was a real beaut, pride of our LLC). He felt nylon was a poor choice for hanging as it offered too much stretch. I was leaking blood something awful, wondering why no one was helping me and how I knew of this man's thoughts when I figured I must've died. Perhaps I should've bristled at that, but I hadn't even noted the crossover, so there wasn't much to fuss about. The man had took me, or some part of me I guess, to be kept as a plaything or a prisoner or a witness, perhaps. I found myself above the scene, watching my former bossman ask my keeper who he was. He opened his mouth to my crew, the oak, the sky, the sward I'd fallen upon in righteous battle, and spoke his name. His was a terrible name, a ball of bright destruction. When he lit out of town, his name rang like a funeral bell.

My keeper squeezed over as a Freightliner roared past, a buffeting wind nudging him closer to the edge. He pumped his fist in that *toot-toot* gesture. The trucker either didn't notice or chose to neglect this core job responsibility. My keeper unsnapped the breast pocket of his mechanic's jacket, a blue polyester number featuring a patch with SUNSHINE AUTOMOTIVE embroidered above the silhouette of a car.

"He denied me my reward," the man said into his pocket. "I am left wanting." The man had spoken to his pocket before but its contents remained unknown to me. I spun and bobbed and craned my neck but I had no neck to crane and no eyes to see.

"Next time," a small voice replied. "There are always more."

"Truth."

The man trudged down the mountain road, his boot heels cracked and embedded with road gravel, bearing down on the town like a summer avalanche.

He paused at the corner of Mulberry Street and surveilled the row of houses, their mailboxes standing at attention curbside. There warn't a single mulberry tree in sight, I'll tell you what. The familiar whining sung out louder here, echoing through the emptied neighborhood. Where the street dipped downward, the man spied the top of a white pickup truck. He seemed pleased by this. He hummed a David Bowie song and shuffled down the sidewalk. *Gee my life's a funny thing / Is my harp too strung? / Just like you / For fifty more?* His recollection of the song was wrong and fractured. I knew it better than he and sought to help, to perhaps find my way into his good grace, but whatever words I formed did not seem to reach him.

The GreenCare LLC truck was defiantly parked in front of a duplex, blocking the street, surrounded by orange safety cones which declared Important Work Was Underway. I laughed. The man leaned into the open tailgate and assessed the nature-wrangling tools neatly clipped to steel racks. His cracked lips approximated a saxophone solo as he unsnapped a Corona RazorTOOTH® Folding Pruning Saw. He ticked his fingernail along the curved blade. Six teeth per inch. He headed around the side of the duplex, newly beheaded grass sticking to his boots.

In a small backyard of criminal blandness, a scaper worked his way along the base of a vinyl fence with a Husqvarna 430LS grass trimmer. The scaper's back faced our way, an edifice of muscle wrapped in a crisp white polo shirt, his attention focused on his whip-stick. I screamed bloody murder at him, begging for him to turn, to see, to comprehend.

"Halloa," my keeper said quietly. The scaper was deafened by his battered STIHL® Pro Mark™ ear-cans and the Husqvarna's 1.3 hp X-Torq® engine, its whip-line lashing the fence 8,000 times per minute. The man studied the scaper's deeply tanned neck and I moaned and writhed at the end of my tether. He stepped forward, still counting off saw teeth with his thumbnail. *Tooth-tooth-tooth-tooth-tooth-tooth.*

"Halloa," he repeated. "Halloa-hey."

I cried out and spun away but the man would not let me avert my eyes, would not let me blink.

———

My keeper testified in the GreenCare LLC headquarters to their bossman, encircled by an agitated crew of scapers. In the center of the circle their comrade's body settled on the concrete floor, slicked red, his neck cut right-around. Two crew members in white polos crouched by him, reverently wrapping a shroud of DeWitt Pro-5 Weed-Barrier landscape fabric around their fallen brother. Someone had placed his blood-spattered Husqvarna in his stiffening hands, as a knight might be buried with his broadsword. Jim Westfield tongued the wad of tobacco under his lip and sighed.

"You happened upon our man in the Hatfield Meadows, you say?" Jim asked, hands on hips.

My keeper nodded and repeated the story as he'd just told it. "Aye, I was out walking the dike. Bird watching, as is my morning routine. From that vantage I saw him, or what was once him if you pardon, dumped on the edge of a field, his truck idling in a ditch."

"And you figured to bring him straight to us?"

"Some matters of justice are not for the police."

Jim scratched the side of his nose and considered the tale.

A stocky scaper stepped forward, the lenses of his Oakleys swirling blue and yellow and pink. "The stranger speaks lies, Jim. This is a Dunphy trap, I am sure of it."

Jim raised a calloused hand. "Easy, Ski." To my keeper he explained, "Our LLC has occasional… *disagreements* with our competitors over at Dunphy & Sons."

"*Competitors?!*" Ski cried. He swiped the bloody trimmer out of the dead man's shroud and pointed it out the open bay door. "Those mulch-eating dogs will pay dear for how they done JayJay!"

Jim raised his hand towards Ski again. I suspected this to be their regular way. The bossman turned to my keeper and gestured towards the patch on his jacket. "I assume you're name's Sunshine?" Sycophantic chortles reflected off push mowers and seed spreaders and barrels of Roundup.

"Mister Automotive to you," my keeper said, dry as a buried bone.

Jim grinned serious. "You done right and honorable by us, Sunny. How may GreenCare LLC repay your discretion?"

"A job," Sunny said. He tilted his head towards the trimmer in Ski's clenched fists. "I'm sure-handed with a whip-stick."

Ski choked out a strangled sound and cried "It is unright for an outsider to slip into a dead brother's boots like this!" He turned to the assembled scapers. "This weed ain't half the edger what JayJay was." Murmurs of agreement.

"If he was as skilled as you say," Sunny said evenly. "Then how did Dunphy take him so easily?"

"YOU SON OF A—" Ski bellowed. He leapt at Sunny as he pulled the Husqvarna's Smart Start™ cord. The compact engine filled the building with a shrieking peal as Ski charged. Sunny dropped to a crouch and grabbed the trimmer above the handlebar, catapulting the burly man to the floor with his own momentum. Ski rolled, his Oakleys skidding across the concrete, and howled with rage. Sunny spun the trimmer's harmful end towards the kneeling scaper and jabbed. A precision strike claimed a swath of Ski's goatee without breaking skin. The big man fell back on his ass, stunned, rubbing the shameful patch of untanned chin.

Sunny cut the engine and the room pulsed with silence. "Dishonor!" a scaper hissed from the sidelines.

"Settle," Jim growled, resting his hand on the Husqvarna's two-stage air filter. Sunny lowered the trimmer. "It is business, my dear scapers. We are in *business*. A full job schedule looms before our LLC." He raised his voice, addressing his men. "Lawns to mow. Hedges to trim. Mulch to spread. Parking lots to leaf-blow." A few of the men whooped. "All that matters is the cut, the trim, the lop."

An old feeling rose up in me at that talk. Scaper talk. Oh! How I longed to slice at a living thing, to name a thing a weed and poison it, to park sideways in the street and rouse a sleepy neighborhood with the clamor of the job. Sunny eyed Jim evenly.

Jim turned to his half-goateed employee. "Mister Laski, your crew is on the Cherry Street job," he said. "Dennis, you're on Hancock with the newbie." He gave Sunny an appraising look. "We are scapers. We scape."

––––––

He was Sunny now. Not just a name, but a *becoming*. The man slipped into it as he'd slipped into the mechanic's jacket at the Goodwill off the highway. When-where was that? Some time-place before my crew strung him up. Names blurred, time stretched, the connective tissue doubled back and faded.

"Jim's orders be damned, I'll be cocked sideways if you imagine taking up JayJay's whipper today," Dennis declared, stepping off the Proline Tandem Axle utility trailer. He shoved a Makita EB7650TH leaf blower at Sunny. Three-point-eight horsepower, six hundred and eighty cubic feet of air moved per minute. I could not remember my mother's face but I remembered that. "You're on cleanup," Dennis said. "Go blow." The other scapers laughed, three deep orange faces, white teeth, wraparound sunglasses. Sunny slung the Makita's shoulder straps over his white polo. Under the green leaf logo on the left breast, the name Miguel stood out, embroidered in gold thread script. A spare shirt, a dead man's shirt. Miguel had fallen the previous spring, Sunny had been told, a casualty of a bloody border dispute with Fiorella Lawn and Plow over in Southampton.

The client's house stood silent, a cedar-shingled ranch nestled among hydrangea and holly. Dennis and AdRock leaned on their accelerators, sweeping GreenCare's matching Scag Cheetah zero-turn rider mowers across the front lawn, past a mail-order plaque that said "The Donegans ~ 15 Hancock" in raised letters. Bobby-Boy and Gregster, armed and earplugged, made for the back perimeter.

Sunny fired up the Makita. He cleared a centerline down the middle of the driveway, forcing gravel and leaves to the sides. It was a shitter's job, I felt. Below this man's honor, if his handling of that whip-stick on Ski proved any indication of rank and experience. But he took to the task. Sunny allowed his mind to wander and I wandered right along with it. When he looked down the street, his gaze pierced through the neighborhood as if it was not there, conjuring a time before the forest got taken, before the meadows were leveled and seeded.

"A lovely valley," a small voice agreed. It was the pocket voice. It should have been inaudible over the revving engine, but we both heard it clear as a porch windchime. "Here there once stood a meadow of bent yellow grass and moths, grubs and finches, secret corridors near the ground which hawks could not peep." I could see the meadow the voice described, a ghost place laid over reality. There but not there, like me. I called out to the voice but got no reply.

Sunny worked his way around the side of the house, along

a walkway to a back patio. Eyes watched him through sliding glass doors. With a flick of curtain, a face receded into the shadows. Sunny took his finger off the Makita's trigger and let it wind down to a dry-throat halt. *A satisfied customer,* he thought as he removed his ear plugs and tucked them into his tool belt. *Surely one with accolades and tales to share with us. I flinched at his use of the word 'us.'* He tapped a dirty fingernail on the glass.

An old man reluctantly slid the door open. His pockmarked face framed a yellow-tipped mustache and an alcoholic's nose. A can of Pabst in one hand, he assessed the devil at his back stoop with basset hound eyes.

"Halloa, Mister Donegan," Sunny said.

"I've already paid your goddamned company, Miguel. I won't do it again," Donegan stated. A slight waver in his voice undercut his gruff delivery.

Miguel smoothed the front of his polo shirt. "They stick you with a double-charge before, sir?" he asked the homeowner.

"Double. Triple," Donegan snorted, taking a slurp from his can. "We don't want your kind in this town. None of us want you here." Miguel squinted at his coworkers. Along the back property line, Dennis set up his mowing perimeter, the sun haloing off the Scag's Tri-Plate Velocity Plus™ side discharge cutter decks. Bobby-Boy flattened the top of a hedge along the west fence with his RedMax SRTZ2460 Extended Reach Hedge Trimmer, his back to the house. "I used to mow my own grass," Donegan continued, admiring his backyard. "I enjoyed it. Got me out of the house, kept my old body moving." He slapped his belly. "I've got a perfectly good mower gathering dust in the shed, y'know."

"What brand have you?"

"*'What brand have you?'*" Donegan mocked with a pinched face. "Christ, what is it with you landscapers and your old-fashioned gibberish?" The old man seemed mad enough to spit on his own slippers. "*Toro* this. *Black and Dickhead* that. *How art thy friggin' rake?* You sound like goddamned fools."

I'd not seen my keeper mocked and I feared for the homeowner, but Miguel took it in stride. He frowned at the patio. Tightly arranged concrete pavers, colored and shaped to look like brick. "That we do," he agreed.

The old man took a long swig. "I saw them stop a neighborhood boy once. Ten, twelve years old," Donegan said in a lower voice. "He was pushing his dad's mower down the street, knocking on doors, looking to do some honest work. Isn't that the *entrepreneurial spirit?* Isn't that *America?*"

I felt Miguel's disposition go awful dark.

"What got done to the boy?"

"They broke his fingers," Donegan whispered, the waver creeping back in.

Miguel's eyes narrowed. "That is America," he murmured, his gaze locked on them pavers. "Who did the deed? GreenCare or Dunphy?"

The old man barked a hollow laugh, spittle on chalk-dry lips. He shook his head with a mighty sadness. "There's no goddamned difference." Donegan slid his patio door shut and drew the curtains.

My keeper studied his reflection in the pollen-dusted glass. Did Donegan see Miguel the same way Jim Westfield saw Sunny? Did either reckon the man I saw, the one who done me with loppers and put me up here? I wondered if m— I recoiled with a shriek, spinning back as far as my tether would allow. His eyes were on me in the reflection, a bottomless stare devoid of color and ruth. I writhed and begged him to stop, let me loose, put an end to me, anything. He pulled his gaze out of me like a fishhook.

Bobby-Boy scurried around the corner of the house, crouched low. "A Dunphy crew!" he hissed, tugging on Sunny's shirt sleeve. "I set my lookers right on 'em!" Bobby-Boy karate-chopped the air in a northeasterly direction.

"Condos next block over! Let's have at 'em! Let's get those fucks what did JayJay! Rally up! Rally up!" He ran low across Donegan's lawn to alert Gregster and AdRock and Dennis.

"A clash is imminent," Sunny murmured, his eyes mercifully cast down.

"Is it not always so?" the small voice replied.

————

Dunphy & Sons Lawn & Tree Service worked methodically across the Hidden Acre condominium complex — mow, trim, cleanup — their neon yellow-green t-shirts piercing to the eye even in the midday sun. The GreenCare LLC crew squatted behind a Honda Pilot parked across the street and schemed.

"A pincer movement," Dennis explained with matching hand gestures. "Bobby-Boy: you, Gregster, and the newbie go around the west side of the building. Me and AdRock'll close off retreat to the east."

"Shouldn't we hold 'til reinforcements can be got?" Sunny asked.

Gregster shoved him. "We strike while striking is within reach! For JayJay! Does the sight of Dunphy blood upon the sward distress you?"

Sunny rocked on his heels and steadied himself. "They ought be cut low for how they did your man."

Bobby-Boy gripped his RedMax trimmer. "Damned right."

Sunny and Gregster followed Bobby-Boy, mimicking the chubby man's crouch-run posture as they moved silently along rose bushes lining the condo's pool. At the corner, Bobby-Boy mimed for Gregster to go left around a recycling shed and for Sunny to stick close. Gregster handed Sunny a Barnel Telescoping Pole Saw, nodded in a way that implied brotherly trust, and disappeared into the roses.

Bobby-Boy caught a flash of neon t-shirt and crept out from cover. His Wolf-Garten Anvil Pruners flexing in his meaty fist, he stalked a Dunphy scaper, a boy in a baseball cap, as he raked out under an evergreen hedge. My keeper stepped lightly behind Bobby-Boy, extending the pole saw's handle and locking the blade at ninety degrees. When Bobby-Boy wound up to strike, Sunny thrust the pole over his shoulder, tapping the boy on the back of the head with the pole saw's pulley. As the boy turned, Sunny twisted the pole and heaved it back, burying the saw blade in Bobby-Boy's throat. The Dunphy boy stood agog as the chubby man dropped to his knees, his neck burbling blood like a fountain. Sunny pressed his hip against the pole and forced the blade sideways, tearing out Bobby-Boy's throat-apple. The scaper collapsed onto the grass, his expression softening from shock to confusion to an open-mouthed nothing. Is that how I'd looked under the hanging tree? The Dunphy boy paled before Sunny, gripping the rake handle in weak defense.

"Ryan," Sunny whispered, reading the boy's t-shirt. "For the love of your LLC, pick up his pruners. The GreenCare dogs are upon you."

———

Beth Dunphy leaned against the Chevy's tailgate and wiped her brow with a sweat-damp kerchief, her hair pulled back in a ponytail, the same style my sister preferred. My heart swole at her memory, 'til I remembered I'd no heart and no sister. This is not how I'd envisioned death. It was a confusion.

"A GreenCare turncoat?" Beth asked, arms folded, eyeing my keeper.

Ryan squeezed my keeper's shoulder. "Aye," he said. "Miguel turned on GreenCare and saved my life. His warning saved us from a slaughtering."

Across the Dunphy & Sons Lawn & Tree Service parking

lot, Beth's crew slid a body out of a pickup truck bed and onto a makeshift stretcher. A Hidden Acres casualty, jagged wounds muting the corpse's neon tee. I'd seen Gregster go at him with the RedMax. "Half-saved you, anyways," Beth mumbled. She assessed the stranger. "What's your game, Miguel?" she asked. "Why help us?"

"I hold no love for you," Miguel admitted. "I love only the work. All that matters is the cut, the trim, the lop. I am a scaper. I scape."

"A scaper true," Ryan whispered.

Beth rolled her eyes at the boy. She'd grown up with scaper sloganeering and horseshit. "If you have a tale, spit it," she told Miguel. "Before my impatience causes me to act rashly with my box-cutter."

Miguel nodded. "A GreenCare trimmer got dead out on Mulberry Street this morning."

"It had naught to do with us," she said forcefully. "Though I'll not shed a tear for 'im.'"

"Aye. I reckoned it to be Fiorella Lawn and Plow and said so. But the GreenCare bossman had other ideas. He used it as a provocation, a false pretense for making war with your LLC."

Beth spat on the asphalt. "Jimmy Westfield stirring his idiots into a fuss."

"I find no honor in his ways," Miguel continued. "It is against the code which all scapers abide by."

"Grand pronouncements from a turncoat."

"A necessary treachery," he said soberly. "I am unproud." He knelt before the woman and I followed him down like a fishing bobber. "I wish to pledge myself to your LLC. May I have audience with your father?"

Beth snorted. "Rich Dunphy is dead, as are his ampersand-sons Dougie and Seth. Ryan and I are the remains of the Dunphy bloodline, a grand-nephew and a daughter previously unworthy of truck-side and shirt-front commemoration."

Ryan Dunphy dropped to his knees next to Miguel. "I vouch for this man, cousin," he said. "I owe him a life-debt."

"Your words do me honor," Miguel said, his gaze cast downward.

Across the lot, a bearded scaper with a gash on his forehead supported a comrade with a leg injury as he hobbled into the Dunphy warehouse. Beth's eyes followed the spatters of blood trailing into the big double doors. Their ranks had been hit hard. "War is upon us," she muttered.

"It is," Miguel nodded.

Beth sighed. "How would you serve the scant remains of clan Dunphy, Miguel?"

Miguel stood quickly, sending me bouncing at the end of my tether. "Let me go back," Miguel suggested. "A spy. Let us destroy the pigs from within the pen."

Beth massaged her temples. My keeper sensed she didn't care for the idea. But her LLC was undermanned and inexperienced—Dunphy & Sons had little chance in a conventional turf war. She dug a business card out of her jeans pocket and flipped it at the GreenCare traitor. Miguel snatched it from the air. She pointed towards the front gate. "Bring me something good."

Miguel tucked the card in his tool belt. "I will send word." He bowed low and stood his ground.

"You've sidestepped my box-cutter, Miguel," Beth warned. "Why tarry within swiping range? Go."

"I beg pardon," Miguel said, folding his hands behind his back. "But you'll agree I'm conspicuously unscathed for surviving today's skirmish."

Beth Dunphy nodded and punched Miguel in the face.

My keeper paused on the steep sidewalk, his GreenCare shirt clinging to his wiry frame. The day had turned humid and mean. He touched the cut under his eye, wincing. The Dunphy woman's ring had been sharp.

"The police will arrive soon," the small voice said. My keeper—bleeding, sweating, and dressed for labor—could not travel undisturbed for long, not in an upper-class neighborhood like Highland Avenue.

"The righteous man walks without fear." He spoke this as if he was quoting something, but I knew it not. He leaned against a tall iron fence surrounding a McMansion. He eyed the bloated lady, busy with dormers and windows and cheap siding, a stretch of driveway winding around the back of her hulking shape. Miguel scratched his chin whiskers. "Put your lookers and thinker upon this, friend."

A meadow vole wearing a small vest climbed out of the man's tool belt and scurried up his shirt front, perching at attention on his shoulder. "You're soaked with sweat," it observed, licking its paws. The owner of the small voice was a cute enough critter, the sort I'd've mowed over in my life previous. I was overcome with an awful remorse at the thought. What sorrows I've served! The man rested his forehead against the iron bars and pointed at the house. "Lawn's unshorn. A telephone book lays beyond the security gate. The occupants are surely absent."

The vole extracted a small pair of spectacles from his vest pocket and squinted at the house. "An excellent candidate," the creature nodded. "I spy the side venting of a gas furnace and water heater, there, by the chim-a-ney."

"And there, in the lawn. Do you clock 'em?" the man asked. I recognized them from life before. Orbit Hard Top fixed sprinkler heads, 30psi. They blanketed the property, every eighteen feet across the sward.

"An expensive inground system. Zoned grids," the vole said, sniffing the air. "Surely I smell a WeatherTRAK ET Pro irrigation controller. I'll bet my whiskers." I thought it a wonderful treat for such a precious small creature to know the tools of a scaper. Never have I been so enamored with a critter. I reached to pet it softly, and a soft pet it was, as my hands proved less than a cloud. It seemed it looked up and acknowledged my presence regardless. Big emotions churned my innards—or however a gutless soul might describe the feeling. "A cherry snare," the vole said. "Set apart from meddlesome neighbors, fenced in.

The man who put me nowhere extracted Beth Dunphy's business card from his tool belt and placed it in the vole's tiny paws. "Two phone calls." He gestured at the phonebook in the driveway. "GreenCare's in the book." He crouched and extended his arm through the iron bars. The little fella skittered down and hopped into the mulched flower beds on the other side.

"A cherry snare, indeed!"

"Do you have your little bag of tools?" my keeper asked. The meadow vole patted his vest pocket and nodded. I wondered who might be in *his* pocket.

"We'll rejoin soon, Sunny-Miguel," the meadow vole said.

The man winked at his old friend. It was joyless, the wink of an executioner.

———

Ski backhanded Sunny, hurt on top of hurt, right across his cut cheek. My keeper, bound to an office chair in the GreenCare LLC warehouse with a knot of extension cord, remained silent.

"What happened to you at Hidden Acres?" Jim Westfield asked from the shadows. "I lost two men out there today."

"We ought not have given him trust!" Ski spat.

"Me and Bobby-Boy got ambushed," Sunny said. "Gregster was trigger happy on his whip-stick. We lost the element of surprise."

"Liar!" Ski lunged at him with a pair of Fiskars PowerGear

Bypass Loppers, a nicer pair than the ones that done me. "I'll cut out your lying tongue!" Two GreenCare scapers restrained him.

"Bobby-Boy and I got separated," Sunny continued. "One of the Dunphy pigs chased me down on his Exmark Lazer Z X-Series zero turn mower." Sunny sketched the scene in his mind and it played out for me like a movie. I admired the way he tumbled clear of the Exmark's UltraCut™ Series 6 deck. Had it not happened that way? His past was a malleable thing. "I retreated into the woods behind the condominium complex, meaning to circle 'round."

"You ran as would a coward!" Ski bellowed. He swiped at Sunny again, his meaty paw snapping my keeper's head back. My tether kinked and stretched, tossing me about the steel latticework of girders criss-crossing the warehouse ceiling.

The office phone rang. I watched Dennis answer the call through a safety glass partition. "I sought to return, to stand with my GreenCare brothers," Sunny continued, licking his split lip. "But I got spun around amongst the firs and pines and stumbled out the wrong side—"

"A scaper lives and dies upon his sward!" Ski barked. The rest of the crew shouted a Marines-like *oorah* in response. "You dishonor our limited liability company, our customer service, our name!" Ski twisted the front of Sunny's polo shirt in his fist and cut a jagged piece out with his lopper blade. "You are not worthy to carry our logo upon your cowardly breast." He dangled the sweat-soaked green icon between his fingers. I could see Miguel's name below it, spattered with Sunny's blood. The men howled.

"Enough theatrics," Jim said, waving a hand for silence. Dennis came out of the office and leaned close to his bossman, whispering and gesturing at a legal pad he'd scribbled on. "Prick up your ears, scapers," Jim announced. "We've a new client. Highland Avenue." A murmur of excitement rippled through the assembled men. "A neighborhood we been hungry for, aye," Jim nodded. "An uptown job. Top priority." Jim considered Sunny, slumped in the office chair. His expression was calm. "All hands on deck."

"You can't mean *him!*" Ski cried. "Surely you can't! Since we laid eyes on 'im, we lost JayJay and Bobby-Boy and Gregster!" Ski wagged a finger at Sunny's battered face. "Treachery lurks behind them black eyes, I swear to it, Jim!"

Jim whistled. Dougster stepped forward and loosened Sunny's bonds. "As you say, brother Ski, we're down three scapers. And lo, a big job looms. An army needs soldiers as an abattoir needs cattle." He turned to his men. "ARE WE HERE TO LIVE COZY OR ARE WE HERE TO SCAPE?"

"SCAPE!" the men shouted. Sunny shouted, too, rubbing his wrists as he rose from the chair.

"AND SCAPE WE SHALL. We bunk here tonight and roll out at 6 a.m."

As Jim Westfield turned towards the office, Ski grasped his forearm. "I do not trust him, Jim."

"Then watch him with hawk-eyes, Laski," Jim said quietly. "If he does not stand true, cut him down."

———

GreenCare LLC rolled up Highland Avenue in a convoy of white pickups and rattling black trailers. As they turned into the McMansion's driveway, the electric gate slid open. Jim Westfield drove the lead truck, Sunny tucked between him and Ski on the wide bench seat. My keeper's face was a sight, battered and swollen. He wore his mechanic's jacket once again, as Ski objected mightily to him donning another GreenCare polo. We swayed in the truck cab as Jim squinted at the morning dew sparkling across the front lawn. Behind us, the gate slid shut.

"Decent turf," Jim said into a walkie-talkie, assessing the

job. "Some thin spots creeping along the northerly hedge will need your touch."

"And touch it I will," Dennis replied over the radio.

"I'll have weed control along the stone pathway, as well." An affirmative grunt on the walkie. "I want you boys geared up and on the move while I go lay my charms on the client." Ski snorted. Jim gave him a wink and sipped from his large Dunkin. Sunlight opaqued the bug-spattered windshield. It wasn't 'til Jim steered us into the shadow of the McMansion's four car garage that we saw Exmark zero-turns rolling off Dunphy trailers. Like GreenCare, it seemed their whole LLC had turned out for the Highland job.

"Hone your edges, gentlemen," Jim murmured into the walkie, his voice tight.

"Treachery!" Ski cried. He grabbed Sunny by the collar.

"Stay your hand," Jim cautioned, weighing the situation. "We might need him yet." Into the walkie: "No one moves without my say-so." He spun the steering wheel on the heel of his palm and slid a machete out from under the bench seat.

Beth and Ryan Dunphy stepped forward as the white pickups fell into formation alongside Westfield's, blocking the driveway, boxing them in. "A beautiful morning to cut some green," she called. Her tone was hard as rebar.

"A fine neighborhood to shake out of bed," Jim smiled, stepping down from the truck.

Ryan squeezed his lopper grips, eyeing Miguel's bruises as Ski dragged him out of the truck cab. "Miguel!" the boy called. "Are you all right?"

"Your fouled lips are not to speak the names of our dead!" Ski snarled.

Ryan leaned towards Beth. "I don't understand."

"Don't let them muddle you," she told her cousin. "Stay sharp."

"It seems we have a scheduling conflict," Westfield called

to Beth as their crews spread out in offensive lines.

"We get the call, we do the job," Beth replied.

Jim nodded grimly and sipped his coffee. "It seems we both got the same call." He scratched his scalp, the machete dangling from a leather strap around his wrist. "I feel we've been manipulated, though I can't quite parse the thinking of it." He motioned to Sunny with the blade. "This your handiwork, Sunshine?"

Sunny raised an eyebrow and half-squinted, the closest I'd seen him approach a smile. Oh, it filled me with a retching unease. I felt a countdown had commenced, a hollow knuckle-rap on the side of a mower's fuel tank. An urgency was upon us. A series of pops echoed across the property as sprinkler heads snapped open. A few scapers flinched out of instinct, wary of a dousing. Most glared hard at the scaper facing them, hate blazing through their Oakleys, knowing that one or the other was likely to die on this green. The Orbit Hard Tops emitted a dry hiss, a leak in the system I reckoned, and no spitter-spatter of water commenced. It certainly did my ratcheting nerves no good, I'll tell you.

"Why do this?" Beth asked Miguel, motioning to the assembled crews. "We'd've gone at each other's throats eventually without your interference. Why put yourself in the middle of it?"

My keeper closed his eyes. "A scaper lives and dies upon his sward," he said in a low voice, like he was soothing a baby. He tilted his head, listening to the grass grow under his boots. I swear I heard it too, a high keening sound. My ears tuned to other things: Worms chewing dirt under the driveway, a squad of ants tearing at a wasp's carcass, privet tangling a stone in a rooted fist. It was a cacophony, Nature, of no order or pattern I could discern. Sunny bobbed his head some, finding the rhythm of it, perceiving what I was deaf to. He opened his eyes real slow, and I'll be damned if he wasn't a bit teary around the lashes. "I wish you dead," he told his audience. "The lot of you." It was a simple truth. Pure as an unplowed driveway on a winter morn.

Jim Westfield shook his head. "Who the hell *are* you?" he asked.

I strained against my confines. The dread question had arrived.

Sunny opened his mouth, but Ski held little interest in hearing him out. The scaper charged forward, jerking the Smart Start™ cord on dear departed JayJay's Husqvarna 430LS trimmer, his battle-cry cut short as fire bloomed from the whip-stick. In that long moment, I saw blooms all around us, expansive bursts of red and orange and yellow. Air became fire, flesh cooked, and the LLCs charged at each other through the flames. Behind us, the McMansion blew apart, an eruption of timber and insulation and plastic and vinyl. I understood then. The sprinkler system had been piped to the gas lines.

Sunny crouched low as debris rained down. He sidestepped a burning scaper, an anonymous shape of flame and flesh. Dougster chased after his brother, attempting to extinguish him with a Worx WG520 Turbine leaf blower. I lurched and swayed above the carnage as Sunny dodged Jim Westfield's machete. The bossman swung blindly at the thick blanket of white smoke covering the property, hoping for a lucky hit.

"WHAT ARE WE TO YOU?" Jim hollered, his voice ragged from smoke. He was on his knees choking before I lost sight of him.

A Wright Stander X™ spun in a tight circle, Dennis on the mower's standing platform, his belt snagged on the control arm. He lolled in my direction, his face a mess of seared meat with a bit of gleaming bone outlining an eye socket. Dennis's jaw moved open and closed as the mower rolled across the steaming lawn towards a burning gazebo. Through the haze I saw the licks of flame blazing out of the ground, every eighteen feet across the sward. The sprinkler heads were spitting fire, by God.

Jim's truck exploded—*BA-DAT!*—leaping into the air on a plume of black rage. At any other time, it'd've been loud as hell. In this chaos it barely registered. The Ford spun and landed wheels-up next to the collapsed garages. From under the crushed cab, I saw Beth Dunphy's arm, saw the ring what cut Miguel under the eye.

"VILE WEED!" Ski charged at Sunny and slammed him to the ground. He pulled us close to his crisped and blackened skull, his Oakleys full of fire. The scaper bellowed an animal sound and raised a pruning saw over his head. Sunny let his arms hang limp, and I felt this might be the end of him. There was a neon blur in the mayhem and a Dunphy scaper lunged, plugging a pair of Fiskars PowerGear Bypass Loppers into Ski's chest. It was Ryan Dunphy. Ski stared through my keeper and spoke a mouthful of blood. He slumped forward, dead.

The boy dragged Ski off Sunny, each lurching step driving the blade deeper into the man's rib cage. "LIFE DEBT PAID, MIGUEL!" Ryan cried. The boy fell backwards and the big man's dead weight rolled onto him. Ryan struggled weakly, his arms sticking to the melting driveway. "Who are you?" Ryan begged. "Why did you come here?"

While Ryan Dunphy smouldered, dying men sought vengeance and demanded murder, their hands grilling like hamburger meat on the melted grips of their tools. Tendrils of fire whipped in an updraft, spinning an inferno high into the sky like a beacon of doom. The Highland Avenue property consumed itself. My keeper—the man of many names, the purging scythe—he passed through the flames and was gone.

———

The man trudged down the hill, smoke rising from his

shoulders and hair. Two doors down Highland, the meadow vole dashed from beneath a hosta. The creature hustled to match the man's pace, clambering up his pant leg and back into his jacket pocket. Behind us, the sky was black.

"Halloa, little plumber!"

"You're pleased with our work?"

"Oh, beautiful morning! Oh, beautiful Earth!" he shouted, grinning, his eyes dead on me. Those lookers set me wailing and those biters set me clawing at the walls of my floating womb. It was then a rage of confusion lashed out at me. Faces flashed past, tinted memories, another life. I saw yards I'd never scaped on streets with strange names. It was Ski and his shameful goatee, tethered, caught up with me. We flailed in our confinement. I tried to soothe him, to explain there was no hope for us. *No hope takes the pressure off,* I wanted to say. *It is as good as freedom.* I said all that but my voice was Ski's voice was our keeper's voice was no voice at all. I was pushed back into the fabric of the womb, and there I found the others what came before me. Crowded and sour and full of clamor, we wrapped ourselves around Ski and pressed in tight.

Sirens swole in the distance as the lot of us turned onto Grandview Street, a row of old-money houses facing a steep drop overlooking town. Beyond the rusted guardrail the valley stretched wide, a bowl of green canopy and shingled roofs. The wink and shimmer of windshields. Church steeples. Telephone poles. Darting sparrows.

"What battles take place before our eyes!" the man cried to the waking households, tears upon his cheeks. His broken boots glided over the sidewalk, carrying him forward, his progress outpacing his footfalls as he descended into the valley, faster and faster and faster.

●

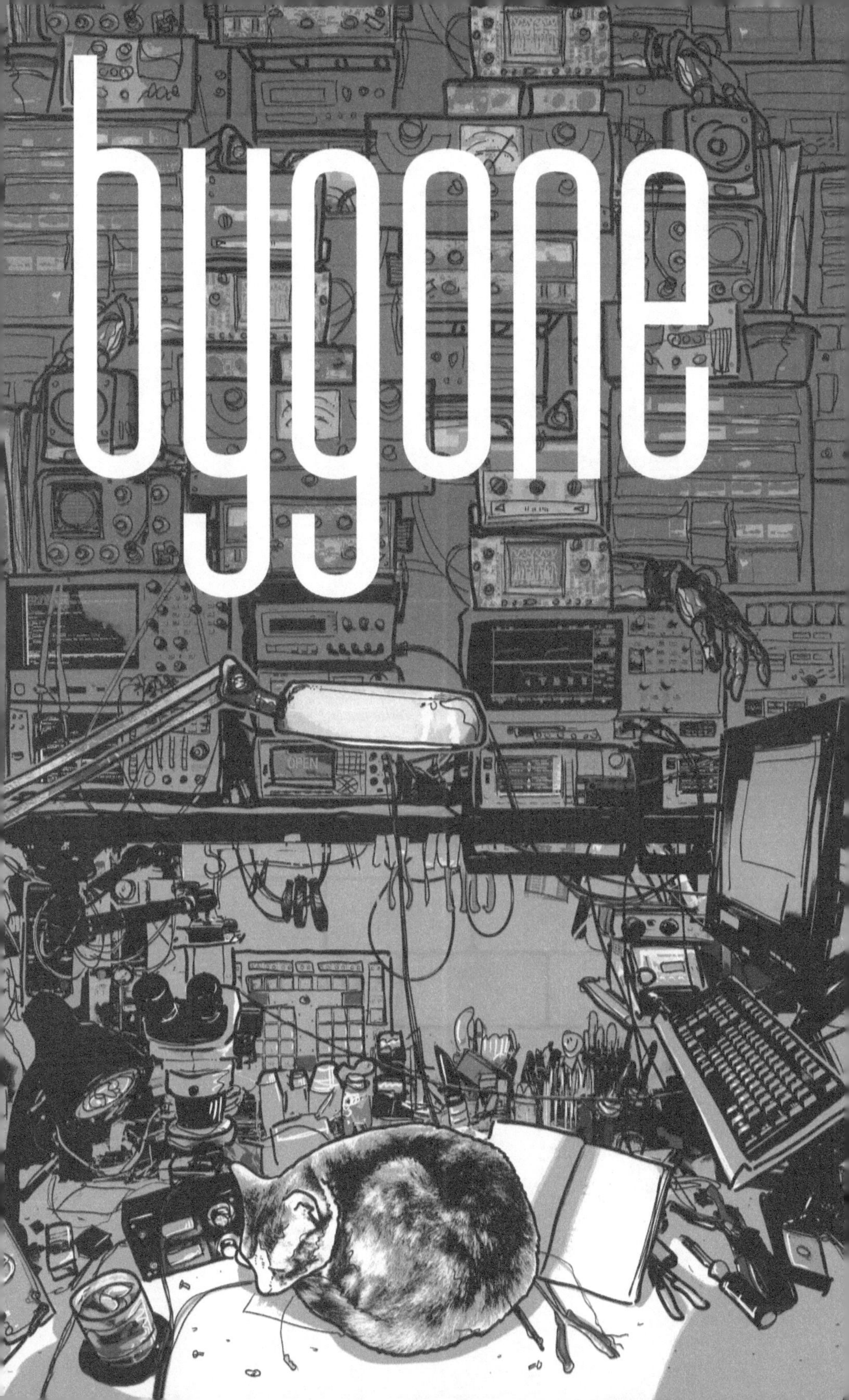
bygone
OPEN

BYGONE

7. LEAVING

Someone had scrawled something on his forehead awhile back. Ghost letters now, indecipherable. His left earlobe has been bitten off, the seams along his joints separated and frayed. He wears brand-new sweatpants and a novelty t-shirt ("I'm not STUPID!!!"). No shoes, no socks, no hairpiece. The bot, shoulders back, smiles at tire kickers and answers questions from potential bidders. The hilltown auction doesn't have many.

Tryan, arms crossed, pretends to contemplate a bid. Her dust-covered leather creaks in the empty warehouse. "Re-skin this one," the geezer next to her opines. "Could be made presentable enough."

She glares at the man through jagged bangs. "You could use a nip and tuck yourself." The man harrumphs and moves on to the next lot.

Tryan tugs at the bot's waistband and inspects the

hacked-back skin around his crotch, an attempt to down-play the worn and stained edges. The metal chassis beneath is dull. Where a human's sex parts would be, a cracked plastic insert covers an interface panel.

"Worked the sex trades, huh?" She lets the sweatpants snap back.

"That's right, yes," he says. "Purchased at auction six years two months nineteen days ago. Previous to that I was a personal assistant to the CEO of—"

"Looks like six rough years."

"I served a variety of functions at the Starlight Entertainment Center."

She prods the clear plastic bag on the folding table next to him. "My, you've got all *sorts* of attachments," she says, mock-scandalized.

"I served a variety of functions at the Starlight," he says again.

She rubs road grime off her glasses with a dirty thumb. "How are your stats?"

"Mobility is at an overall score of 68.2%. Left knee is dis-engaged. Right knee is compensating. Spine, elbows, and wrists are functioning normally."

She offers a noncommittal *hmmm*.

"Power core is at 59.8%. OS and firmware are six years two months nineteen days out of date."

"Kept you offline, huh?"

"The Starlight staff was less than attentive to maintenance issues."

"You're very politic."

"As I mentioned, I was a personal assistant previous to my engagement at the Starlight."

"You're an old model who's seen better days." She assesses the bargain hunters roaming the makeshift auction hall. Lots of overalls and broken boots. "You're gonna wind up working out in a field. That'll be the end of you."

The bot shrugs his 62.3% operable shoulders. "My next assignment will likely be as challenging as my last."

Tryan smiles and taps her boot against his calf. "G'bye, bot."

"Goodbye, miss."

———

She steps out into the sunlight, the featureless wall of the abandoned regional food processing plant stretching off into the weedy distance in both directions. It will collapse soon. They all will.

"Hola, Tryan." Sev says. Her bot stands guard over her old Shuangxi Marauder, strategically casting his shadow over the bike's vinyl saddle.

"Hola, hola," she says, squinting up at her polished steel friend. The robot tilts his head, fine motor movement around his mouth suggesting a smile.

"How was the auction?" he asks.

"Nothing in the boonies today, Sev," she says. "Met one of your cousins in there, though. Entertainment veteran. Looks like he's been rutted half to death."

"Yikes." He holds out her helmet collar. Tryan snaps it around her neck and adjusts her glasses. She puts her palm on Sev's chestplate. Hot.

"You're a hella handsome piece of work, you know that?"

"Awww!"

She powers up the low-slung bike, the antigrav hubs lifting the cycle into riding position. She hugs the chassis as Sev climbs on behind her. She throttles the bike forward. Humming electrics, wide spokeless rubber on loose gravel. Her favorite sounds.

———

The cat navigates the workbench debris: hip rotors, wrist assemblies, face bits, computers, torches, dirty dishes, multi-tools and monotools. He climbs into a cardboard box next to Tryan's vise and nests in a salvaged wiring harness. His name is Daniel.

Tryan throws her helmet collar across her workshop and slaps at the light switches. She glances at her calendar, a retro paper thing so old it's useful again. The month is lousy with Sharpied Xs. Tomorrow is circled, and inside the circle it says FUCK.

"You still leaving?"

"You know I am," Sev says, pulling the bay door closed. Tryan drags her feet across the concrete floor to her bed, a mattress ringed with boxes of bot parts and precarious stacks of salvaged tires. She flops onto her comforter, burying her face in the mass of superheroes printed on it. She groans into Superman's chest.

"Easy," Sev soothes, retrieving the discarded helmet collar from under the workbench. He hangs it on the bike's handlebar where it belongs and pauses to stroke Daniel's back. Both the cat and the bot could do this indefinitely, but there is work to be done. Sev gently corrals Daniel aside and attempts to tame the workshop mess.

"Stop fucking with my stuff," she says, rolling onto her back.

"Stop fucking up your stuff," he counters. He holds up two spare fingers that match his own. "This is valuable mech, Tryan! These things are military grade! You gotta keep cat hair and gunk outta the joints!"

"Flip yourself off for me, please," she says, rummaging through a box by her foot. She extracts an antigrav hub she stripped off an old Nippon bike. Tryan jabs at it with a multitool. "Have you made any more plans for up there?" she asks, eyes on her work.

"Haven't thought that far ahead." He sweeps his

magnetized palm across the benchtop, collecting metal shavings and stray screws. "I don't want to overthink it, I just want to go."

"You think you'll get shit from anybody?"

"I think I'll get shit from lots-of-body," he laughs. Tryan pries at a piece of aluminum shielding. It pops free and spins across the room. "You could come with me, you know," he says, crouching next to the Marauder. "It's not like you're not invited." He lies on the concrete and explores under the bike with her grandfather's paint-spattered flathead screwdriver.

"It's your trip."

"You don't want to go anyway."

Tryan snaps and releases the spring clamp on her multi-tool. "You always leave me."

"So you keep telling me." He chips at road gravel wedged into the bike's undercarriage. A chunk of asphalt refuses to budge. The bot grumbles, emoting his version of aggravation. "Our infrastructure continues to deteriorate," he declares. They pry and chip in silence. Daniel pays them no mind.

"You're my favorite," she mumbles.

"You're my favorite, too."

"I worked hard on you."

"And look how well it paid off!" he cries, pointing at himself with the screwdriver. She laughs. He sits up with a programmed groan. "What about you? What're you going to do after I'm gone?"

"Pine."

"Uh-huh."

She twists the core free from the hub assembly and places it on top of her mini fridge. "That's a good core."

"Uh-huh."

Tryan dumps the detritus of the mechanism back into the box and strips off her road gear. She crawls under the comforter and Sev turns off the overheads. He switches her old drafting lamp on and continues organizing her workbench.

She flips through a few different entertainment streams on her dev, a never-ending torrent of timekill scrolling across her heads-up display. She sighs and takes off her glasses.

"Come to bed," she says. "I'm lonely."

"In a minute," he says. In a minute, he does.

———

Tryan accelerates through downtown Prescott, pointing the bike towards the highway. Main Street is dead-quiet. Like most of western Massachusetts, most of New England, most of the United States and the world, it is mostly abandoned. They ride south towards Bradley Air & Space in silence, Sev's head looming over her shoulder. She pushes their speed a little more than she should. If Sev were capable of worry he might worry, but the highway proves to be tolerably maintained, clear of large obstacles, even patched here and there within the last decade. Tryan focuses her attention on the asphalt, the wind, the fat tires bouncing and kicking up debris. Anything but the bot wrapped around her like a roll cage. She hurls the powerful machine down the road.

———

Abandoned cars line the Bradley Connector median, pushed aside and rejected. The more valuable models were stripped or hauled away a generation ago, leaving these orphans to collect pollen and sink into the grass. Tryan knows damned well they're picked over, but still can't resist eyeing the junk. Scavenging is practically her only hobby.

Near the security checkpoint, she switches the power-plant off and rolls the Marauder up to the rear bumper of a waiting transport van. Sev disengages from the frame and holds the bike upright. Kids in the back of the van gawk at Sev's chromed presence. They wave and he waves back. Tryan wipes her glasses on her shirt and flips them off. They burst into giggles and flip her back, three howling children and six tiny birds pressed against the rear defroster. The line moves briskly, security loose and perfunctory. When Tryan rolls the bike up to the checkpoint gate, they encounter a guard with a scuffed tablet and a sunburned neck.

"Sharp old bot," he says. "You rig that yourself?"

"Uh-huh," Tryan answers.

"I'm no skin fan, either," he says, opening a blank form on his tablet. "They're fuggin' creepy."

"Mmm."

"Air or space?" he asks.

"Space," she says. She opens Sev's transport docs on the bike's display and flips them to the guard's tablet. He scrolls through them.

"You only got one ticket booked. You leaving this pretty boy behind?"

"Ticket's for pretty boy."

The guard squints at the bot and consults his tablet. "I'm not seeing any property transfer here..."

"He's an independent."

The guard raises an eyebrow. "So he's leaving and you're staying?"

"Just you and me on terra firma." She grins aggressively at the man, all teeth, and stomps her boot heel on the blacktop. "Maybe we can repopulate the planet together."

He raises the gate and waves them through.

———

There is a medium amount of bustle at the pick up/drop off area, maybe twenty or thirty people, enough to make Tryan anxious. She parks the Marauder in front of a large video monitor playing an Exodus Corporation ad loop. *Traffic, crowds, and advertising all in the same day. Jesus.* "Goddamned humans," she gripes.

"You're a pestilence," Sev agrees, dismounting.

"I feel like a pestilence."

"You'll live."

"I feel like I might not."

He waits on the curb while she fidgets with her glove. He has no luggage. Neither do most of the other departing passengers. It costs hella extra.

"Aren't you coming in?"

"Nah," she says to the glove. "I gotta get back. I got stuff to do."

"The hell you do," he laughs. "I don't take off for another hour. Keep me company, then you can watch the rocket launch."

"Rocket launches aren't very interesting," she says, peering at the cloudless sky. He laughs again. It's a good laugh. She coded it herself. "How are your stats?"

"High 90s across the board."

"Damn straight."

Another pause.

"Don't take shit from anybody," she tells him.

"I will miss you, Tryan," Sev says. The girl scrunches up her face and says nothing. He steps back. "Go."

She goes.

———

Tryan rips down the outbound lane of the Bradley Connector. She forgets the bike is even there.

———

"We've got a long night ahead of us, Daniel," she whispers, scooping the cat off her stool and stealing his warm spot. She keys the hardware lock on the workshop terminal. Passphrase for security level one. Passphrase for security level two. Tryan scrolls through her archives and loads a massive file into active memory. The cat situates himself on her lap while progress bars jog across the screen. She cups Daniel's tiny head in her hand and waits, surrounded by broken things, locked in a cinder block box in an abandoned building on an abandoned planet. Daniel headbutts her wrist. The screen goes black.

A voice chirps out of the speakers. "Hola, Tryan!"

"Hola, Eight."

2. LAG

It is cool in her grandfather's garage, the door open, the sun not yet set over the pines. Tryan double checks the readout on the tester hooked into her second bot's open chest panel. He is a Brandon model (mostly), with a few used parts bodged into the unskinned chassis.

"**Have you completed the modification?**" Brand asks, his voice routed through the old workbench computer.

Tryan bites her lower lip. "Should be all set. I followed the tutorial. The controller upgrade should solve your weird lag issues."

Outside, a bluejay shouts about the shelled peanuts Harry has left spread across the patio table. In the distance, more bluejays shout back. Distracted, Tryan wonders why her grandfather encourages the birds. They're mega annoying.

"**Good,**" Brand responds.

Tryan rolls her eyes. The lag has been driving her crazy for weeks. If this controller upgrade doesn't solve the problem, she's going to chuck the whole damned rig into the Swift River and start over. She unclips the tester and tosses it on the workbench.

"'Kay. I'm powering you up." She pushes her thumb under Brand's jaw and finds the boot switch. There is a jarring pop and the bot crumples to the concrete floor, thick white smoke rising from its chest.

The girl rubs her temples and steps into the driveway, reciting a steady stream of whispered fucks and shits. The bluejays are still yapping in the backyard. Tryan wants to shoot them and set the yard on fire and tear out the pines with her bare hands.

From the workbench, Brand's voice calls through the smoke. "Did it work?"

4. SOLDIER

The burning soldier catches her eye immediately. She recognizes the silhouette in a friend's boyfriend's image feed (photo caption: "SWAMP PARTY! #botfire"). Tryan consults a model database on her dev and confirms the chassis profile as Military/Enforcer, only ten or fifteen years old. She flips the photo and the datasheet to the living room wall monitor, giddy, dancing around her grandfather's house while the old man and her bot wait for an explanation.

"Solid old tech," Harry nods, leaning back in his recliner. "Looks like hell, though."

She *pfffts* at him. "Surface damage. Remember the wreck I pulled these arms from?" Tryan asks, squeezing Four's bicep. The bot flexes his arm mechanics. "That was a hit and run. This is nothing."

Harry squints at the monitor again and rubs his chin stubble. "I suppose you might be able to salvage a few useable components off it."

"Salvage!" Four says, his arms raised in victory.

"Salvaaaaage!" Tryan whoops, mimicking her friend's pose.

———

Tryan grabs the geotag from the photo and she and Four are packed and out the door by mid-afternoon. They stock up on supplies downtown, foraging through the aisles at Jane's old hardware store. The woman had moved away the previous fall, a sick cousin in Ohio or something. She'd left the doors unlocked. She knew she was never coming back to Prescott.

They make good time on the Marauder, shovels banging around in the bike trailer all the way through the Berkshires. An hour past the state line, on the edge of a dead town named Ripton, they find the dirt road they're looking for. Tryan ventures down a few overgrown paths, steering the bike through deep muddy ruts. At the third dead end trail, she swears at the night sky. Four brings the satellite map up on her dev.

"GPS isn't super helpful when there aren't any roads," she grumbles, blinking the graphic aside.

Close to midnight, they roll into a rough clearing crammed with junker sleds and teen beaters. Beyond a grassy hillock, she sees the pulsing light of a bonfire. The old soldier's outline juts out of a pyre of burning pallets, buried waist-deep in hardened swamp muck. All eyes are on Tryan as she powers down the Marauder's electrics. The bike folds into its parked configuration as Four sits upright behind her.

"A kegger!" he says, scanning the group of teenagers watching them.

"Go get lost in the dark."

"*Fun!*" the bot says, disengaging his ankle bolts from the bike.

Tryan hangs her helmet collar on the handlebars. "See if you can connect and wake the old geezer up," she texts as Four recedes into the shadows. "Guess I'm gonna have a brewski?"

———

Tryan perches on a mossy log set back from the group,

trying to look as cool and unapproachable as possible. She hadn't expected to run into people, so her newly formulated plan was to simply wait them out. She faces the fire, her attention focused on her heads-up display, and watches a video of a container ship breaking up above a moon base. Tryan zooms in on the different sections of the ship as it implodes. She scrubs the footage back and forth, examining the hull as it collapses and uncollapses. Vehicles and cargo containers and grav generators spiral off into space. Tiny bodies convulse and go still.

A boy sits on the far end of the log. He is a few years younger than her, afflicted with aggressive acne and a voice like a blown tweeter. "You have, uh, pretty eyes," he stutters.

"I know."

"Old-style devs. Don't wear rets?"

She taps a finger against her black plastic frames. "More reliable, brighter display, doubles as goggles." She's had to explain this before.

He motions towards the parking area. "Old bike, too. You're hella retro."

"I use what works."

Silence.

"You have, uh, pretty hair."

She laughs and squints at him through transparent video. "You're not very good at this, are you?"

The boy looks at the ground in search of a clever thing to say. There's nothing there. Tryan imagines his dev is a flurry of insults and lewd comments from his friends circling the fire a few meters away.

In a second HUD window, Tryan keeps tabs on Four's communication with the soldier. He's crouched somewhere in the underbrush, attempting to access the crippled military hardware with a steady stream of old military access codes.

"FZ81938274330BDY01920-49-291"

"UNAUTHORIZED REQUEST."

"GPT1094829873QPT01929-48-667"

"UNAUTHORIZED REQUEST."

"It's in deep standby mode, broadcasting with a fried antenna." Four tells her over the comm. "The signal keeps dropping."

"K," Tryan texts back. "Keep at it." She sighs and turns to the boy. "What's your name?"

"Wil."

She motions towards a group of kids drinking next to a stack of splintered pallets. "Get us some beers, Wil."

He scrambles to score some beer from his friends. She hears laughter, and after a few minutes of teasing he returns victorious.

He offers her a Miller High Life. "You have, uh—"

Tryan holds up a finger as she accepts the can. "Let's just sit," she says. "In silence." Wil nods. They sit and watch the summer effigy burn.

———

Fifteen minutes later, "AUTHORIZED.   F24901 REPORTING FOR DUTY" appears on her HUD.

"Boo-ya!" Four hoots in her ear.

"Ffffinally," she texts, leaning forward. "Pull its stats." Raw data fills her field of vision.

"Looks rough," Four assesses. She scans the overview: missing arm, undefined motor failure below the waist, mangled internals. A survivor of a transport crash eight years ago.

"It defaulted to a homing protocol," she texts. "*Return To Base.* He tried walking home."

"Aw, like a puppy!" Four says. "A very dumb puppy." Tryan suppresses a smile. Her bot's anima improves every day.

Wil notices her unfocused HUD-stare. "You watching something good?"

Tryan blinks and shrugs.

"That rig's been stuck hip-deep in a swamp for almost a decade, Tryan," Four says in her ear. "Aside from the damage these junior pyros might have caused, we're looking at an unstable power core, a full payload of compromised ammo, a fragged OS, and multiple hull breaches."

She eyes the ugly pile of MIA military tech, soot-black and motionless. The fire has burned low enough for her to make out graffiti scrawled across the bot's chestplate. *POX. 845 Crew.* A blue skull.

"What would you like to do?" Four asks. For everybody's safety, Tryan knows the old soldier should be detonated in a quarry. She has little doubt they should walk away from this salvage.

"I want it real bad," she mutters.

"Huh?" asks Wil.

"What would you like to do?" Four asks again.

"I'm *thinking*," she snaps at both of them.

Tryan soon discovers that the local kids' capacity to stand around and stare at burning shit runs deep. Apparently not a lot to do in this town. After nursing her beer for ten eternities, she takes Wil's hand and leads him into the bushes. *The only thing worse than being bored is being bored and horny.* Tryan tells him what to do and how to do it, and she has a fine enough time with him in the shadows. When she's done, she sends the boy stumbling away.

Back in the clearing, two kids dismember another pallet, nails squealing as they twist the boards free. "These little shits are gonna go all night," she complains to Four as she zips up her leathers. She decides her wait-them-out plan isn't going to cut it. "We'll come back in the morning. Find me a dead neighborhood we can crash in." Four pulls up a satellite image of the surrounding area on her dev. Tryan pans across the map as she heads back to the Marauder. A farm boy steps into her path. He's a bit older than the other kids. Bigger. Heavier.

"Sup," he says, stepping too close. Beer breath.

"Sup," Tryan replies flatly, her gaze boring a hole through his well-tanned forehead.

He motions towards the bushes she and Wil had just visited. "Have a nice time?"

"Do you need assistance?" Four texts.

"I'm good," Tryan says quietly, eyes locked on the boy. The townie kids are silent and attentive.

"Bet you are."

Tryan thinks of seven sharp replies and decides to not waste them on this slab of stupid. She sighs and steps around him. The boy pivots on his boot heel and blocks her retreat again.

"Don't get between me and my bike," Tryan says.

He leans over her. "And what if I do?"

By the third syllable of that sentence, a piston-loaded steel baton is already dropping out of her jacket sleeve and into her palm. By the fourth it is extended, and a moment after he speaks the last word, the boy is twisting in the mud, wailing, clutching his knee in agony. Tryan collapses the baton against her thigh and eyes her gaping audience.

"Someone should probably take him to the hospital."

She continues to her bike at a casual pace, careful to appear calm and not bursting with adrenaline. Four emerges from the shadows between an old Honda and a hover van.

"Making friends?"

"Get on the fucking bike," she says in a quivering whisper.

———

They cut through the marsh until they reach the rail line she'd seen on the satellite map. Tryan tears ass down the tracks, the Marauder's fat tires thudding against the old railroad ties. Echoes bounce across the marsh as she maxes the throttle. The electrics pulse. A few kilometers south, she slides the bike down an embankment and into a cul de sac of empty houses.

Four kicks in the front door of a split-level cape with a wild front yard. He illuminates the living room with the task light embedded in his chestplate. The house is a time capsule of a family who left everything behind. Tryan pokes around the kitchen. Photos on the fridge door, a child's drawing, an Employee Of The Month award from the regional processing plant. *Offworlders now*, she thinks, shaking her head. A squirrel rustles in the cabinets under the sink. Four stands in the splintered doorway, motionless, waiting for her to abandon her half-hearted exploration. She checks the garage for anything of value (*always* check the garage) and the basement for tools. Nada. She drags her boots back into the living room and drops onto the couch in a *whompf* of dust. Her bot dims his light. "Set an alarm."

———

They're back at the clearing at 5am. The old soldier stands guard over smoldering boards and crushed beer cans. Four unhitches the trailer and rolls it up to the fire pit. "This isn't going to be a pain in the ass at *aaaallllll*." He's been experimenting with sarcasm lately. Tryan hasn't been able to fine-tune the subtlety yet.

"Is it online?" Tryan croaks. She is coffeeless and couch-sore and not full of chit-chat.

"SIR YES SIR," the soldier bleats from a damaged speaker deep in its chest.

"Sir, yes sir!" Four echoes.

Tryan unstraps a shovel from the trailer and offers it to Four. "No, let me," he says. This time, his sarcasm is on point.

She drops heavily onto the log and checks the soldier's stats again. Four scrapes charcoal and melted trash from around the soldier's hips. "It would be quicker if we cut the legs," he suggests.

"You know what those are worth?" She leans back and closes her eyes. "I want it all."

Four digs into the ashy soil, clearing a shallow trench around the soldier's hips. A tree root has grown through its exposed thigh mechanism. Four jabs at it with the lip of the shovel.

"DROP YOUR WEAPON," the old soldier commands, turning on dirt-packed bearings to stare at Four with empty eye sockets.

"Whoa, now," Four says, patting the soldier's remaining shoulder. "Easy, old fella."

Tryan opens her eyes in time to see the soldier's alert level escalate on her HUD.

"PERIMETER SECURITY THREAT," the soldier announces, seizing Four by the arm.

"Let go!!" Four shouts. He smacks the soldier's head with the back of the shovel.

"Four! No!" Tryan leaps forward as defense protocols scroll across her dev.

"DROP YOUR WEAPON," the soldier repeats.

"Sorry, sorry," Four lets the shovel clatter to the ground. "Weapon dropped," he confirms, still struggling against the bot's solid grip. Tryan claws at the soldier's blackened hand. Its mechanics are in wretched condition, but still heavy duty, still military grade. Tryan is keenly aware how her bot compares to the military model's specs, and she doesn't like the match-up.

"Can you shut it down?" she asks.

"No," Four says, straining against the soldier's grip. "It switched into a defensive mode. System's overloading."

"Stand *still*, goddamnit," Tryan grunts. Her bot complies.

She shifts into worst-case scenario thinking, circling behind Four, calculating how quickly she can disconnect his arm.

"I shouldn't have hit it with the shovel," Four concludes. "In retrospect that was an error."

"Shut up. I'm working." She tugs at his aluminum shoulder panel, the sharp edge cutting into her fingers. She ignores the pain.

"It's gonna pop, Tryan."

"We can do this." She unholsters her multitool and severs a wiring harness.

"Negative," Four says. "It takes six minutes thirty seconds to disengage an Electrodyne 440 shoulder assembly. The soldier's core temp is rising steadily and will redline in approximately five minutes."

Tryan struggles to recall articles she's read about power core failures and blast radiuses. She jams her multitool under Four's shoulder blade and clamps onto the first of nine locking caps. The blood-smeared tool slips from her grasp.

"Shit!"

"DROP YOUR WEAPON," the soldier repeats.

"SHUT UP!" she erupts.

Four rotates his head 180 degrees to face her. "He's right. Drop your weapon." He points beyond the marsh with his free hand. "The railroad tracks. Head south. Go." He nudges her towards the bike. "I'll see you when you come back to pick up the pieces."

Tryan blinks hard, frustrated, trying her damnedest to make sense of the scene: her big prize, her best friend, beer cans, a goddamned swamp. *What the hell happened?*

"I got greedy."

"Yes," Four says.

"You're not supposed to say yes," Tryan says, holstering the bloody multitool.

"Noted."

She confirms that Four's anima is backed up to her server.

She steps towards the bike. "I'm sorry."

He nods. "Noted."

Tryan speeds away from the clearing, maxing the Marauder's electrics. She plows the heavy bike through reedy mud, cutting a path straight south. Tryan hits the rail embankment at full throttle and the Marauder lands on the tracks hard. The sound of the explosion blots out the machine gun patter of the tires against the railroad ties.

6. INFERNO

The card perched on the bot's shoulder says cherry, brazilian rosewood, and ebony. Its body panels are hand carved and polished. The brass jawbone gleams under the parking lot lights. The 40BDL is an antique, a quarter of a century old and tricked out in a wonderfully impractical way. Tryan waves a hand at the bot's face and gets no response. Display only. Shame. It's hella pretty.

She strolls through the cruise night crowd at the Turnabout Diner, surrounded by bots, bikes, luxury cars, industrial vehicles, and whatever other hardware the hilltown gearheads felt like dragging out of their barns to show off. She passes between a pair of custom sleds hovering above the asphalt. Further down the row, a gleaming fire engine overshadows a one-person subspace glider. Across the aisle, an automated bricklayer and a 100-year old tractor. Tryan runs a finger along the hood of an IC roller that smells like french fries, a grease conversion. Her dev IDs it as a 1977 Mercedes 240D. Next to the Merc, Six minds her bike — a Shuangxi Marauder 3000A, the last generation of wheeled bikes. She'd left it in riding position, the antigrav units suspending the frame between fat, hubless tires.

"Hola, Tryan," Six waves.

She knocks on his chest plate affectionately. "Any

admirers?"

"Some city dudes tried to buy me out from under you."

"You're all mine, you handsome beast." Six is her sixth major rig, a B-series chassis with a lot of A-series bits bodged in. He's the best boyfriend she's ever built. Tryan reaches up and places her palms on Six's angular cheekbones. He leans forward so she can kiss his chin.

They mount up around midnight, Six bolted behind her as she eases the bike out of the diner lot. She winds up the Marauder's electrics, showboating a little, the hubs howling and pulsing white and blue. A few of the geezers hoot their approval as she kicks up a spray of gravel. Then she's gone, her wheel glow receding down Route 20 until the dark woods of western Massachusetts swallows them up.

———

Tryan opens her eyes to blackness. She's on her back, sore and cold. She gropes for her blanket and claws at dirt instead. "Six," she groans, her voice thick in her ears. The bot doesn't answer. *Am I hungover? Did I even drink?* "Lights!" she barks at her workshop's OS. Instead of the overheads turning on, the Marauder's headlight flickers on a few meters away. Tryan props herself up on her elbows and frowns at a row of decapitated saplings along the edge of a road. *Outside. I'm outside?* "Six!" she calls again. No response.

Tryan rubs her forehead and her palm comes away bloody. She unclips the half-deployed helmet collar from her neck and limps over to her bike. The Marauder is on its side, its tires twisted in a jumble. "Up 'n' at 'em," she says, a phrase Harry sings through her bedroom door some mornings. She taps the cracked touch screen and the bike hums to life. The hubs right themselves and the frame snaps back into alignment.

Tryan rests against the saddle and loads the bike's black

box program. She scans the video footage from the forward cam, pausing at a flare of approaching headlights. *After the diner.* She nods, her head clearing. *The ride home.* She leans in close to the bike's cracked screen and scrubs forward frame by frame. Tryan sees an object — A pipe? A baseball bat? — swing out of a gray sled's open window. There are a few frames of tree branches, then black. She massages her neck and checks the timecode. Fourteen minutes ago. Someone jacked her shit fourteen minutes ago.

Tryan logs onto her workshop network and loads Six's anima backup.

"Are you okay?" his voice crackles out of the bike speaker. "Where's my rig?"

"I dunno. I'm not getting any location data on it."

"Someone zapped me before I could get my feet under me," he says, reviewing his last log events. "Data suggests an 80,000 volt cripple stick."

"Smash and grab," she mutters.

"Here's the bike audio after you got knocked out." Six plays a sound file. Tryan hears the distinctive sound of a field disruptor followed by a heavy metallic clunk. Tryan leans close to the speakers. Two or three men confer under their breath. She hears metal dragged across the asphalt — Six's incapacitated body. A trunk slamming shut. An engine whines and departs.

Tryan looks up and down Route 20. *North or south?* "What's the stereo field on the audio?" she asks, struggling to keep her focus. "Can you tell which way they went?"

Six compares the waveform to the bike's orientation. "South."

She presses her fingers into her eyes, sending color blobs dancing across her vision. She shakes her head and squints at the night sky. A crisp white moon filters through the tree canopy. "ID the sled's headlight style. Crossref with the engine profile."

Six pulls data from an online library of schematics and sound signatures. "Headlights are a three-up configuration. Power plant is 94.3% likely a Nippon Sequential Drive, luxury model, running on modified Class B lifters. I can narrow it down to a list of thirteen possible models, all of them small and fast."

"Crossref with your diner footage," she says. "Look for something gray or silver."

Six analyzes hours of backed up video in an instant. "Bingo." He flips a video still to the bike's screen: the diner's parking lot, a POV shot looking towards a silver sled parked between an old Mustang and a trailered speedboat. "The city guys," Six confirms, sending another still: the two men that wanted to buy him. Tryan ignores it. Their faces aren't important.

"A modded silver 2068 Nippon Eoan sled heading south with a seventeen minute head start," she states, sliding her leg over the saddle. She winds up the electrics. The hubs pulse. "I want that rig back."

<hr>

Tryan catches sight of the Nippon twenty miles down 91. The sled accelerates as soon as her headlight crests the horizon.

"What's the plan?" Six asks, his voice faint in the rushing wind. Tryan barrels down the breakdown lane, scattering a blanket of pollen as she closes the gap. The Nippon swerves to block her approach.

"No plan," Tryan hollers.

Six checks the bike's stats. "Easy on the Marauder. It sustained damage on—"

She ignores him, switching the comm to the public frequency. "You've got my rig. I want it back."

Five local randos respond, none of them the driver of the

luxury sled. Wiseass jokes and trolling. She cuts the audio.

"Getting close to Springfield," Six warns. "We don't like cities, remember?"

Trappers and slavers. Vultures and throat-slitters. "We don't," she agrees. She banks the Marauder across two lanes, a dislodged undercarriage panel grinding along the road. She kicks it loose and accelerates, approaching the Nippon from the driver's side. *Now what?* She nudges the sled's rear fender. The driver cuts the wheel, rocking the Nippon into her lane. Tryan reverses the electrics, tires chirruping, and falls back fast.

"Should I remind you you're not wearing a helmet and already have a head injury?"

"No."

"Tryan—"

"I'm not letting that rig hit the city, Six. We worked too hard on it. Those shitbrain scavs don't get to part it out."

"I want it back as much as you do, T. But could we—"

"Can you connect to the chassis det pack? Are we close enough?"

"Aww," Six groans.

"Can you?"

Six pings the detonation pack buried in the rig's torso. "It's broadcasting. But is there any other—"

She squeezes the bike's grips. "Engage the Dante."

"DANTE SEQUENCE EXECUTED. DET PACK INITIATED," Six bleats, his anima overridden by a core system-level voice modulator. "DET PACK LINK SUCCESSFUL. PASSKEY?"

The Nippon surges forward. Tryan glances at the map on the cracked screen. The city exit is a few kilometers ahead. "Don't take it," she warns the driver through gritted teeth.

"DANTE PASSKEY INCORRECT. PASSKEY?"

The hover sedan swerves smoothly across three lanes. She keeps her distance, zigzagging the road bike to avoid debris.

She's got no plan for this. No goddamned *plan*. She punches the screen. "FUCK!"

"DANTE PASSKEY INCORRECT. PASSKEY?"

She exhales slowly and presses her bleeding knuckles against her t-shirt. "Inferno."

"DANTE PASSKEY ACCEPTED. ABANDON ALL HOPE YE WHO ENTER HERE. CONFIRM ACTION?" The off ramp sign flashes past her. The Nippon drifts lazily to the left—a dope's attempt at a fake-out—and lunges across the Pike at the last possible moment. The driver maxes the powerful Class B lifters and the sled jets down the off ramp. She holds the bike steady. The silver roof sinks beneath a blur of guardrail and weeds.

"CONFIRM ACTION?" Six asks again.

She exhales through clenched teeth. "Confirm."

There is a ground-shaking double explosion: the sharp staccato of Tryan's rig self-destructing, quickly subsumed by the thunder of the Nippon's powerplant ripping apart. The off ramp flashes brilliant orange and fiery red as she decelerates. Beyond the median, a plume of fire and smoke blooms. Glowing tatters of upholstery swirl in the updraft as flames spread to nearby treetops. Headlights appear at the bottom of the ramp: city scavs already zeroing in on the burning wreckage.

She rests a boot on the guardrail and presses her palm against her forehead again. A dull throb grows in her skull. Six is on the comm, telling her to get moving. "Nothing for you, assholes," she mutters, smearing tears and blood across her cheek. "Nothing."

3. KEEPER

Tryan squats, attempting to pry the bot's shin plate off without scratching it. She jabs her multitool into a seam below his kneecap.

"Ouch!" Tres emotes, recoiling.

"That didn't hurt," Tryan tells him.

" Sí."

"Then stop complaining."

"Your request contradicts an earlier request to express emotions. When we—"

She glares up at the bot. "I can't have you saying 'ouch' every time I poke your innards." She taps the multitool's rubber grip against his thigh. "Find a middle ground, willya?"

He nods. "I will no longer say 'ouch'. I will also exclude variants 'ow,' 'ahh,' and 'that hurts' from my lexicon."

"Now you're just being sarcastic."

"Am I?" He seems pleased by the prospect.

The girl stands, swatting nonexistent dust from her jeans, a gesture she has subconsciously picked up from her grandfather. She drops the shin plate onto his workbench. Harry's garage is overstuffed with geezer cruft: electrical relays to forgotten technology, moldering cardboard boxes full of dead memories, leftovers from a carb rebuild, bundled magazines stacked on top of a pinball machine in the corner. As a functional work space, the garage falls somewhere between hella-cool and near-suffocating. She's been considering taking over the old brake shop closer to town.

Harry opens the door to the kitchen and leans in the doorway.

"Hola, Harry," Tres waves.

"I need you to go to Janey's to pick up the new generator," Harry tells his granddaughter.

"Why didn't you have her deliver it?"

"Because I have an able-bodied granddaughter with an able-bodied bot—"

"Gracias, Harry," Tres salutes.

Harry salutes back. "The truck's up at Linda's, I think." Linda, their closest neighbor, is four silent blocks north.

Harry lends out the pickup to whoever asks, leaving Tryan to hunt it down when it's needed.

"I gotta go all the way over *there?*"

Harry shrugs. "Grab a different truck, I don't care." He eyes the workbench covered with components. "Whaddaya pulling him apart for this time?"

"I had a malfuncSHIN," Tres says. Tryan's been teaching him about puns.

Harry groans and gives the bot a critical squint. "Tune his gyro, hah. He's listing to port like a leaky canoe."

Tryan tilts her head. "Whaddaya talking about? He's *perfect!*"

"Check it against a level." Harry steps back and swings the door shut with his cane. "Be back before dark, hah?" he calls through the wall. She listens to his slippers shuffle across the linoleum.

Tryan presses the ancient garage door opener mounted above the workbench. She loves the sound of it. Taut chain, groaning springs, old tech that refuses to break. Her hoverbike waits in the driveway, a bright yellow Cyclone IV she liberated from a mostly picked-over Southampton dealership. "I guess we've got a delivery." She pats Tres's belly affectionately. "C'mon Leaning Tower Of Pizza. Mount up."

———

Fifty thousand birds chatter and squawk along the ledges of Main Street's crumbling storefronts. Well, maybe not fifty thousand, but a friggin' annoying amount. Tryan squats on the Toyota's tailgate in front of Jane's hardware store, scrolling through a comedy feed on her dev. Jane leans in the entryway and talks about the birds like she's glad they're around, but she's also a little deaf. While Tres lugs the generator out of the back room, the woman fumbles a Chesterfield out of her shirt pocket.

"How's your gramps?"

Tryan blinks her feeds aside. "You talk to him more than I do."

"Well, I'm asking *you*."

Tryan bites her lip and replies in tech rat terms. "His mobility's down. 60%. 65, tops."

Jane lights her cigarette. "He puts on a show when he comes by, but I can tell he's hurting. I could scayeh up one of those scoots for 'im." She mimes a steering-handlebars motion. "Take the weight off that damned leg."

"Those are lo-fi," Tryan insists. "I keep telling him to get one of those biomech limbs."

"Those are a bit hard to come by down heah, m'dear," Jane says, gesturing with her cigarette skyward. *Offworld.* She steps aside as Tres appears behind her. He turns and crab-walks the crated generator through the doorway "And they cost money the coot doesn't have, anyway"

Tryan shrugs. "Well, he *looooves* that cane."

"Lying is bad," Tres says.

The woman snorts and exhales a blue-tinged cloud. "Harry's got too much pride for a scootah. Stubbun bastard."

"Sí," Tres says. He lowers the generator onto the Toyota's tailgate, rear leafsprings creaking, and slides the crate across the gouged bedliner.

Jane pats the bot's shoulder. "This one's a keepah," she tells the girl.

Tryan buries a smile in the hollow of her shoulder. After a few years of trial and error, she's inclined to agree, but only to herself. Her third rig, kinks and glitches aside, is hanging together all right. His anima has been deepening in odd and occasionally surprising ways. Tres is almost fun to hang out with. "I guess," she shrugs.

"I heard you two almost burned down the garage," Jane says with mock sternness.

Tryan grins and rocks on the tailgate. "This genius tried

testing a battery with his power coupler."

"It didn't hurt," Tres says, holding up his hand. Two electrical contacts glimmer in the center of his blackened palm. "And in my defense—"

"Thpppptt!" Tryan raspberries. Thumbs down.

"You gotta watch these bots like they're toddlahs," Jane laughs. "But all in all you've bodged togethah a fine rig," Jane proclaims, watching the bot ratchet a strap over the generator. "Naht too shabby."

"Thanks," Tryan and Tres both reply. Tryan slides off the tailgate and slams it shut.

"Harry tells me you're giving up on school, yeah?"

"It's slowing me down."

Jane smirks. "Can we make a hair appointment for ya?" she asks, raising her chin towards Tryan's tangled mop of hair.

Tryan tugs at her bangs and clicks her teeth together. "Not long enough to bite."

"Some folks get haircuts fah fun, y'know."

The girl shrugs.

Jane shakes her head. "Anyway, talk to Harry. Talk him into one of the scootahs, hah? I'll poke around the old folk's place up on Perkins and see what's lying around."

"'Kay." Across the street, sparrows lining the old restaurant's roofline get into some kind of bird disagreement. Jane smiles and squints at the cloudless day.

"What's your plan for the rest of the aftahnoon?"

Tryan tilts her head towards the Miss Prescott Diner, the only functioning downtown business besides the hardware store. "French fries."

Jane knocks on the tailgate with a calloused knuckle. "Attagirl."

———

Tryan leans on the truck's back bumper, extracting another

beketchuped fry from the to-go container. Tres crouches in a nearby parking space and examines a colony of ants as they expand from a crack in the asphalt like a living shadow.

"Those are unhealthful," Tres comments.

"The ants or the french fries?"

The bot turns, a rudimentary frown crossing his facial mechanics. "The french fries, Tryan." He analyzes her wordless response: a withering stare, an arched eyebrow, a slow blink. "Ah, willful ignorance for comedic effect."

She tilts her head and grins. "Good boy."

A dust-covered kid trudges around the corner cradling a cardboard box, his unlaced shitkickers dragging along the sidewalk. *Danny Tetrault.* Tryan mentally hangs herself from the nearest telephone pole. She doesn't know the farm boy well and doesn't want to. Her grandfather once opined the boy was dumber than a box of screws. She liked that. It fit.

"Hey," he mumbles, raising his chin towards her.

Tres looks up from the ants. "Hola," he waves.

"Wasn't talkin' to you, fag-a-tron," the boy sneers. Tryan squints from under her bangs and resists a sarcastic retort. "Check it out," Danny says to her. He lifts a kitten out of the box, an undernourished calico with wide eyes. "Found it in the liberry basement."

Tryan's gut reaction is to snatch the animal from the stupid boy's stupid calloused hands. She knows this approach would yield poor results. Careful to maintain a front of utter disinterest, she says, "You don't seem like a cat person or a book person."

He snorts. "I was busting up some old tables. Oak."

Tres stands, casting a late day shadow across Main Street. He holds his finger out to the squirming kitten, who latches on to one of his chrome-plated knuckle joints. Danny jerks the cat back. "Keep yer rut buddy outta my face."

Tryan exhales slowly. "Ease back, amigo."

"Si, amiga," the bot says, retreating a step.

Tryan smiles at the boy and puts on the best Casual Girl Voice she can muster. "Whatchya gonna do with the kitty?"

Danny shrugs in that way only a budding thirteen year-old sociopath can. "Teach it to fetch. Cook it on the grill. I dunno. Nahahaha."

"You shouldn't harm animals," Tres says, tilting his head. "That is lo-fi."

Tryan winces. "Tres—"

Danny's face creases down the middle. He steps to Tres. "You tellin' me what to do with my own shit?" Tres, a foot taller, looks down at him impassively.

"Living beings are not property—" the bot begins.

"Hey," Tryan interjects. She holds up her to-go bag and shakes it like a prize. "Danny. C'mon. Trade you fries for the kitten. My gramp'd get a kick out of it."

"Your gramp'd get a kick outta a bunch of dicks in his ass," Danny scowls.

"Sure," she nods, agreeable as she needs to be. She points at the Miss Prescott. "I'll buy you lunch. Seriously, how much ya want for the cat?"

Danny shakes the kitten by the scruff. "This cat? *My* cat? Who says he's for sale?" He slaps the kitten hard on the head, a cruel parody of petting. "This little guy's my best friend." The kitten meowls low and long.

Tryan abandons charm, her hands curling into fists. Time for a different tack. "Cut the shit, Danny."

"Stop, please," Tres says.

"Stop what? *This?*" Danny winds his arm back in a poor pitcher's stance, the cat writhing in his fist. The boy's eyes are focused in the distance, the patch of sky above the diner's roof.

"NO!" Tryan shouts.

Tres steps forward and straight-arms Danny in the sternum. The kitten tumbles into the bot's outstretched hand as the boy flops spreadeagled onto the broken sidewalk.

Tryan folds her arms in satisfaction and nods. "Nice catch."

"Nice CATch," Tres corrects. The cat clambers up his arm and perches on the base of his neck.

She rolls her eyes and strolls over to the still boy. "Sorry, Danno," she says. "No lo-fi horseshit on our watch." Danno doesn't move.

"The hell's going on?" a voice calls. Carrie, one of the waitresses, leans out of the diner's entrance. A handful of customers are on their feet, gawking through the dirty windows.

"It's nothing," Tryan says. "He was going t—"

"That the Tetrault kid?" Carrie asks. "Is he all right? Is it his heart?"

"His heart?"

"He's got a heart thing, I don't know," Carrie says. She turns inside the door. "Call the ambo."

Tryan kneels next to Danny. "His heart?" she says again. Tres leans in and checks the boy's pulse.

"Uh-oh."

"What'd you do?"

The bot holds out his palm, the two electrical contacts gleaming in the late day sun. "I gave him a little zap."

"You *tased* him?"

"A little?"

Customers stream out of the diner to stare at the boy on the ground. A farmer holds a finger to his ear and speaks into his dev. "Yeah. Fronta Miss Prez. Bot just killed a kid."

"Shit," Tryan whispers, her mind racing. *Get in the truck, head for the hilltowns. Then what?* "Shit."

"Tryan, I'm sorry," Tres says. "He was going to harm th—"

On the far side of downtown, the police station alarm bleats. The gawkers freeze. Carrie puts a hand on Tryan's shoulder. "Hon, we've got to get clear…"

Tryan leaps to her feet and shouts at the farmer. "Whudja call the friggin' drones for?"

"Tryan—" Tres says.

"It's the law!" the old man shouts back.

Jane hustles down the sidewalk, scanning the sky. "What in hell is going on?" she calls.

"Tryan," Tres repeats. The girl spins to face him. The bot offers her the kitten. "I'm sorry."

The cat leaps to her, claws out. She gazes at the dots of blood rising on her tanned arm. A single thought loops in her head, blotting out everything else: *What is happening? What is happening?*

The birds are silent, gone, fled the scene. A high, whining sound rises above the sound of the siren. Tres turns and runs down the center of Main Street. His gait is graceful and well-tuned, but she'll be damned if Harry wasn't right: the bot lists ever so slightly to the left. Tres's construction-grade torso explodes before anyone even sees the drone. His beautiful head is lost in the mess. The custom legs she had shipped up from Florida stop propelling the burning chassis forward and the whole rig topples in the crosswalk. The kitten digs its claws into Tryan's shoulder, tiny needles demanding her attention. The alarm cuts out abruptly. The drone hovers overhead, monitoring the scene as diner customers murmur and capture video while they wait for the staties to arrive.

Tryan frowns at her friend's executed remains, a twisted mass of tech and time and love. One of Tres' power cores pops like a pistol shot. The drone circles and drops a blob of suppressant foam onto the burning rig. Jane's hand is on the back of Tryan's head, stroking her tangled hair. The woman says something in a soothing tone. Tryan stares down the street, her face orangy-red in the late day sun.

"I forgot to put his shin guard back on."

5. SPLIT

"I *told* you we shoulda taken it down last summer," Harry

says, shaking his head. His helper bot Max stands next to his mobility scooter and shakes its head, too.

"Whaddaya mean 'we'?" Tryan eyerolls. She kicks the scooter's plastic bumper. "I haven't seen *you* up many trees lately, Harry." He toots the scooter horn indignantly and scowls.

The massive elm bough rests on her grandfather's garage roof, solar panels and shingles buried under a jumble of summer green. Last night's storm had snapped the old cables holding the main trunks together. The sound from inside the house had been terrific.

"Think Sync can handle this?" Harry asks, waving a hand at the downed limb like it was a spill on the kitchen floor.

Over the top of her dev glasses, she peers at the trunk's fresh wound. "Give him a chainsaw and a day or two, I guess."

"I'll help, Harry!" Max pipes up. The bot is a meter and a half tall and tends to tip over serving lemonade.

"Thank you, Maxy, but I think this is more Sync's speed," Harry says. Max salutes. Harry leans on the scooter's handlebar. "Tryan my dear, this situation needs to be sorted pronto. We need to replace those panels before the battery grid gives out. I've got ice cream in the freezer."

"That is a priority," she admits. Creamery goods were rare in the valley and not to be squandered. "Could we pull the panels off the Fletcher's place?" she suggests, motioning to the roof peak rising from a mass of black swallow-wort next door.

Her grandfather harrumphs. "Bill Fletcher was a cheapskate and an idiot. Those panels are garbage, I assure you. Look at that fence!" The warped fence bows towards them, barely containing the dense vegetation that used to be the Fletcher's side yard. "I told him to get the premium pine!" Harry whinges as if this is a current feud. The Fletchers moved offworld nearly a decade ago.

Tryan tunes him out, panning across a satellite map on

her dev. She scrolls across the valley, trying to recall recent solar panel sightings. "What's the old government contractor place in Northampton?"

"L9. They made laser scopes f—"

"Yeah, yeah." She rotates the map. "Last I checked, they still had a few big panels on the roof."

Harry grins, a retired engineer who appreciates an excuse to install industrial grade hardware in a residential building. "If we're gonna do it, might as well do it up right."

"Again with the 'we'," she mumbles.

"The structure is essentially sound," Sync announces from the shadows. Tryan's bot pushes a dangling gutter aside and emerges from the garage's slightly askew back door. "Three trusses will require repair. I'm sorry, Harry. The pinball machine took a hit."

"Goddamnit," Harry grumbles.

Tryan grasps Sync by the hips and rests her forehead against his chestplate. "Feel like a road trip?"

———

Tryan eases Harry's pickup through the remains of L9's demolished security checkpoint. The building's glass facade is long gone—smashed in and kicked out. The truck rolls over the remains, tires grinding the safety glass beads into the asphalt. The parking lot is littered with flattened computers, shattered solar panels, and two giant HVAC units. Of all the sorts of people in the world she hates, Tryan especially hates vandals. *Dumbasses wasting useable tech.* She switches off the Toyota's powerplant and squints past the cracked visor. "Let's see what's up there."

"Yay! Free stuff!" Sync claps excitedly. It's an annoying sound, but she doesn't have the heart to tell him to knock it off.

———

They hear the girl bellowing before they even reach the roof entrance. She is scream-singing an original composition over the edge of the building, down Hospital Hill, towards the library. The girl, maybe six or seven, turns when the rusted door hinges groan.

"Hey, kid." Tryan drops a milk crate of tools onto the rubber roof membrane.

"Hola," Sync nods, a coil of steel cable looped over one shoulder and a portable winch balanced on the other. He trudges towards the panels on the west side of the building.

"They can aaaaall hear me," the girl tells them, waving her arm towards town. She wears a lime green vinyl raincoat, cinched tight, and pink rubber boots. A fine combination.

"Sure." Tryan agrees. She squints at the tree line and dials up her glasses' tint. "You up here alone?"

"You betcha."

Tryan sits on the milk crate, the gray rubber roof surface squishing slightly under her. "Whaddaya doing?"

The girl spins idly, her blonde curls catching in her mouth. "Singing and throwing stuff."

Tryan approves of this recreation. "Excellent. I'm Tryan."

"Kinda name is *that?*"

"It's Ryan with a T in front of it."

The girl raises her fists and grunts. "Me! Sadie!"

"Hi, Sadie."

The girl watches Sync examine the solar panels. "That your bot?"

"Yup."

"That's *my* human," Sync chimes in, gesturing to his friend.

"What's his name?"

"Sync."

The girl gives Tryan a you're-not-fooling-me side eye. "Kindaaa naaame is *thaaat?*"

"He's my fifth bot. Five, Cinco, Sync. Get it?"

Sadie isn't impressed with Tryan's clever naming scheme. Most people aren't. "What're you doing up here?" the girl asks.

"We're salvaging panels."

Sadie holds out her hand. "How much you gonna gimme for 'em?"

Tryan lets half a grin slip out. "Oh, are these yours?"

"You betcha." She steps to the edge of the roof and spreads her arms wide. "All this is my Queendom."

Tryan laughs. "Queendom?"

"My ma says it's a queendom."

"That's a bold declaration."

Sadie turns towards the crumbling college campus down the hill. "MIIIIINE!" she bellows, fists shaking.

Sync assesses the remaining solar panels. "Weather damage, vandal damage, maybe some little queen damage," he informs Tryan over the comm. "There might be an unmolested candidate on the far end."

"Get crackin'," she texts back. He drops the coil of cable and wades into a wide, shallow puddle covering the far corner of the roof.

"So how much for a panel?" Tryan asks Sadie. "You want dollars?"

Sadie scrunches up her nose and points at Sync. "I want *him*."

Sync reaches underneath a panel and tugs at its wiring harness. He unsnaps a connector and plugs it into the data port on his wrist. "Kids love me," he says. "They can't help it."

"But he's my best boyfriend," Tryan tells Sadie. "You want me to trade in my best boyfriend for a dirty old solar panel?"

"Even tradesies."

"But I put a lot of work into him. I built him myself."

The girl is unconvinced. "Camman!"

Tryan stands. "Hokay, well, I might need to write you an IOU, Queen Sadie." She squints at the bot as he stands. He's a handsome son of a bitch. "That a good one?"

"I ran a diagnostic," he nods. "This one seems functional." He flips the data to Tryan's dev but she trusts his decision. She heaves the milk crate onto her shoulder. "It was nice meeting you, your majesty. You should head home now. We're gonna lower that bad boy over the edge and I don't want you too close."

Sadie follows. "I wanna watch."

Sync fires up a plasma torch and focuses the flame on the upper bracket of the solar panel framework.

"I really don't want to see you catch on fire, Sadie," Tryan says.

"*Camman!*" Sadie follows.

Tryan drops the milk crate next to Sync. "Well, maybe I do a *little*," she mutters.

Sync cuts through the two lower brackets and the solar panel droops. "You're going to make a wonderful mother someday." He braces the front edge of the heavy panel against his hips and raises it towards him. Sync's heel sinks into the roof surface, the rubber membrane giving a little too much. "Tr—"

"Sync!" The roof splits open and swallows her bot and the panel. Tryan loses her footing as the membrane tears free from the rotted roof surface and she waterslides down after him. They drop into an office cubicle. Tryan smacks off the edge of a desk and lands on the concrete floor. A tangle of rusted girders, wallboard, and water-soaked insulation rain down on them.

"Ffffaaaahhh!" Tryan curls into a ball and clenches her knee. Her broken glasses slide off the bridge of her nose as she writhes on the thin, musty carpet. "Sync," she groans. She sees him wedged between a crumpled filing cabinet and a cubicle wall, his chassis folded backwards, bisected under the bulk of the shattered solar panel. *Goddamnit.* Tryan flops on her back, ready to wallow in her lousy luck when she remembers the girl. *Where's the girl?* "Sadie?" she shouts, the exertion rousing a new pain in her ribs. "Sadie!" She drags herself towards a filing cabinet compressed under a steel girder. "Are you under there?"

Overhead, a flap of slick roof membrane dangles from the side of the hole. A blonde head appears over the lip. "Hello, lady?"

Tryan twists around and holds up a hand in warning. "Stay back from the edge. Stay back, okay?"

"That was *a-may-zing*," Sadie gapes.

Tryan rolls onto her side and calls to Sync again. Her best boyfriend's eyes are dark.

Max corrals twigs and leaves with an old rake while Harry circles on his scooter, supervising the bot's front yard clean-up. The Toyota bounds around the corner, its electric power-plant humming, and lurches to a halt in the driveway. Sync bounces around in the truck bed and comes to rest leaning awkwardly over the rear fender.

"Hey, big fella! What took ya so long?" the old man asks. Harry lifts himself from the scooter, steadying himself on the pickup's tailgate. Sync's legs are missing, hydraulic fluid pooling in the bedliner. "Jesus on the cross!" he calls to his granddaughter. "You chopped 'im in half!"

Tryan shoulders the passenger door open, her face smeared with sweat and dust and blood. She slides to the edge of the bench seat, her left leg splinted with pieces of drop ceiling frame and a computer power cord.

"You hurt yourself!" Harry exclaims.

"Yeah, Harry. Gimme the damned scooter."

Sadie leans over from the driver's seat, tiny fists pounding on the steering wheel. "I've been promised ice cream!" she shouts.

Harry frowns, guiding his granddaughter out of the truck cab. "You stole a kid!" he hisses.

Tryan grabs hold of the scooter's handlebar. "Kneel, you fool." She drops onto the padded seat with a grimace of pain. "You're in the presence of royalty."

8. NOR'EASTER

She reverses the sedan's thrusters, slowing to navigate around the tree growing in the middle lane of the Mass Pike. The woman makes eye contact with a squirrel squatting on a low branch. It marks her passage. She nods. She is a visitor in the Land Of Squirrels and respect must be paid. She fires the antigravs, kicking up a spiral of pollen and gravel, and continues west.

A prerecorded message transmits on the public channel. "**Welcome to Wild Acres, a private concern managed by Pioneer Trust LLC,**" the AI says in a Bland Pleasant Female voice. Tryan shakes her head at the stock Michelle anima. "**Please upload documents and state nature of business.**"

Tryan flips her credentials from her dev. "Personal," she says to the sedan's passenger compartment. A few chirps of data burble on the comm line. To Tryan's left, beyond the guardrail, a deer bounds across an overgrown field.

"Thank you," the AI says. "**You have been granted a provisional twelve hour pass through Wild Acres. Please exit through a border checkpoint by 09:00 UTC or you will be fired upon.**"

"Friendly!" Ghost says in her ear.

"**Say 'yes' to agree to terms,**" the AI continues. The full Terms Of Service contract scrolls across her ret display. She blinks to clear it.

"Yes."

"Hey, check it out," Ghost says, opening a popup window

in the corner of her heads-up. "There's a live satellite feed." Zoomed in from low orbit, she watches their rental sedan cruise down a faded strip of highway, a gray line cutting through two dense swaths of evergreen. She wiggles the steering wheel and watches the sled on the video rock back and forth. No lag. She wonders what sort of firepower they have aimed at her.

————

An hour later, Tryan coasts into the former township of Prescott, Massachusetts. The sedan skims above the grassy strip that has subsumed Main Street. The diner side of the street is choked by scrub trees and bittersweet. The row of brick storefronts that housed Jane's hardware store is gone, collapsed and swallowed by nature. She idles the sedan at the main intersection, tracing the various animal paths through the swaying yellow grass.

"Sort of pretty," Ghost comments.

She gestures with a gloved hand. "Mosh pit for ticks." She turns the sedan towards her grandfather's house.

————

As best as she can recall, things in her grandfather's ranch house are as they'd been left, unmolested by scavengers. Not too surprising, considering the region's dwindling population over the last decade. Tryan retrieves a canvas bag from a coat hook, gives it a shake, and tries to sort out what holds meaning. She isn't sure she'll have many clear answers.

The living room is musty and open to the elements, milkweed fluff drifting through the broken picture window behind the water-damaged couch. Tryan takes Harry's moldy pipe from the coffee table. From the hall closet, his heavy old Navy coat. She pops the memory card from his tablet and puts it in her jeans pocket. Things to scroll through later, or not. Harry's stout helper bot stands at attention, plugged into a long-dead charging station between the peeling table and the trash can.

"Maxy," she murmurs. She rubs her thumb along his grimy brow, remembering when she'd kludged together a couple busted Brandons for her gramps one Christmas. Not a bad job for a 16 year-old tech rat.

"He was a good worker," Ghost says, which is about the nicest thing you can say about a housekeeper model.

Beyond the kitchen window, the yard has disappeared: grass, garden, and patio consumed by the encroaching forest. Tree trunks thicker than Tryan's wrist press against the sliding glass door by the stove. She steps carefully towards the hallway, noting how steeply the floor slopes towards the center of the house in rippling waves of cracked hardwood. She imagines tree roots probing the old house's stone foundation, pushing further inward every year. "Nature's coming for this place," she says.

"Quite a bit of deterioration," Ghost agrees. He offers her a VR overlay of how the house looked nine years ago. She swipes it aside.

"Lo siento," he says.

Tryan slips photos out of filthy picture frames. A young Harry on a fishing boat (no shirt, a can of Pabst in each hand), her parents leaning against the gleaming front bumper of an old IC ground car (she tells herself she's more interested in the car than the humans), Tryan's third grade school portrait (pigtails, poofy sleeves, tooth gap). An allergy warning blinks on her ret. The med implant in her neck doses her with an antihistamine shot on top of her painkillers.

Ghost reviews her health stats. "How are you feeling?"

She shrugs, then pauses to search for a truer answer. She tucks the photos in her jacket.

"Alone."

———

The security keypad on her workshop door is dead, the lock mechanism fused with rust. Tryan braces herself against the building and twists the handle. It snaps off with a rattling pop.

"Ho! Easy on the hardware," Ghost says in her ear.

She peers under her glove, flexing the intricate latticework of micromech in her palm. "It's fine," she says dismissively. She jabs her steel thumb into the mangled lock. Bits of metal skitter across the concrete floor inside. She heaves the bay door up on its dry rails. A raccoon dashes past her and hustles into the underbrush.

The workshop is dark and still, the high windows opaque. Her Marauder leans against the center support column, right where she'd left it a decade earlier. Tryan runs her glove along the dusty saddle, her eyes on the workbench.

Ghost whistles appreciatively. "Handsome devil," he says.

Eight hangs from the workbench rack, a one-armed enforcer-grade torso suspended over the cluttered benchtop. His face half built, his eyes dark, the bot is a work in progress left incomplete. Tryan ejects the dead power core from his chest and tosses it into a milk crate. She rummages in a bin and retrieves a spare core reporting 12% juice on its meter. She slides it into Eight's power slot and twists it. He boots up.

"Hola, Tryan!" Eight says brightly, pivoting on the rack clamp between his shoulder blades. "Network error. I have been offline for—"

"Eight, I know. Calm down."

"I am calm." The bot cranes his head forward. "Your appearance has noticeably changed."

"I know," she says. "I've been away for awhile."

"This is an understatement."

She touches his cheek. "I know."

"You keep saying that."

Tryan leans forward and whispers where a human ear would be. "I know."

"What happened, T?"

Tryan leans against the stool and pokes idly at an elbow joint. The tech surrounding the rack was old even back when it was new to her. Now it was beyond obsolete, bordering on retro. "There was an accident. Nine years ago. Harry had trouble breathing and I had to drive him to the hospital in Northampton, remember?"

Eight nods. "I remember when you got the call. There was a snow storm."

"Turned out to be the worst nor'easter in fifty years. Bad visibility. Bad everything." She shakes her head slowly. "Shouldn't have been on the roads in that old pickup." She smacks her fist into her palm. "Route 2. A three-up long hauler plowed right over us."

"Shit," Eight says.

She sifts through the benchtop clutter and grabs a multi-tool. She notes the slight tremor in her hand, her bio interface failing to compensate. *Needs some adjusting.* She flips the tool's pressure clamp open and closed. "Harry didn't make it."

"Tryan, I'm so—"

Tears run down her cheeks. "And I lost a few important bits." She folds back her collar, revealing a steel mesh shoulder panel. Eight gently reaches out and touches the seam between her mech and her skin. Tryan raises her gloved hand and flexes her fingers.

"Very Luke Skywalkery," the bot says. She smiles and slips the glove off, entwining her finger mechanics with his. "Nice grip," Eight nods appreciatively.

"Biomech. 1400EL series from Kulakov Engineering," she says. She realizes the company didn't even exist the last time Eight was connected to the world. "It's top of the line stuff."

"Are you okay?"

Tryan frowns at the cracked concrete floor. "Lost my left arm, left leg, right foot. Got a helluva head injury." She runs a finger along a faint scar traveling up her forehead and into her hairline. "I'm half bot now," she says. "So that's cool, I guess."

"How are your stats?"

She smiles and wipes her eyes. "High 90s across the board."

The half-bot nods again. "After your accident, you didn't return."

Her jaw tightens. She tries her best to not hear it as an accusation. "I was in a coma for awhile. Then they transferred me to Boston. Multiple surgeries. Physical therapy. By the time I felt whole again, I was three years older and had become a city girl."

"Are you still rigging?"

She lifts a boot to the stool and rotates her mechanical ankle. "I sort of became my own rig after that." The bot nods. "I had you backed up to the cloud." She taps a finger against her temple. "Your anima is still running. You're part of my OS now."

"Nine?"

She smiles. "Gave up on the numbering thing. I just call you Ghost."

"Hola, Eight!" Ghost calls from a speaker embedded in Tryan's skull.

"Hola, Ghost!" Eight replies. Their voices are identical, their cheeriness at odds with the current reunion.

"This is weird," she says.

"It is," they reply in unison. Tryan cackles.

"Enough about me," she says, clearing her throat. She gestures around the dark workshop. "What happened after I…" She pulls her glove back on. "Left?"

Eight shrugs his shoulder. "The workshop network went down during the storm." He points at the collapsed ceiling along the back wall. A triangle of daylight shines through a jagged hole. "Lost the data uplink and solar on the roof. The battery grid lasted almost two months. I ran on standby mode for an additional three months after that."

She steps around a stack of bike tires and crouches next to her raccoon-shredded mattress. The cat door to the parking lot is pushed in, choked with poison ivy. Tryan asks the question that has weighed on her for a long time.

"Was Daniel trapped in here?"

"No," Eight replies. "The autofeeder lasted awhile. Then he started foraging during the day." The bot wiggles his fingers. "He'd always come back for petting." Tryan blinks back tears. Ghost monitors her heartbeat. "After awhile, he stopped coming back."

Tryan nods. "He was a good boy," she whispers.

"He was."

She rubs her sleeve across her face. "I hope he knew I loved him."

"He did," the bot says confidently. "Did you go to Harry's?"

"Grabbed a few things. Tchotchkes and photos. I dunno why I bothered."

"Some things are important, Tryan." He points at the bed. "Take your box."

Tryan rolls her eyes. "Fine." Stepping over a clump of moldy laundry, she slides an Adidas shoebox out from under her nightstand. In bold Sharpie, the lid declares "PRIVATE!!!!" She runs a finger along the lettering. Her writing is different now because her hand and brain are different now. She tucks the box under her arm. "I'm not opening it."

"Just take it. You'll want it later."

"I *ammmm*," she grouses, feeling very much like her surly teenager self.

"Are you happy?"

"We're doing okay." She taps her finger against the med implant in her neck. "I'm sipping antidepressants."

"You used to make fun of people with those. Ret implants,

too."

She blinks slowly. "I used to make fun of everything."

"We've got a flight booked," Ghost interjects. "We're going up next week."

"Offworld?" Eight asks in genuine-sounding disbelief. "You're *leaving?*"

"Massachusetts has been sliced up and sold off to the corporations. Shuangxi bought Boston." She picks at the worn edge of the box. "I've got friends—"

"Congratulations."

She flips him off. "Anyway, we're getting kicked out of the city so we decided to go up together." She points generally towards space. "I've got to go soon," she says. "After 9:00, I'm a trespasser."

"The valley has been purchased by a conservation trust," Ghost tells Eight.

"That's nice," Eight says.

Tryan shrugs. "Depends who it's being conserved for, I guess." She steps towards the exit. "You want to be left on?"

Eight looks around the dim shop. "Doesn't seem like there's much to hang around for." He points at the workbench rack holding him upright. "*Hang* around."

"I got it."

"Good one," Ghost says.

The right side of the bot's face grins. "Gracias." Tryan looks him in the eye, searching for some hint of hurt feelings behind the lens. She sees glass, plastic, metal. Her friend's soul never resided precisely there. He places his palm over the power core in his chest. "You should get going."

"'Kay." She runs a finger along the bike saddle again and moves towards the bay door. "You would've turned out great," she says over her shoulder. "One of the best."

"Damned straight," Eight agrees. "Take care of my friend," he says.

"I will," Ghost replies.

"Adios, Tryan," Eight calls.

Tryan wades through the waist-high grass, her progress noted by a groundhog and satellite surveillance. Cottonwood seeds drift along the late afternoon breeze. Ghost adjusts her antihistamine dose. She climbs into the rental and switches on the powerplant. The field that used to be a parking lot ripples as the sedan rises.

"Too many memories here," she mutters.

"That's not a bad thing, dummy," Ghost says.

Tryan snorts and wipes away fresh tears. The woman says a silent prayer for her cat and her friend and her grandfather and her home and points the sedan east.

———

Eight listens to the antigravs fade into the distance until they are indistinguishable from the wind blowing through the pines. He looks at the cat door. The nor'easter had blocked it with snow for months. Daniel's autofeeder had only lasted a week or so. Surely, Tryan could have guessed these things. They were logical conclusions one could draw. These were the dicier moments of human interaction for Eight, navigating the intentional blinders people sometimes chose to wear. He thinks he handled the situation correctly. The bot sighs, the pensive one from the Emotive Expression add-on pack Tryan gave him when he was Sync.

Between the cinder block wall and the mattress, Tryan's comforter lay in a ball. He can't see into the rumpled folds from the workbench, but Eight knows there is matted fur and a small pile of bones curled up inside, waiting in a polyester nest.

"Good boy," Eight says to the empty workshop. He twists the power core in his chest and goes to sleep.

1. STARTER

The girl bounces the Ford off a utility pole, the compensators sending it into a dizzying spin towards the middle of the road. She laughs and drums on the steering wheel as the lux sled reorients itself to the lane.

"**That was unsafe,**" Cameron says, steadying himself against the dashboard.

She punches her passenger on the shoulder. "It was supposed to be." Tryan activates the autodrive and steps out of the idling car. She strolls towards Main Street, abandoning her bot. Cameron switches off the powerplant before the car can take off towards some old preset destination. He catches up to Tryan at the corner. She leans against the crumbling brick of the old credit union, squinting across the intersection.

"Out-of-towner," she says, raising her chin towards the Miss Prescott Diner. A man reclines on his parked hoverbike, dust-covered leather baking him in the afternoon sun. He rests his head on the instrument cluster, dev glasses tinted black, his fingers laced around the milkshake parked on his stomach.

Cameron tugs on her shirt sleeve. "**Stranger danger!**" Tryan is already pulling away.

———

"Hey," the man calls, even though she's still crossing the street and he's facing the opposite direction.

"Proximity sensor," Tryan says.

He sits up and looks at her through tinted devs. "Yeah," he smiles. "How'd—"

Tryan nods towards the man's bike. "Cyclone series. I've watched videos on 'em. Dev-integrated proximity sensors."

He laughs. "Little tech rat, huh?"

Tryan doesn't know the slang but likes the sound of it. She shrugs.

"**Good afternoon, sir,**" Cameron says, waddling up to the curb.

"This is my bot Cam," Tryan says.

The man grins around his straw. "I've met Cam before."

Tryan scrunches her nose. "No suh."

"I mean I've met bots like Cam before. I've met a lot of Camerons."

"Oh." Tryan knows Camerons are cheap models, but it had never occurred to her to feel ashamed of this fact until just this moment. She lets her bangs fall across her eyes.

"I'm Pegg. What's your name?"

"None of your fucking business," Tryan responds coolly.

"**Stranger danger!**" Cameron repeats, pointing at the biker.

Pegg laughs again and holds his hands up in surrender. "Right, cool. That's fine, tech rat. Cool." The out-of-towner squints at Cam's three quarter scale stature, his coarse hairpiece, the plaid shirt she'd picked out for him this morning. "I liked stuff like this when I was your age, too."

"What stuff?"

Pegg shrugs. "Toys. He's a toy."

"Cameron's cool!" Tryan says defensively.

"**I'm cool!**" Cam agrees. He flashes a double thumbs-up. Tryan winces.

Pegg leans forward. "No disrespect. I just mean when you really get into bots, these off-the-shelf units get really frustrating to work on." He slides his devs down his nose and stares into the bot's dead eyes. "Camerons have cheap motors, surplus controllers, slow processors, and plastic joints. They're fun, but they're junk." He winks at Cam. "No offense."

"**I'm cool!**" Cam repeats. He does a little jig. Tryan rests a hand on his shoulder until he stops. Her cheeks are red.

"The great thing about Camerons is they're easy to pop

open and see how stuff works. Grab a utility knife and slice the crappy skin job off 'em. Bodge in a few parts from a Brandon. Mess around with some of the aftermarket kits. It's fun. He's great, really."

Tryan nods. She'd bookmarked a few kits already, unsure of how to proceed. "You have a bot, too?"

Pegg nods. "Back home, yeah. Custom rig. It's great watching the anima develop into a real personality and not just be a bunch of triggered responses." Pegg turns to Cam. "Right, cool dude man?"

"I'm **cool!**" Cam enthuses. An electric guitar sample wails from his internal speaker. *Diddle-dah-diddle-da-da-daaah!* Tryan has never heard him do that before, but senses Pegg has.

"Please stop it," she says quietly.

Pegg takes a long final drag from his milkshake and tosses the cup into Miss Prescott's trash can. "Sorry. I gotta hit the road anyway." He clips his helmet collar around his neck. "Nice meeting you, Cam. Nice meeting you, tech rat."

Tryan steps back as the Cyclone's lifters whip up a spiral of dust. Pegg drifts the bike away from the curb before hitting the throttle harder. The bike rockets down the weed-cracked street and disappears.

Cameron points at the settling dust. "**Stranger danger!**"

Tryan is already dragging her worn sneakers down the sidewalk, kicking a rock ahead of her. Cameron marches dutifully in her wake. His servo motors whine, his joints squeak. She notices how his clunking footsteps perfectly describe his awkward gait. Further down Main, she sees Jane smoking outside the hardware store. She waves.

Tryan will go in for her daily visit. She will meander the crowded aisles of the shop and rummage through the shelves and bins as she always does. And then she'll buy a utility knife.

●

ENTERING

INC.
1994
THIS TOWN

SPEED
LIMIT
50

THIS TOWN

Scott Sullivan holds his breath, teetering between the next step and the last. He tilts backwards and his ass hits the ground hard. A cardboard box spirals from his hands, emptying itself in midair and distributing its contents across his driveway. Flat on his back, Scott groans, waiting for the first reports of bodily injury. He appears unbroken.

"What are you doing out there?" Lindsay calls from their new kitchen.

"Loafing," he croaks. She doesn't look out the open screen door, doesn't notice his foolishness on display. He props himself up by his elbows. Old journal pages flap in the afternoon breeze, water damaged gig posters drift across the lawn, a guitar capo rests on his belly.

"Rock and roll," he mutters.

———

He balances the overflowing box on his Twin Reverb, which he has parked next to the water heater. Someday, there'll be a small home recording setup here. It's one of Scott's big plans for the new house, a plan *waaay* down at the bottom of a daunting to-do list.

Scott attempts to stuff the stack of memories back into the box so they can be re-forgotten. He smooths out a Bowery Ballroom flyer from 1996. He doesn't remember playing the show, but there's his name, right there. A Trocadero flyer from '94, a Bay State show from '92. A coffee-stained 'zine with a drink ticket stuck to it. A flyer from 1993, when he opened for They Might Be Giants, "Scotty Sullivan: MTV Star, True-ba-dore, Drunkard" handwritten in Sharpie below the Pearl Street logo. Scott leans back in a ragged armchair, his back stiffening, aware he should already be chewing ibuprofen. He slips a journal out of the stack, a CVS notebook with "NORTHAMPTON DEC 1997" written in ballpoint on the cover. He flips it open, the scent of stale cigarettes wafting off the pages. A *Maximumrockandroll* clipping flutters into his lap. He drops the album review into the box unread.

"You down there?" Lindsay calls from the top of the stairs.

"Yeah." He frowns at a note in the margins of the next page. "Unpacking."

"We should get going in ten," she reminds him.

"Yup," he agrees. He squints at his drunken scrawl, decoding his overly-affected block letters: S's shaped like lightning bolts, E's written as triple-stacked dashes. Habits he'd shed years ago. "WHEN YOUR SOBER," he'd written, "FIND THE NIGHT MAN." He reads his instructions again, intelligible but nonsensical.

Upstairs, he hears Lindsay rattle the screen door latch. "Babe," she calls. "I think we're gonna need to replace this."

Scott tosses the notebook on his amp. He adds the screen door to his mental to-do list, well ahead of the basement recording studio. *WHEN YOUR SOBER FIND THE NIGHT MAN.*

———

Three days later, against his better judgment, Scott steps inside the Dunkin Donuts on King Street for the first time in sixteen, seventeen years. He'd abandoned Dunkin coffee back when AOL was still mailing out CD-ROMs, when *Seinfeld* was still on, when he didn't know what coffee was supposed to taste like. He assesses the pink and orange room, the video menu boards, Fox News blaring on a flatscreen. *Things change, I guess.*

The line moves quickly as the caffeine delivery team efficiently serves their customers. Scott orders his classic Sully order, medium-one-cream-one-sugar. He throws in a jelly donut for good measure, because fuck it. Before the change hits his palm, the cashier is already talking over his shoulder to the next customer in line. He shuffles aside with his styrofoam cup, loathe to disrupt the flow of commerce.

"Fuckin' moron!" a voice mutters. Scott blinks hard, his lips pressed tight, and turns towards Mike. *Of course. How could it not be Mike?* The old man hunches at the window counter, passing judgment on a reckless left turn in the intersection beyond the parking lot. He's out of uniform, obviously. He hasn't worked here in what, a decade, probably?

"Mike," Scott says, dragging a stool next to him.

"You know it," the old man responds. He nurses a small coffee, the senior discount beverage of choice.

"You showing these kids how to do the job?"

Mike waves a hand towards the busy counter. "Pfftt."

"You're looking good," Scott nods. The old guy is thinner, skin sagging, and lacking his trademark mustache.

Mike peers over the top of his bifocals. "Horseshit," he replies. His New England accent turns it into *hawshet.*

Scott laughs. "Hunred puhsent."

Mike leans back. "I know you," he says, wagging a finger. "Scotty Sullivan," Mike nods. "I remember you. I talked to you a couple of weeks ago at the Bay State."

Scott tilts his head. *Oh, man.* "I don't think so, Mike. The Bay State's been closed for almost fifteen years."

"I know that." He takes a sip of coffee, his eyes following a Subaru around the corner. "You were drunker than shit."

Scott drops his gaze and grins. "That was my speciality back in the day." He fiddles with his cup lid, the little tab not staying where it's supposed to. Scott cautiously sips the molten coffee and grimaces. 'One sugar' in Dunkin-land is more sugar than he consumes in a week.

"You were a goddamned mess," Mike says, not unkindly. "Took one to know one."

"Yeah, I seem to recall you being, uh . . . rosy-cheeked."

Mike holds out his cup. "Cheers."

They tap styrofoam.

"You were a late-nightah," Mike says.

"Yeah. My post-gig destination. Roll in drunk and belligerent at 2 a.m. for a coffee from The Night Man."

"The Night Man," the old man grunts.

"You still got that name tag?"

"Why in hell would I keep a goddamned name tag?"

Scott laughs, embarrassed. "I dunno, you were sort of a local icon."

"I was a drunk who got shitcanned for drinking on the jaub."

Scott sips his coffee. "How you doing now?"

He shrugs. "More on the wagon than off. You?"

Scott squints at the ceiling tiles. "Sober fourteen years or so." The 'or so' is a ruse. He knows the number to the day.

"'Membah the U-shaped countah?" Mike asks. He points at the Dunkin workers assembling chicken wraps.

"Yeah, yeah. You or Linda would stand in the middle and

hold court."

"Linda!" Mike muses. "The mouth on that one. She could talk paint off a wall."

"Yeah, and the regulars. Doris and Francis and the guy with the captain's hat! He always had that hat on!"

"Bobby Carbone. He died in '08."

"2008? What was he, a hundred?"

Mike shrugs.

"Man, I dunno how many times I fell asleep in those booths," Scott muses.

"More like blacked out. I remember youah brother always coming to collect you. You'd leave that car pahked in the lot for a day or two."

"My Cougar!" Scott says with pride.

"Thing was a heap."

"That car was a *classic.*"

Mike snorts and stares out the window while Scott takes a bite of his donut. He remembers them being bigger and less stale. "I've been waitin' for you to show up heah. I thoughta you once I figured things out a little," Mike says. "You're the right kind of townie. I found you and told you to find me when you sobered up. I guess it took you awhile to get the message."

Scott shivers in the air conditioning. Mike motions towards his half-eaten donut. "That thing got delivered by a truck early this morning. You remember we used to make 'em here? Fresh every day, right in the back room." He points past a cardboard display of a cartoon man jogging with a to-go cup. The man's tie flows over his cartoon shoulder as he chases a cartoon taxi. "Remember the window?"

"Yeah," Scott says, rolling with the abrupt subject-change.

"I want you to do me a favah," Mike says. "I want you to stand over there and try to remembah the window."

"What are you talking about?"

"Go over there," the old man over-enunciates. "And try to

remember the back room window."

Scott hits his weirdness limit. "I should get going, Mike."

"Oh, don't talk to me like I'm a goddamned child," Mike squints. "Go, I don't give a shit. You're a stubborn prick, you know that? I had to tell you seven damned times to write yourself a note!"

"Mike, I don't remember ever seeing you at the Bay Sta—"

"Just go stand behind the fucking cahdbaud thing! Ten seconds! Ten lousy seconds!"

Scott flicks his thumbnail against his cup lid. "Jesus," he mumbles. *What am I doing here?* "Fine."

"Superb," Mike grunts.

Scott sweeps sugar granules off the counter and crumples his bag into a ball. "Seeyuh, Mike." He tosses his trash and stands between the door and the display, knowing the old man will be watching. He turns to protest one last time, but Mike's attention has returned to the intersection.

"Alllll righty then," Scott says under his breath. With a quick glance at the cashier, he steps behind the cardboard display. The graphic on the wall depicts more cartoon people from all walks of life enjoying Dunkin Donuts products. He remembers when this wall was beige, with tile running along the lower half. The weird little window was to his right, offering a view of the donut fryer. You could watch the baker work if you were here early enough. Was the window glass? Plexiglass? Plastic? Scott frowns as his memory gains focus, as the cartoon consumers fade away and the window emerges from the wall. He touches the chipped metal sill and flinches. The cahdbaud display, gone. He's standing in a Dunkin Donuts in 1995. The room is silent.

The walls are decorated in brown and orange and tan, booths along the front wall. Bobby Carbone sits at the U-shaped counter in his red track suit and captain's hat, laughing at a Clinton joke. Mike stands in the center of the U, a bigger, younger, mustached Mike. Familiar Mike.

"The Night Man," Scott whispers.

Mike looks up with a grin. "You know it! What'll it be?" he calls across the room.

Scott has no goddamned idea what to say.

Mike wags a finger. "Medium one cream one sugar, right?"

A quiet affirmative sound comes out of Scott's open mouth.

"Thought so." Mike waddles towards the coffee makers, humming a tune. Scott stares at his name tag. 'MIKE - NIGHT MANAGER' it says, the -AGER blacked out with a Sharpie.

"Superb," Mike says, pressing the lid onto the cup. "Dollar nineteen."

"Did we, uh," Scott rasps, finding his voice. "Were we talking before?" He points at the row of empty brown booths, where someday there will be a long counter.

Mike shrugs. "I talk to folks all day long."

Scott shakes his head. "Just now, I mean," he clarifies, trying to peer into this middle-aged man's eyes, to find the old man he just saw.

Mike grins at Bobby and shakes his head in amusement. He has a nice little buzz going, buoying him through another Tuesday overnight shift. "You here for your car, kid?"

Scott turns towards the front windows. The entire room is reflected back at him. He peers through his own fluorescent-lit ghost to the darkness beyond. It's late, snowing, the traffic signal blinking yellow. His 1967 Mercury Cougar waits for him next to a mound of dirty New England snow, the road salt nibbling at her edges. Scott moves towards the door, his legs on autopilot, an unseen hook pulling him along.

"Dontya want your cawfee?" Mike calls, more curious than bothered.

A frigid blast of wind whips snow in Scott's face. The Night Man has neglected his shoveling and sanding duties, and Scott's sneakers fly out from under him immediately. He whacks the back of his head on the door frame and every-thing goes blinding white.

"My God, are you okay?"

A woman's voice. Scott squints up at her, a businesswoman's silhouette in the bright summer sun. She offers him a hand up. "Nah, I'm . . . Slipped on the, uh . . ." He squints at the lot. A Prius sits where the Cougar was, his Honda Element parked two spaces over. He picks himself up off the sidewalk, embarrassed and confused. "I'm fine, thanks." Scott watches the woman walk inside and join the line. He cups his hands against the glass to look for Mike, old Mike, but the window seats are empty. He swipes at the gravel stuck to his palms and inspects the rip in the knee of his jeans.

"Well, this is fucking *perfect*," he mutters.

———

He tells the story the same way he'd describe a dream, an incredulous narrator dutifully relaying the facts. His brother's side of the phone call is silent.

"You drinking again, Scotty?" Kevin finally asks.

"Christ, no!" Scott declares, as he picks at his salad. He's at The Roost, the cafe next to the truck-eating bridge, his phone wedged between his ear and shoulder. "Clear-headed and sober as shit."

"You sure this isn't some kind of late-game breakdown? You were a goddamned mess after the tour and Julie and everything."

Scott closes his eyes, focusing on a faint hum on the phone line. "Don't talk to me like I'm an asshole, Kev."

"Well, you *were* an asshole."

"That's true," he sighs. A Smithie at the next table scrolls through Instagram. Like. Like. Like. *Doesn't she have any goddamned standards?*

"You said you saw the Cougar?" Kevin asks.

"Swear to goddamned god, Kev. Gold, vinyl top, covered with snow."

"I remember that thing on the Pike. Handled like a sideways rowboat."

Scott laughs.

"You were off the rails for a stretch, man," Kev reminisces. "Remember the time you drove yourself home? I still don't know how the fuck you managed it, you were so shitfaced. Left me in a goddamned snowstorm to boot, you prick." Kevin likes to bring these stories up. Featured attractions in the Scotty Was A Real Mess exhibit. Thanksgiving is always a blast.

"Yup."

"'Member when you and Jules were up at the quarry?"

"I get it, Kev. Drunk brother. Dark times. I get it. We all get it."

"You gonna tell Lindsay about this?"

Scott laughs too loud,. A piece of red onion flies across his table. The Smithie gives him a look. "Might keep this one under my hat for a bit." The hum intensifies. "Listen, Kev. This connection is shit. I'll let you go. Talk soon."

Kevin puts on his serious brother voice. "Call me later, Scotty. I wanna know you're okay."

"Will-do." End Call.

On the cafe stereo, a half-assed band whinges about something pointless. Behind the weak songwriting and too-slick production, Scott can still hear the damned hum. He abandons his attempt at a healthy lunch and dumps his salad in the trash. The hum is louder near the trash can. It's a familiar sound he can't quite place. The hook is in him. He can't let it go. He kneels down, pretending to fuss with a shoelace, and listens. The hum emanates from behind the bus bin cart. He leans forward and knocks a stack of Coors over. The clatter and clack of glass bottles echoes through the liquor store.

"Jesus!" he shouts, steadying himself in the corner packy

that used to be next to the truck-eating bridge. Pop's Liquors is cramped: walls lined with refrigerator cases, high shelves, windows covered with sun-bleached cigarette ads, a stained drop ceiling.

"What are you doing?" the owner yells, stepping down from the counter. He is Indian and definitely not named Pops, but Scott has always thought of him as Pops. It's difficult for Scott to not call him Pops.

"I'm *so* sorry!" Scott says, picking up a toppled case. At least two bottles have cracked, soaking beer into the much-abused carpet.

"Put it down. Get out." Not-Pops states.

"No, really, I—"

"You are a drunk. I do not have time for you. Go. Get out of my store."

Scott recalls he may not have been the most welcome customer here in the nineties. He pulls a wad of bills out of his pocket. "Listen, lemme pay for the beer. I'm so sorry, truly. I must've leaned wrong or something."

Not-Pops takes the money. "You sneak in here, you make a mess. Last week, you're in here saying 'birdy num-num' to me. You think I'm stupid? You think I don't know Peter Sellers?"

Scott is horrified. "I'm *so,* so sorry, sir. I used to drink—"

"Used to!" the store owner laughs. He picks up a case and sets it upright. "Get out. Go away now. I have no time for you."

Scott heads for the door, giving his mess as wide a berth as he can manage, apologizing again to this man he has probably slurred apologies to a hundred times before. Not-Pops looks at the money in his hand and throws the bills on the floor. "Monopoly dollars. You are a funny man."

Scott pauses at the threshold, every idiotic time travel movie coming back to him at once. "I—No. It's—" He sighs, defeated. "Real money." The refrigerator cases hum in disbelief.

"Birdy num-num! Very funny! Goodbye!" the owner waves, moving towards Scott, forcing him backwards. The door swings shut and he's standing outside the Roost.

———

A week stumbles by. Scott sleepwalks through work, avoiding downtown Northampton, postponing errands. Lindsay offers to buy him lunch twice, and twice he talks her into eating in Easthampton instead. When she requests a Friday date night, he knows he's caught, curving towards some pre-written fate. The hook is in him again, buried deep in his sternum. A big hook, a butcher's hook, dragging him back towards town. He listens to her restaurant suggestions. He knows where they'll end up. Of course. Lindsay's mom got them that gift card. Dread settles in his bones as he cheerfully agrees. The Sierra Grille. It opened back in '03. It used to be the Bay State.

———

He hears the echoes as soon as they walk in the door: the mushy, distant sound of a Marshall combo cranked too loud, a poorly tuned bass, dull cymbals crashing. He smiles at his wife and ignores the rumble of his past. The hostess escorts them to a high table in the front room. The echoes reverberate through whatever twenty-year time hole lurks in the back room of the Sierra Grille. That was where the bands played—Hospital For The Dead, Chicopee Kick, Lonesome Stuntmen, fifty more. Scott asks about Lindsay's day. He tells her about arranging his new office at the house, his struggle setting up the wifi router. Dead-boring talk, anything to stave off the darkness overtaking the room, old shadows dulling the restaurant's lights. For the first time in seven-odd years, Scott Sullivan needs a drink.

He forces conversation for ten minutes more before excusing himself. He walks past the bathrooms and into Sierra's rear dining room. He can picture the old wall-mounted light fixtures, red cloth napkins draped over the bulbs—somebody's attempt at ambiance. The smell of cigarettes permeates every surface of the room: the wood paneling, the flowery wallpaper, everyone's clothes. The volume rolls in like a tidal wave. The room is sweaty and stuffy, loud and obnoxious.

"Sully!" Anders hollers in his ear, slapping him on the back. He pushes a PBR into Scott's hands. "You look like shit! When'd you get back, rock star?"

"Just now," Scott yells. A hardcore band from Connecticut wrecks shit in front of the pink-curtained bay window while bodies shove into each other. Not a lot of townies here tonight. Anders hollers something about Scott's music video. Scott nods and navigates around him, towards the bar. He sees Julie sling her purse over her shoulder as her group of ladies abandon their table.

"Jules!" he calls, pulling free of the audience.

"Scott, you big fuck!" she beams, all teeth. She opens her arms. "Gimme a goddamned hug!" He squeezes her hard, smelling her hair and resisting the urge to kiss her. Her body language is wrong, her hair is wrong. Scott struggles to place himself in the right time. *We aren't going out yet, we haven't broken up yet, she isn't dead yet.* "Easy does it, fella," she says, pushing gently on his shoulders. He releases her, his eyes wet.

"Sorry, Jules."

"I thought you were out on tour," she yells over the band. "Didya sell piles of CDs?"

"Oh, *yeah*. A veritable *mountain*," he says dryly, giving a thumbs down. She laughs. He feels his guts drop into a bottomless pit. *Julie.*

Tanya Dussault tugs on Julie's sleeve. "We were heading over to Hugo's because this—" Julie motions towards the commotion in the back room, "—is a fuckin' shitshow."

Candace and Beth wave at Scott and head for the door. "Come drink with us!" Julie says.

He's spent the past week sussing out the apparent rules of this weirdness. It had to do with places. Doors booted you out. Back. Forward. Whatever. "I think I've got to stay here. Hang out and talk with me."

She laughs and covers both ears. "Are you retarded?" He cringes at the nineties. "Not a fucking chance, Sullivan!" Julie backs away, still laughing, Tanya steering her towards the door. "Gimme a call next week! Lates!"

And she's gone.

Scott peers through the plastic plants crowding the front window, watching the girls disappear into the night. Behind him, Mike sits at Julie's table. The old, present-day former Night Man. Scott is too overwhelmed to be surprised. *Of course. Sure. Why not?* "I haven't seen her in a long time," he croaks, dropping into an empty chair.

Mike nods. "Great way to see old faces," he agrees.

Scott pushes his palms into his eye sockets and stares at the empty pint glasses between them. "What'd you do to me?"

"I didn't do anything to you. I just showed you a thing I found."

"What are you doing here?"

"Same thing you are. Filling in the gaps."

Scott scratches his jaw. "I don't know what that means, Mike," he says numbly.

Mike shrugs. "I'm not sure I do, either." He stares at Scott for a long minute. "Listen, you used to overdo it drinkin', just like I did. I know that much about you."

"I did," Scott nods.

"Blacked out a lot, I bet."

"I've got a few blank spots, sure," Scott says.

Mike leans in close. "I think these" —he taps a fingernail against an empty glass— "are the blank spots."

Scott opens his mouth, but there's no good response to that statement. He closes it again.

"It's August, 1994. The 17th," Mike says, tilting his head towards the bartender. "I peeked at Jerry's paper when I came in. I can't say for sure, but I'm guessing that right now, '94 me is unconscious, lying in his own piss on the floor of my old apahtment over on Graves Ave. It's how I spent a lot of my weekends back then. What do you suppose you're doing right now? A hot Saturday night in the summer of '94?"

"August 17, 1994," Scott muses, shaking his head. "Goddamn it. I know right where I am," he sighs, picturing the flyer. "Trocadero, Philadelphia, opening for Lush." *Julie said it. I'm out on tour.*

"Had a few drinks that night, didya?"

Scott snorts. "They kicked me off the tour the next day, I think. I was a fucking wreck."

"Blacked out?"

"Way out."

"And here's that lost time." The old man places his hands on the smeared tabletop, fingers spread. "I'm up the street in my apartment. You're in Philly. We're both out cold."

Scott considers this, trying to reconcile Mike's theory with his grip on reality as of late. "This is fuckin' crazy," he whispers, squeezing his eyes shut.

Mike shrugs. "Sure. That's what you said when we talked last month. I was back here and I ran into you. The younger you, 1997 you," Mike says. "We had the same goddamned convahsation we're having now, except you were shitfaced and not listening. So I made you write yourself a note."

"Find the Night Man."

Mike nods. "Took you a month to get the message."

"Twenty years." Scott nods. "Are we time traveling?"

"Eh," Mike leans back. "Time watching, maybe? I dunno. I don't think we can change things. Whatever we do, it's already happened. Near as I can figure, this has all passed." He waves his hand at the wood paneled walls, the paneling that was ripped out during renovations in the early aughts and buried in the landfill up on Glendale Road. The landfill that has been closed for years.

"Should I bother trying to warn people about 9/11? That big tsunami? Trump?"

Mike shrugs. "You could try. But youah the drunk singer and I'm the drunk donut guy. Things sort of work out so no one's going to take what we say very seriously."

Scott laughs hopelessly. "So we're sort of . . ." He twirls a finger. "Participatory spectators."

"You're the college boy."

"SULLIVAN!" a voice bellows. A tanned boy strides in, gold crucifix, tight shirt. *Who the fuck is this?* The kid menaces over Scott, a compressed steel spring lubricated with testosterone and cologne. "You grab my sister's ass at Meyer's last week you fuckin' faggot?"

Scott squints. *What a shit-show.* "Probably?"

Sucker punch.

———

"Whoa! Are you alright?" the Sierra hostess asks. She is crouched over him.

"Jesus!" Scott blurts, grabbing his nose as he rolls around on the carpet.

"Sir—"

"I, uh, jeez—"

"You fell—"

"Honey! What happened? Are you okay?" Lindsay is there.

He's on his feet, confused and embarrassed, steadying himself against the wall. "Clumsy. Bumped into a tabl—"

"Your nose is bleeding!"

He's a bit preoccupied for the rest of their date.

———

Scott slouches on the front porch, his morning coffee resting on a stack of old notebooks. He skims a beer-soaked journal from 1998, scribbling notes on a scrap of paper. He turns the rippled pages, cataloging parties and binges, trying to pinpoint times and places he may have blacked out. What he'll do with this data, he isn't sure. His twitches when his phone rings.

"Checkin' up on you," his brother says. "Making sure you still exist."

"I still exist."

"You see The Night Man again?"

Scott bites his pen cap. "For the sake of not opening an extremely large can of worms, let's say no."

"I don't like the sound of that, bro."

Scott shrugs and redirects. "Kev, you remember when you me and Julie tried to go up to the Quabbin?"

"When the Cougar overheated and we ended up on the side of the road in Ware? Sure. Fun day."

"That was the day you hit on Jules while I went on the water run."

"Ah, camman!" Kev laughs. "She was fulla shit! I mean, no disrespect to the departed."

Scott doodles in the margin of the journal. "She was pretty fuckin' great, though, huh?"

"You're dwelling a lot lately, Scotty. Seeing ghost donuts and ghost cars and whatever."

"Yup," he agrees. "Maybe I'm playing catch-up. I haven't done a lot of . . ." He draws a spiral. "Reflection."

"Whelp, for the official record, I'll say Julie was a peach and your car was a death trap piece of shit."

"That car was *not* a piece of shit!"

"I recall it sitting in my side yard for two and a half years, dear brother."

"Well, sure," Scott admits. "It was a piece of shit *then*, yeah. But *before* that."

"Oh, yeah, buddy," Kev says. "It was a real show piece 'til you took it out in the Meadows and put it over a rock wall." Scott groans at the memory. "Snapped a shock tower."

"Subframe, too," Scott adds. "Hell of a car."

"That thing woulda been worth something today if you'd taken care of it."

"I wasn't taking care of much in those days."

Kev pauses. "Just tell me you're not drinking again."

"I'm not, baby brother."

"Tell me you're not crackin' up."

Scott sips his coffee and watches the mail carrier walk up his neighbor's driveway. He hasn't met any of his neighbors yet. "Jury's out."

"I'm *so* sorry about last night," Scott says to the hostess. "I took some strong allergy medicine."

"No problem, sir! I *totally* get it," she says, organizing menus. "This summer's been *terrible!*"

"I may have lost my flash drive last night. I had it in my pocket. I was wondering if I could—?" he motions towards the back room.

"Absolutely! Go right ahead."

The afternoon sun streams through the Sierra Grille's big windows, making the room too bright for his memory of the place. *I don't think I've ever been here during the day before.* Kevin kneels, pretending to look for a thing he did not lose. He can already hear echoes of applause. *This gets easier every time,* he thinks, an observation which both satisfies and worries him. Someone pushes past him in the crowd. He hears fingers slide across amplified guitar strings.

Dennis stands at the mic in his rumpled suit and tie,

clapping around a Miller Lite bottle. "'Nuther hand for Shannon and Justin!" There is cheering and clapping. Scott claps, too, slow and loud. Habit. *Support the scene, man.* "The open mic extravaganza rolls on. We got a slew of talented folks coming up in a bit," Dennis says, shielding his eyes against the single light pointed at him. "But I'm gonna break format here for a sec, cuz I want you to help me get a special guest on stage right about now."

Shit.

"Scotty Sullivan, everybody!" Dennis announces, pointing his bottle at Scott. The crowd whoops. "Sully, c'mon, brother!" Dennis cajoles, holding up a Strat. "One song." Scott steps forward and takes the guitar. "Heading out on his first headliner tour, folks," Dennis says. "Huge deal, right? Give him a hand!"

Scott digs a guitar pick out of his pocket. Julie is in the crowd with Tanya and the rest of them. He smiles at her but he doesn't think she smiles back. The light is in his eyes. He turns up the reverb on the abused Peavey perched on a chair behind him and strums the Strat. It sounds terrible.

"All right," he says into the mic. "Settle the fuck down." He clears his throat. "This is for Jules." A few <u>awws</u> from the audience. He looks again and can't find her. He strums a C chord.

"Oh I ain't gonna make it."

The crowd hoots and howls at the lyric, a song they've heard too many times. But hell, now it's on the radio—*Boston* radio—and there's a video on MTV, too. Even the jaded scenesters manage to get behind his minor hit. It's a rallying call, a thing worth cheering for.

Scott sings and thinks about Jules. About what a saint she was for putting up with his bullshit, about how smart she was to bail out while the going was good. He remembers her as an innocent person caught in the wake of his mess of a life, a side character in the larger narrative of his rise and fall. She dumped him (and was right to do so), earning the flawed genius another wound to tend.

But it wasn't *quite* that simple, was it? Wasn't it truer to say Julie moved to Chicago that summer to *escape* his bullshit? Can't he recall a phone call where she said *precisely* that? He didn't put her on a 10-speed bike that morning, and he wasn't driving the garbage truck that ran her over, but he most definitely helped put her in Chicago, didn't he? In her story—the series of events making up *her* life—he had to admit he featured in there pretty prominently, right?

His fingers form chords and his lyrics come out of his mouth, sober and somber and clear. The song is twenty years rehearsed and performed, imprinted into his guts. He gives it to the room, smooth as whiskey. The audience is rapt, the local hero burning like a fistful of road flares in the corner of a dark room. *Their* room.

Julie sobs by the back door while Tanya rubs her shoulders. She's crying because he's leaving for tour tomorrow, the big tour, the headliner tour that's gonna Hindenburg spectacularly. *But she's not crying about that, right Scotty?* She's crying because he just dumped her. Rock-and-roll man wanted his freedom on the road. He'd been a frightened boy who didn't know what to do with the love she kept pushing on him, so he'd bailed.

A tear runs down his cheek as Julie's friends coax her out the back door. He watches and keeps playing. The same hook of time that's been dragging him along pins him to the stage like a bug specimen, compelling him to finish his minor hit. The hook stops him from running into the snow-covered back alley. No patching things up, no apologies, no begging her to not-go so she can be not-dead. The hook pierces his body and the song pours out of the wound. His tears and cracked voice cement his legend as the sensitive drunk troubadour. He loves that legend, that role, that lens he can bear to see himself through. Townies have told him about this performance over the years, one of many Sully stories he couldn't recall but nodded along with anyway. All part of the mythos of Scotty Sullivan, a mythos he could buy into without ever remembering.

He sings the last chorus, the crowd howling along. *"No, I don't think we're gonna make it,"* they bleat. The last chord rings out and the room erupts. He hands the Strat back to Dennis, desperate to get the fuck out of the cheering, noise-filled decade. A hard slap on the back. Get ya a beer? *Beer! Beer! Buy the fucking alcoholic a beer!* He waves the offer off, keeps moving. "Since when does Sully turn down a drink?" someone barks.

"Since 2001!" Scott shouts, head down. They laugh at their lovable drunk and his nonsensical horseshit.

The next act starts a song and Scott fades to the back of the room, into the shadows between the napkin-covered light fixtures. The booths in the back are piled high with winter coats, guitar cases, and empty bottles. In the shadows, he sees a familiar pair of boots dangling out of the furthest booth, the Doc Martens he bought on Newbury Street when he was in college. *Someone punch me,* he wishes. *Someone push me out the goddamned door. Someone let me off the hook.*

Scott wanders into the front room and slumps at the same table he and Mike had sat at the night before. *Or was it twelve years ago? Whatever.* He pulls his phone out of his pocket. 2:30 in the afternoon, no cell tower to connect to, no wifi. The Molson clock near the door says it's past midnight. He begins shredding a damp coaster, concentrating on his fingers and their busywork. *Am I sitting at the Bay State doing this? Am I crouched in the corner of Sierra Grille in a coma, or did I disappear? Is time passing there? Am I married to Lindsay or haven't I met her yet? Is this my present or my past? How do I opt out of this shit?*

His brother pushes through the front door, a wintery gust and his ex-girlfriend following him in. It's young Kev.

Mullet Kev. Ripped jeans Kev. Whipped by Heather Kev. "Where's he at?" he calls to Jerry. The bartender arches an eyebrow towards the back room. Kev and Heather trudge past Scott's table, stomping snow off their boots. He slouches lower. Maybe he doesn't need to worry about being seen, because they never saw him, so there's no way they could see him, right?

Kev and Heather emerge from the open mic crowd a minute later, Sully hanging between their shoulders. The audience serenades them with chants of "SULL-Y!" Kev pretends to be amused. Heather doesn't bother. How many times did his little brother have to haul his ass home, bail his ass out, back in these good old days? Kev and Heather walk the drunk out the door and into the cold night.

Scott contemplates a drink, just one or seven, wondering what kind of *Inception*/Russian nesting doll shit he could conjure up if he got blackout-drunk in a time-rewind of being blackout-drunk. He stares at the little ceramic heads mounted over the bar: a sea captain, a leprechaun, a sheikh. Outside, a guttural rumble that twists his heart, a sharp nostalgia-ache he's had just about enough of, for Christ's fucking sake.

Scott tips his chair back and peers out the front window. Kev and Heather bicker on the sidewalk next to his idling Cougar, his gold-and-rust baby. They've wrangled Sully into the passenger seat and now Kev wants to get the fuck home.

"I drove you out heah in the middle of a snowstorm," Scott hears Heather say. "The least you could do is walk me back to my friggin' cah." She motions towards Main Street, and Kev's mullet nods a reluctant affirmative. He pats the Mercury's peeling vinyl top and says "Back in five." Sully fogs up the passenger window, out cold. They shuffle up the sidewalk, another argument brewing. *Two more years of misery, then she'll dump him,* Scott recalls. *Thank fuck.*

Scott watches the puffs of exhaust from the Cougar's

tailpipe. *The heater core in that car was for shit*, he thinks. *They'll be home before it warms up.* He's at the door, dangling a foot out in the winter night. Will his sneaker land on a hot summer sidewalk? Does it matter? Is he done here or not?

"'Hey, bozo! Close the fuckin' door!" the bartender shouts at his back.

"Sorry, Jer!" He hops over the threshold and lands ankle-deep in snow. The wind cuts through at his thin shirt.

"Fuck." He hops up and down. "Fuck!" He jams his hands into his pockets as the hook drags him around the front of the car. Motor oil cooks on the manifold, the smell sweet and familiar and unbearably sad. *Shit.* The door hinges howl like hunting dogs. Scott drops into the ripped vinyl seat.

Scott rests his palms on the frigid steering wheel and looks straight ahead, delaying looking at his passenger for a few more seconds. He pokes in the ashtray, jabbing at cigarette butts and pennies and guitar picks. He inspects the shit job he did installing the CD player. Scott presses the eject button. *Click, whir.* Built To Spill's *Keep It Like A Secret* slides out. He exhales a white puff of breath, turns, and takes a good hard look at himself. There sits Scotty Sully Sullivan, out cold in the cold, his face mashed against the passenger window.

"How we doin', Sully?" he asks himself. "How we holdin' up? How'd we turn out?" The blower fan groans as snow accumulates on the windshield. He flips the wipers on. Inadequate for the job, along with the heater and the engine and the brakes and the owner.

"We let this old car down," Scott says. "We let Jules down. We let this town down." He rests his head on the wheel, the engine vibrating through his skull. He eyes the sleeping drunk. "I let you down." He weeps, snot and tears smearing his numb face. "I'm awfully sorry about that, Sully." He wants to punch or hug this dipshit man-boy. Maybe both at once. Squeeze the stupid right out of him.

"We're not out of the woods yet," he says, clearing his throat. "To be honest, we're not even all the way *into* the woods yet. You got three more years of this coming down the pike."

He buckles the lap belt and revs the straight six. "I vote we take the ol' Cougar down to the Meadows and try our damnedest to crack the shock tower a little ahead of schedule," he announces. "Any objections?" Sully doesn't say a word. Scott nods and shifts the Merc-O-Matic into Drive. Northampton is silent and white in the rear view.

"Hold on, kid," he says, letting the Cougar roll out into the unplowed street. "It's gonna be a real shit-show."

Scott Sullivan drives himself home.

●

POP OVERRIDE

Explosions, Martin thinks. *I want to watch shit blow up.*

He peers over the uncombed heads in front of him, scanning the movie listings above the ticket kiosks. The entertainment center's official name is the Shuangxi Sector E19 Double Happiness Consumer Expanse, but everyone still calls it the mall. Martin stands in the heart of it, at the entrance to Plexent Corp's massive cineplex of forty state-of-the-art immersive theaters: rumbling audio, wide spectrum surround screens, full menu, full bar, waitstaff, deluxe chaises with optional genital manipulation.

As he crosses the threshold, Martin's dev links to the Plexent network. His heads-up display refreshes, the newsfeed replaced with behind the scenes clips, corporate tie-in promotions, and movie trivia. He saves them for later with a blink and shuffles forward in the queue, the plastic soles of his Homeaway Active Lifestyle Slippers shushing across the marble floor. He decides on *Expendables Reborn*, a reboot of the classic action film starring CGI simulations of the original cast. He waves his hand across the kiosk sensor, his ID chip communicating with Plexent servers, with a satellite, with his creditor. *Handshakes and encryption keys and authorizations, oh my!* Martin N*4493 Stout purchases one movie pass.

A woman in a crimson jumpsuit materializes out of the milling crowd and greets him. "Hello, sir." She is tall, her leather-padded frame a striking contrast to the slouching pajama-clad theatergoers around them. Martin is on guard, unaccustomed to strangers talking to him.

"No soliciting," he says with a stutter. "No thank you."

She smiles generously. "C3 Regional Brand Engagement Representative. Plexent Corp in conjunction with C3 would like to offer you a complimentary fountain drink." She taps the plastic snack caddy strapped across Martin's chest with a data chit. "We're beta testing a new flavor."

"A new flavor?" Martin asks, reaching for the chit. "I've tried them all. What's this one?" She presses it into his palm.

"An exclusive preview for Premier Guests only," she says with a wink. "Redeem at the C3 bev station inside." She spins on a boot heel and strides away, quickly consumed by the crowd. Martin marvels at the chit. Aluminum, with the C3 logo embossed on it. Below that, the word PREMIER. He rubs his thumb across it.

Sunday afternoon. Explosions. Boasting rights on an exclusive beta flavor from C-goddamned-3. *Check, check, check.* He squeezes the chit in his fist, barely cognizant of the shit-eating grin spread across his face.

———

"This is gonna be great," Reva says as she crouches behind a *Street Riot: Class Warfare* arcade cabinet. Kjell leans against the game, watching Martin wander towards the crowded concession area.

"Fuckin' sugar dope," he mutters, shaking his head. "I could see him drooling from here."

"Ah, stop it," Reva says. On the arcade screen, Player One launches a tear gas canister into the face of a union protester. Concussion, 300 points. "You can be such a prick." This was true. In the two weeks she'd been partnered with him on FLF missions, Kjell had seldom performed a non-prick act.

"This could be a bigger clusterfuck than E47," Kjell says, eyes narrowed. "I wanna see some consumers get swatted flat."

"Why would you say that?" Reva asks, elbowing him in the shoulder. Kjell grabs her wrist—faster than a human should be able to move—and shoves her against *Street Riot.* Reva counters with equal force, the two exchanging strikes and blocks in an incomprehensible blur of limb movement. "Stop it," she exhales, pushing him back. "Cut the shit."

Kjell smiles and holds his hands up in mock surrender, the elastic membrane of his EXO suit peeking out from his jacket sleeves. "Sure, Reva. You got it."

"Why did you bring up E47? What did you do?"

He tilts his head towards the concession area. "Your dope is claiming his prize."

Reva searches the crowd for Martin's face. *What did you do?*

———

The C3 bev station—a Shuangxi Mark 90—is an imposing 360 degree self-serve beverage kiosk in the center of the concession area, serving close to 700 different exclusive C3 flavors. In the decades since C3 increased their focus on brand building and IP protection, the corporation has taken on an air of urban legend: Brand Enforcement troops confiscating bootleg flavor formulas, strike teams reducing illegal distro units into rubble, license infraction massacres. Mostly crazy sounding shit that probably wasn't true. Probably.

Martin pushes towards the besieged bev station, his snack caddy pressed against a woman's back, maneuvering closer to a bev dispenser. The Mark 90's soothing female AI voice assists twenty customers through twenty speakers.

"… Selection 412: One large Gracious Grape… Welcome to the Shuangxi Sector E19 Double Happiness Consumer Expanse C3 beverage station, brought to you in partnership with the Plexent Corporation. Selection 119: One large Apple Curry Vim… Ice or extra ice?... Selection 440: One large Energy Juice Tea… I'm sorry, I couldn't hear you… Selection 390: Two extra large Spiced Potato Waters… Welcome to the Shuangxi Sector E19 Double—"

Hands grasp at the sleek black edifice, accounts are debited, cups snatched from serving trays. Martin leans in and drops the chit into the seldom-used manual input slot. The machine swallows the data. Martin blushes in pre-social anxiety, his jaw set as he waits for his flavor to be announced, for the pulsing crowd around him to be stunned and awed as he casually drops a Premier Guest beverage into his snack caddy's cupholder.

The humming machine hums a little louder and the multiple AI instances fall silent. The throng of customers look expectantly at the menu boards mounted above the C3 Bev Station. The screens flicker.

When the Mark 90 speaks, the female AI's voice is pitched a full step down, as if mired in syrup. "Selection 666: One complimentary premier Pineapple Charcoal Mango Chutney Fizzy Pop Backslash Loop."

Martin blinks as his drink drops onto the serving tray. It's no ordinary soda cup—it's a thick fancy *plastic* cup, with sculpted ridges for maximum grip, and a lid with a built in jumbo straw. The theater's concession area falls silent, those nearest to him giving him space as he reverently retrieves the

Premier Cup and snaps it into his snack caddy. As his audience watches, he tilts his head forward and takes a hands-free sip. His mouth is full of sparks and carnal umami. Tears form at the corners of his eyes. Ocean waves smash in his ears, slowly recede, and then he is back at the mall.

"It's good," Martin whispers, nodding. People are asking questions, reaching out, touching his sweatshirt, shooting video. He takes a step back. This much attention is too much. He spins around and looks for refuge from the staring crowd. *Restroom. Perfect.* He pushes past the heavy door, the growing murmurs of the theatergoers muted by the soundproofed walls.

"Backslash loop?" Reva says, eyeing Kjell. "That wasn't in your code back at FLF."

Kjell grins. He probably thinks it's charming.

She shakes her head and scans the crowd around the humming bev station. She's lost track of Martin. "Where's our guy?" Plexent security marches into the lobby, five men in light body armor. Their stun prods and glossy boots are a watered-down version of the *Street Riot* cops corralling protesters on the arcade screen. They circle the bev station, barking questions at the crowd.

Kjell stands. "Time to bounce." Reva chases after him as he skirts the edge of the concession area and moves towards the entrance. Behind them, a Plexent guard shoves an uncooperative witness against the bev station and gives him a Level 1 stun. The man makes an undramatic *hhurk* sound. A queue of bystanders turn away, eyes focused on the popcorn patterned carpet, and move quietly towards the main theater corridor.

"What did y—" Reva says. An alarm sounds. Distracted, she stumbles into Kjell. He has stopped short at the main doors, two more Plexant security guards blocking his path.

"IDs and tickets," one demands, his stun prod in Kjell's face.

"We, ah," Kjell says. "We were just in the arcade." Reva sees his hands are curled into tight fists. *This was a bad idea.*

A man in a suit steps between them, his nametag identifying him as the real C3 Regional Brand Engagement Representative. "Have you seen any unusual activity?" he asks.

"There's some sort of trouble," Reva tells the rep in the most-innocentest voice she can conjure, waving generally towards the fracas by the bev station. The AI is talking again, but she can't make it out over the growing clamor of guards corralling theatergoers and the alarm. She wraps her arm around Kjell's waist and gives a medium tug. He's ready to spring, his EXO rigid. *Son of a bitch.* "My husband and I. We're trying to get out of harm's way."

"Yeah," Kjell grins at the C3 rep, shoulders flexed. "Harm's way is a helluva spot to be in."

———

Martin rests his forehead against the tile wall, standing weirdly between a urinal and a tampon dispenser. With no one else in the restroom to see him, he closes his eyes and takes another suck from the special drink in his snack caddy. He lets the carbonation dance on his tongue. He assesses the quantity remaining. *How long can I make this last?*

A popup appears in the center of his heads-up display: "Plexent Patrons: A minor power issue has temporarily closed the main concession area. We apologize—"

The restroom door slams open. Martin flinches as the hydraulic door-slower-thing snaps right off and clatters across the tile floor. It's the C3 Brand Hospitality Lady.

"You—"

She slams the thick door shut, cutting off a burst of clamor. "Did the power go out?" he asks.

"No the power didn't go out." He sees her blink away the same popup. "Don't you know corp bullshit when you see it?"

"I—." Another Plexent popup offers him a 10% off coupon for his inconvenience. He adds it to his account before clearing his screen. "No, yeah. I do," he nods. "Sure."

She wedges a trash bin between the wall and the door. "I couldn't find you out there. I was worried—"

"This is really good," Martin nods, patting the drink in his snack caddy. "Thanks so much f—"

"Thank you. I'm proud of it. But we've got to—"

"What, you made it?"

"Yes."

"I've never met a soda designer! That's amazing!"

"I— well." She blushes. "Yeah, thanks. Buuut—" she points at him and frowns.

"Martin." He offers a handshake. She grabs him by the wrist, spins him like he's made of cardboard, and firmly presses him against the wall. Martin's fight or flight instinct kicks in. His dev sells his heart rate data to an advertiser and he gets a popup for anti-anxiety meds. *I already take those!*

"I'm Reva. Hello. Sorry, listen, Martin. I've got to get you out of here. Things are going a bit sideways out there."

"What's—"

"Have you used one of these before?" she asks. Martin squints over his shoulder as Reva unslings a folded EXO suit from her shoulder. *Strength Enhancement For Recreation And The Workplace.*

"I had a gym membership once and they let us—"

"Great," she says, already holding the compact unit against his spine. "This one runs a little hotter than that. Like, times ten. Stand still." She activates the kit. Elasteel straps unfurl along the back of his limbs, wrapping thin tendrils snugly around his joints.

"A hacked EXO suit?" he exclaims as the machine corrects his posture. He's read about these in the feeds. Criminals doing mighty leaps. Punching cars. Super villain stuff. "These are against the law!"

"So is flavor tampering, but it's what I do." Reva spins him back around.

Martin realizes his jumbo straw is still hanging from his lip. He lets it drop. "This is an illegal soda?" he whispers. "What's going on?"

"We didn't mean to—"

"Who's 'we'?"

She gestures towards the door. "My partner. He coded the chit."

"Well where is he?"

"He thought he could take on two security guards with stun prods. They left him unconscious on the floor so I grabbed his EXO." She nods at Martin. "For you." Martin's eyes grow wide.

"You're a num-num!"

She holds up a finger. "That's a derogatory media slur. The Flavor Liberation Front seeks to—"

Martin leans against a toilet stall. "Jesus, I've read about you! The riot in sector E37—"

"We don't have time for this, Martin. The plan was supposed to be one drink. Your drink. A *fuck you* to the corps so they'd know we could hack them. It should've warranted a response from the mall cops. But—" Martin opens his mouth. "BUT!" Reva winces. "My partner changed the code. The situation has… escalated. C3 is coming."

Martin goes pale. Reva opens the door a crack and peers out. Amid the screaming and shouted orders and alarms, Martin can hear the bev station's calm voice. "Selection 666: One complimentary premier Pineapple Charcoal Mango Chutney Fizzy Pop Backslash Loop... Selection 666: One complimentary premier Pineapple Charcoal Mango Chutney Fizzy Pop Backslash Loop… Selection 666: One complimentary premier…"

"C3," he whispers.

"This is a massive breach of their system. They're going to respond… with force." She drags him over to the door and points his body towards the far corner of the lobby. "Past the theater lines, then turn left down the main corridor. We'll find an emergency exit. When I say run, run. You don't need to push too hard. Let the EXO do the work."

"I don't want—"

"RUN!"

Martin launches himself across the cineplex lobby and into a wall.

————

"Times ten!" Reva shouts, plucking Martin out of the jagged hole in the wallboard. She stands him upright. He sways, space-eyed, squinting at a popup asking him to rate the theater's restroom cleanliness.

"That hurt," he coughs, dust dandruffing off his head. Behind Reva, a Plexant guard slaps a premier glass out of a woman's hand and batons her in the sternum. She drops to her knees and gasps for air, joining ten other people already writhing on the carpet. The bev station is still talking, multiple streams of soda overflowing cupless serving trays. Martin checks his snack caddy. His Premier cup is secure.

Reva shakes him and turns his body towards the theaters again. "Lines, corridor, emergency exit. remember?"

"Mmmyeah."

"YOU!" the C3 Regional Brand Engagement Representative bellows from the arcade entrance. His stun prod is extended and ready for some engagement.

"GO!" Reva shouts at Martin. She thrusts forward, closing

the distance to the rep with a two meter backwards push off the wall. Reva slides across the soda-soaked carpet, ducks the zappy end of the prod, and delivers a brutal EXO-assisted elbow to the man's gut. He folds in half.

Martin dives through the melee, the room seeming to slow down as he tumbles past flying fists and screaming children at EXO speed. He barely avoids the line of theatergoers pressed against the wall, refusing to surrender their place in line for the 1:20 showing of *Righteous Enforcer Priest.* Martin bounces off the movie's lobby display and the trailer starts playing on his heads-up. Reva glides past him, digging her padded shoulder into the wall to brake.

"Keep moving!"

They leap down the corridor, Martin acclimating to the EXO's capabilities. Ahead, the 11:15 showing of *Righteous Enforcer Priest* lets out, squinting audience members wandering into their path.

"Like this!" Reva shouts, not breaking pace. She kicks off the left wall and launches herself into a spiral: one kick off the ceiling, one more off the right-hand wall. She lands on the other side of the crowd in a powerslide, turning in time to watch Martin plow straight through ten or fifteen people. "Or like that," she mutters. She pulls him free from the tangle of limbs and sets him on his feet. He wavers. The only thing holding him upright is the EXO suit. Reva pushes him forward.

Martin, dazed, lunges towards the steel doors. "Coming in hot!" he shrieks. *Isn't that a line from a movie? Wait, was it Righteous Enforcer Priest?*

They slam through the emergency exit, grabbing the push bars for balance as a frigid winter wind whips their faces. Another alarm sounds.

Martin leans forward, chest heaving, shielding his eyes from the snow and grit blowing across the parking lot.

"Shit," Reva gasps. It isn't a winter wind.

A large red gunship lowers onto the cracked asphalt, fore hatch sliding open. Private soldiers in gleaming red armor spread like a pool of blood across the Shuangxi Sector E19 Double Happiness Consumer Expanse West Entrance Parking Area. Impact blasters, military grade EXO suits, carbonation sensors, helmets like Brutalist apartment buildings.

"C3 Brand Enforcement," Reva whispers.

Martin clutches his snack caddy, panic deep in his chest, as a detachment of troops leaps high in the air, their graceful EXO-assisted arcs set to terminate about eight inches in front of his Homeaway Active Lifestyle Slippers. More troops flank left and right, dropping to their knees, blasters steady. *Righteous enforcers*, he thinks.

"Back inside!" Reva cries, tearing the collar off Martin's shirt as she hurls herself back with a massive kickoff. Martin spins like a top, then there's a terrific explosion, and then cinderblocks and blackness.

"Martin?" A gentle voice, a hand on his. "Martin N. Stout. Last four digits 4493. Please sit up. We have several items to discuss."

Martin opens his eyes. Ceiling tiles. He labors to lift his head upright, smearing drool and dust across his cheek with a swollen hand. He stares dumbly at his scraped knuckles, his gaze traveling up his bruised arm to a bright white t-shirt. He tries to read his chest upside down. "C3 Your Flavorite Drink!" *Flavorite?* His brain can't untangle it. He makes a croaking sound.

"Please, drink some water," the man says, setting two paper cups on a table. Martin squints at his crisp gray suit. The room has no windows, one door. Martin tries to turn this jumble of observations into something meaningful. His neck is stiff. Everything is stiff.

"First time in an EXO suit of that caliber, I'd imagine," the suit man says. "Our techs had to cut it off you. Apologies regarding your shirt." Martin remembers his soda, his snack caddy. He touches his chest. "I'm afraid we had to confiscate that, too, Martin," the man says. "Our team members down in Mouth Feel analyzed your soda. Most interesting. Primary synthesized flavor profiles: Pineapple, charcoal, mango, chutney. Secondary flavor highlights: Bone broth, bamboo, wax, tetrafluoroethane. Do you know what tetrafluoroethane is, Martin?"

When confronted with a new word, Martin's instinct is to search it on his dev. His heads-up is blank, his newsfeed empty. No connection. Martin feels an existential unease creep into his gut. He is cut off, alone in this room with this man. He shakes his head no.

"It is a refrigerant used in our Shuangxi Mark 90 beverage station. The data chit you loaded told the machine to reroute a reservoir tank into the beverage maker cylinders."

Martin rubs his throat. "Am I poisoned?"

The man smiles and says "No, Martin. It is non-toxic in such a minute dose. But a unique flavor, no? You gave people something they'd never had before. The head of Mouth Feel sends along her unofficial compliments."

"I didn't make it."

"Of course."

"Where am I?"

The man leans forward. "You are in C3 headquarters. You are in an interrogation room. Our conversation is being recorded." He offers his hand. "My name is Riddhi Raj. You may call me Raj. I am a senior Infraction Investigator here at C3."

Martin rakes his fingers through his hair and winces at a tender spot on the back of his head, some sort of wound. He can't tell how bad.

"Is your head all right? Can you remember the soda flavors

I just told you?"

Martin rubs his eyes. "Uh, pineapple, charcoal, mango, ...chutney." He waves his hand in a small circle. "The refrigerator stuff."

"Tetrafluoroethane."

"Yeah, tetro floro—"

"The Flavor Liberation Front. You've heard of them?"

Martin nods. "Num-nums. Buncha hippie kids."

"That is how they are portrayed in the media, yes. But make no mistake, Martin. They are a dangerous terrorist organization."

"C3 sent a squad of tr—"

"They disrupt commerce and sow seeds of discontent, Martin." Raj sits back but speaks forcefully. "Discontent hurts our brand, hurts our workers. Disruption hurts the economy. Our country is dependent on our economy, Martin, don't you agree?"

"Where's Reva?"

"Your partner is currently at large. We have Kjell in custody."

"Who?"

Raj smiles. "You were wearing his EXO kit. He has already implicated you in the beverage station tampering and named you as an FLF leader."

Under different circumstances, Martin might explode in a panic at such an accusation. But in this moment—this exhausting moment—he leans back and snorts. "Yeah, I'm a num-num." He rolls his eyes. "Out of shape insurance agent is secretly a terrorist leader. Good senior investigating, Raj."

Raj's smile does not falter. Martin's heads-up notifies him of a fileshare invite from Riddhi R. "Open it, please."

Security footage appears in the center of Martin's vision. He is at the cineplex's bev station, dropping the data chit into the slot. *Never take a data chit from a stranger,* he scolds himself.

"This is you, yes?" Raj asks.

Martin watches the short video loop. 4k cinema quality, good lighting, sharp focus. No use denying. "Yeah," he says with a rasp. He peers into his empty cup. "Could I get some more—"

Another fileshare. "This is you, yes?" Raj asks again.

Martin watches another video loop of his EXO-enhanced body slamming sideways into the crowd of righteous theatergoers. He winces and nods.

A third fileshare. "This is you, yes?" His tone is more of a statement than a question.

Martin watches a lower quality video loop. Outdoors, night time. A man walks across a parking lot, his head all sparkle and shimmer. Martin squints and swipes the clip aside. "I can't tell who that is. He's wearing one of those scrambler things."

Raj leans back and folds his arms. "That is you exiting the Sector E47 Hellaburger location last month, third of December, moments after hacking their C3 beverage station." Martin opens his mouth. "Ten minutes before a riot broke out resulting in several deaths and multiple inj—"

"THAT'S NOT ME!" Martin shouts. He'd seen clips of this on his newsfeed. "The num-nums had—"

"It's you."

"The news said your C3 goons stormed in and—"

"The resulting fire engulfed the entire block."

"IT WASN'T ME."

Raj stands and smooths his jacket. He touches Martin's hand. "It's you," he says softly.

Martin locates the panic he'd misplaced earlier. His heart pounds against his bruised ribs as Raj turns for the door. "WAIT!" He doesn't want the polite man to leave. He's not sure who comes in next.

"We're going to find you a more suitable shirt, Martin. You'll be escorted to a press conference shortly. As you've waived your right to a trial, you're free to say whatever you'd like."

"I didn't waive anything!"

"We have your signed CWC Consent Without Consent form."

"I didn't sign that!" Martin yells.

Raj frowns. "You don't need to."

A strangled sound escapes Martin's mouth.

"Your conviction and execution have already been arranged. I'm sorry, Martin." Raj the polite man leaves him alone in the interrogation room.

———

Martin's brain cycles through unfeasible action movie scenarios: *Can I kick the door open? Climb into an air vent? Overpower the next person through the door?* He knows the answers to those questions. He weighs the pros and cons of crawling under the table and throwing up and dying and going to sleep forever.

A heavy thud vibrates in the soles of his feet, which he only now realizes are bare. He emits a breathless squeal. *Was that an explosion?* There is muffled yelling from the floor below. "What now?" he whispers.

Four sharp pops behind him send Martin scrambling over the table. With a sizzle and flash, a perfect square of concrete wall falls outward into the night. Whatever signal-blocking material woven into the walls falls with it—Martin's dev reconnects to the public network, his newsfeed sidescrolling at double speed as it loads. Phrases like TERRORIST ATTACK and THEATER MASSACRE and AMONG THE DEAD whip past. He sees his name. The doom-y feeling in his gut manages to get heavier and drop even lower.

"Martin!" Reva's voice echoes from far below. "Did we kill you?"

Martin steps cautiously to the ledge. He stares out at the city, whimpering as icy winds whip at his thin flavorite t-shirt. Another explosion lights up the plaza below. Two stories below him, Reva is backlit by the orange plume. She spins a hoverbike around and backs it closer to the C3 building. Down at street level, bikers clash with C3 security. *It's a num-num jailbreak*, he thinks. *Jesus, I look even guiltier.*

"What are you doing?!" he hollers.

Reva spins around in the saddle and calls over her shoulder. "Saving your ass!"

"I *know* that!" He turns and shoves the table across the interrogation room, blocking the door. He can't remember which way the door swings but whatever. He lunges back to the hole in the wall, clamping on to the rough concrete edge for support. "I mean what are you doing down *there?* Come up here and get me, goddamnit!" A cab company ad blocks his vision. He briefly considers it before dismissing it.

"No can do," she replies, slapping the bike's airframe. "Standard metro hoverbike. Doesn't go higher than five stories."

"THEN GO GET ANOTHER ONE!" he cries, spit and snot spiralling in the frigid updraft.

"No time, Martin! This is what you get. You're gonna have to jump."

"JUMP? ARE YOU...?" He peers down at Reva's hoverbike, trying to eyeball the distance to the small bike saddle. "ARE YOU GODDAMNED...?" he cries. He can't think of a big enough word to encapsulate his feelings on the matter.

"Come on!" she demands.

"There's going to be a press conference. I can tell my side!"

"They're framing you, man!" Reva yells. "Corp bullshit! You're nothing to them but propaganda!"

A headline flashes across his newsfeed. UPDATE: "YEAH I'M A NUM-NUM!" SAYS DEFIANT FLF LEADER STOUT. It is accompanied by a muted video loop of him sitting in this room at that table. Martin spins on his heel and scowls at unseen cameras. "Fuck!" he cries.

"I'm sorry, Martin! It wasn't supposed to—"

"For a soda? You ruin my life for a goddamned POP?"

Reva shrugs. "I just wanted to give people a new flavor."

"THAT'S STUPID."

"Martin!" Reva points above him. He twists himself around as a C3 gunship appears over the lip of the roofline of C3 headquarters. It rotates, the bold white stripe along the bottom of the red fuselage shimmering in the city lights. It descends towards them. Twenty floors, fifteen. Ten. "Jump!" she orders.

An alarm sounds somewhere in the building. "I'm an insurance agent," he whispers, somehow an accusation pointed at Reva. He backs up a few steps, his bare feet slapping on the floor.

"IT'S TIME TO GO!"

Behind him, the doorknob rattles. Bellowing voices. Table legs scrape across tile. He's already running. Martin launches himself towards oblivion with a maniacal laugh, his fingertips grazing the belly of the descending gunship. *Pineapple Fucking Charcoal Fucking Mango Chutney Fucking Fizzy Pop,* he thinks as he falls into the night. He flails, grasping at air, as a nearby noodle bar offers him $5 off his next purchase. Martin blinks the ad aside, tears clinging to his eyelashes from the cold, and spirals. He can't see Reva or the bike or the city, just streaks of light and that big white stripe bearing down on him. *Fuck it. It was good.*

●

the
bottle
man

THE BOTTLE MAN

The sound of tires sticking to hot asphalt receded as I stepped through the gap in the weed-choked fence. Desperate for time away from the suffocating heat of my apartment, I descended into the woods, following a vaguely-defined path around the lip of a gully. Below, street runoff dribbled from a rusted pipe, zigzagging through rocks and trash on its way to a directionless bit of swamp. Overhead tree boughs squeaked and gibbered. *Sounds like a baby Wookie.*

I pushed through some scrubby brush and slid into a shallow depression in the ground. It was an excavation of some kind, one of many from the look of the pockmarked hillside. I toed some broken bricks and shattered bits of porcelain hidden in the freshly turned soil. Junk was scattered everywhere: sun catching a piece of mirror, a rusted can under an exposed tree root, something plastic and faded fluttering from a thornbush. *Illegal dumping? An old landfill?* I imagined weird old men out here, digging up bottles to sell at the Brimfield Antique Show, charging New Yorkers five or ten bucks a pop. Pun intended.

I crouched to pick at a half-buried piece of milky glass. Was it a sugar bowl from the '50s or a face cream jar from the '20s? My doodad-dating skills were underdeveloped and insufficient. Under the black rot of last year's leaves I unearthed broken soda bottles from local breweries a century gone: Easthamptons and Springfields and Holyokes. The more I found, the more I wanted to find. I clawed at the hard ground, glitter chipping off my nails, and freed an old brown glass medicine bottle. "REGISTERED," it declared in raised letters. *To what, for what, by whom?* I slipped it into my bag, indifferent to the dirt going in along with it, my eyes already on another treasure near my foot. *Taking vintage junk from an old landfill,* I thought as I shifted position. *Am I stealing or picking up litter?*

Slick with sweat, I wrestled another bottle from the ground—a three-sided design I'd never seen before. It was thick-walled and heavy and filled with dry muck. I added it to my bulging inventory, already picturing it washed and shimmering in the sun on my kitchen window sill. I spotted the neck of a matching one near the edge of the shallow pit. *A twofer!* I scraped at the rocky soil to get a hold of the bottle but someone else's fingers were already wrapped around it. That was how I met the Bottle Man.

———

I scrambled back, my heart bouncing around my ribcage like a tennis ball in a clothes dryer set to "Just Found A Dead Body In The Woods/Delicates."

"Whuuuhh," I whispered. It seemed like a reasonable thing to say in that sort of situation. The half-buried hand didn't move. How *could* it? It was dead. *It's not holding the bottle,* I reasoned to myself. *It's just stuck.* I crawled forward cautiously, the July afternoon pressing in, and prodded the bottle. Nothing. I pushed a stick against one of the fingers. It didn't budge. "Whuuuhh," I whispered again.

I used the stick to scrape dirt away from around the knuckles and soon unearthed a dead wrist and a deader forearm. *I should call 911. I should've already called.* This was a crime scene or an unmarked grave or something else I definitely shouldn't be touching. But I kept touching. When I got past the elbow, the arm began to move, helping me dig. Instead of being terrified, I was thankful for the hand. *LOL.* We worked together to free his shoulder and neck, and finally the Bottle Man wrenched his head free from the earth.

His skull was a mash of mud and dried skin, with a rock wedged into his overextended jaw. Broken bottles had been pushed into his eye sockets, bottoms-out. The Bottle Man shook his head and slapped weakly at the rock in his mouth with his free hand.

"GOU!" he said.

"The rock?" I asked.

He pointed at the thing. "Yeh h' rah! G'ou!" He motioned at the rock again, his movements Muppet-like, and let his head drop back into its head-shaped hole.

I slipped the stick into his mouth, seeking leverage between the rock and his back teeth. "This might hurt." The dead man mumbled something, his tone suggesting something along the lines of *Well, yeah.* I pulled lightly on the stick, causing his head to loll to the side, his atrophied muscles still asleep. "Sorry," I said, repositioning. "Let me just…" I placed my foot on his forehead to steady him. "On the count of three, okay?"

He nodded.

I jerked the stick forward on two. It seemed like a thing people in movies do. The rock popped out of his mouth with an awful grinding sound. He reached into his mouth and scooped out a clump of decomposed leaves. The Bottle Man hawked up a gob of black muck and gasped the humid summer air.

"Jaysus, girl!" he cried with an Irish lilt, working his jaw open and shut, left and right. "Ye said *tree!*"

"I'm sorry. I thought—"

"Someone calls 'count tree,' I spect a *one-two-tree!* I'm fair sure that's the point of it!"

"I'm sorry!" I said again. "You wanted the rock out. I got it out."

"Thatya did," he said, his fingers exploring his black teeth. "Holy Fadder, I think ya took the pickets right off my fence."

I stopped myself from apologizing a third time. He gazed up at me with smeary eyes, wiping mud from the thick bottle bottoms with an equally dirty thumb. "Well, are ye gonna leave a fellar half-dug or what?"

"Right," I exhaled. "Sorry." *Damn it.*

We dug. I shouldered most of the grunt work, the Bottle Man pitching in with a hand that gained finer motor control as the afternoon unfolded. It took an hour to free his chest and other arm. The Bottle Man wondered aloud if a good hard yank might finish the job. Dripping with sweat, I wiped my palms on my jeans. I grasped his bony wrists and leaned back. The landfill held him in its grip.

"Maybe if you turn 'round and let me grab onna ya, you could gimme a hoist?"

I took a deep breath. I was dizzy and dehydrated and breathing felt like drowning. I turned and crouched low so the Bottle Man could wrap his mummy-dry arms around my neck. Steadying myself, I exhaled slowly and bolted upright, squat-thrusting in an approximation of what I thought a weightlifter might do. The Bottle Man broke free of the landfill, his spine snapping above the hips.

"Ooooof!" I tumbled forward and landed flat on my face. Rocks and bits of broken dishware jabbed into exposed flesh.

"Y' took my feckin' legs off!" he cried over my shoulder, twisting around to assess the damage.

"Get offa me!" I bleated. The whole front of my body was

a big stinging *ouch.*

"Are ye away in the head, girl? I got no feckin' legs!"

I thrashed around the debris-strewn hillside, attempting to force the half-man off my back. The Bottle Man clung stubbornly on and I surrendered quickly. The heat, the digging—it was all too much. I rolled onto my back, muffling the complaining Irishman beneath me. Above, the canopy of leaves hung dead and still. The birds were silent. Somewhere back towards the trail, the baby Wookie complained.

The Bottle Man wrenched his head from under my shoulder. "Aren't we a manky pair!" he declared, his dead rot shimmying under my weight.

I closed my eyes, red blobs dancing across blackness, and concentrated on not fainting. *Shitshitshit.* My heart was beating too fast. I needed water. I needed to make better decisions.

"Now I bet you're wonderin' why I wa—"

"Shut up."

———

Between the humidity, the direct sunlight, and the relentless charm of my corpse backpack, the walk home almost killed me. By the time I stumbled into the apartment and cranked the AC, I felt I'd heard too much and understood too little.

They'd lynched him in 1811, he told me, a wandering Irishman accused of a petty crime ("Stealin' apples! *Apples* of all things! Can you imagine! Do I *look* like the apple-eating sort?"). The fine Christian citizens of the Pioneer Valley had rolled his body into a shallow grave, in a remote wooded area which later became the town dump. He had no memory of the first hundred years or so, rightly believing himself to be quite dead. A heatwave in the early 1900s interrupted his long moment of nothing. Warmed him up like leftovers. He awoke with broken bottles in his eyes, his body compressed under a pile of refuse and rocky New England soil.

He lounged down there for another century, neither alive nor dead, listening to truck drivers and trash men. The town dump closed, grew over, and was forgotten. Then he eavesdropped on hikers and birds and kids smoking cigarettes. He heard bits of topsider chatter: their hitteler scares and beetle manias and seery where-am-Is. He mentioned these not-quite-right pop culture and historical references in a winking tone that suggested he was putting me on, that of *course* he knew who Hitler was. Or maybe he didn't. I couldn't tell for sure.

"I am parched in every nook of my soul," he hinted as I tracked mud across the kitchen linoleum and flopped into a chair. He wriggled his torso up onto the chair back. "Could go for a long gargle. You?"

I extracted my phone from my filthy glass-filled bag while the Bottle Man jabbered about a den of rabbits he befriended in the 1960s. I took possibly the most unflattering selfie of the Internet age: a mud-caked chick slumped at her kitchen table, dehydrated and exhausted, with a bottle-eyed corpse leering over her shoulder. I captioned it "Met a guy." Got nine likes!

———

I'm not going to discuss the shower in detail here, but it involved a terse negotiation to allow for shirt and bra removal, a maddening conversation about what a loofah is, and too much body commentary. Never mind we're talking about a man two hundred years dead experiencing indoor plumbing for the first time. The whole ordeal proved almost as draining as the digging and the trudge home. When we were done I curled up on my bed, wrapped in a towel and the Bottle Man. As I dozed he kept talking, and I fortunately slept through six hours' worth of dubious tales and nonsensical slang.

"You met him in the woods." Emily said. My housemate leaned against the fridge, arms folded.

"Hiking," I nodded. I assembled a peanut butter and banana sandwich on the narrow strip of counter between the stove and toaster oven. The Bottle Man dangled from my neck, resting my phone against the side of my head as he scrolled through my Facebook feed. He *ooh*ed and *I-never*ed and *praise-be*d at my friends' photos. He seemed pretty easy to impress.

"You brought a guy you met in the woods back to the apartment."

"Correct."

Emily put her hands on her hips like a frustrated parent, a big trigger for me (along with her criticism of my clothes, my posture, and my brand choices). She was a year younger than me and such a goddamned *mom*. I closed my eyes and took a deep breath.

"Jessie," she said in her disappointed mother voice. "Could we speak privately in the living room?"

I gestured at the man hanging off my shoulders. "Clearly we cannot."

"Ladies," the Bottle Man interrupted. "You've a lovely gaff and all, but what say we get a drink, eh? Get to know each other like roomies, like ahh, golden girls, eh?"

I rolled my eyes. "I'm not going out like this," I stated, taking a honkin' bite of sandwich. "Ever."

"Ah, love," the Bottle Man said. "Don't be so down on yourself. You've got skin with blood under it. You've got globby eyes and a thumpy heart." He cupped my boob with a dry gray palm.

"That's not my heart."

"Just sayin' what's the sense staying in when you're so

bloody *alive?*"

That was the nicest thing a guy had said to me in maybe three and a half years. I glanced at Emily. She huffed and stormed out of the kitchen.

"All roight then! A duo it is!" The Bottle Man tapped on my phone's music app. "Let's have a proper tune!"

"*Return to the breath,*" my guided meditation murmured.

"Press stop," I told the Bottle Man.

"Don't y' have any summer jams on this thing?"

"You don't know what a summer jam is."

"I do *so* know what a summer jam is. I've got two ears, don't I?"

"You've got one ear."

"Well, I've got two ear holes and I know what a sum—"

"Press stop."

———

I tried to smooth my dress, which looked baggy and weird with the dead guy's waxy arms criss-crossing it. I scowled at him in the bathroom mirror. "You're bunching it up."

"Aww, we been in here for *ages,*" he groaned at our reflection. I experimented with a side ponytail while the Bottle Man nipped at it. It was somehow playful and not horrifying. I guess you just get used to things. I let my hair fall in surrender and grabbed a handful of bobby pins. Squinting at the mirror, I attempted to build my hair into an intentional-seeming shape.

"Is this normal, all this primping?" he asked. "Are we meetin' a foreign dignitary of some sort?"

I met my own gaze. "I have a can of hairspray and a lighter in my room." I slid a bobby pin behind my ear. "I'll light us both on fire." Clip. Tuck. Smooth. "I'll do it."

The Bottle Man closed his crooked mouth. He watched me fiddle with my bangs, his jaw clicking against my neck.

"You've chose a lovely frock tonight, Jess," he said finally, giving me a gentle squeeze. "'Tis lovely."

———

The Stones blared out of the jukebox, competing with the baseball game on the flatscreen over The Watering Hole's bar. The Bottle Man did his damnedest to shout over all of it. I slouched on a bar stool, fingers laced around a Greyhound, while the Bottle Man bellowed off-color jokes at the regulars. He accepted pint after pint from strangers, eager to down as many as they'd pay for. The beer dribbled out of his ragged torso and soaked the back of my dress. The evening was going about as well as I'd anticipated.

"They strung me roight up that tree!" he cried, a rapt audience of college kids circled close. "Snapped my neck like *dat!*" He attempted a finger snap for emphasis, but his middle finger flopped backwards. Everyone laughed. His head nodded loosely, bottle eyes sauced and delighted, and laughed along with them. "They all stood dar *starin'* up at me!" he continued, searching his dirt filled skull for a modern reference to cement his standing with these pink faced topsiders. "Like I was a *yew tube,* roight?" The small crowd erupted in a fresh gale of laughter, hearty dude back slaps transmitting through the dead man's withered frame to my damp one.

"This is a helluva crew y'got, Jess!" he shouted into my ear.

"I don't know these people."

"A real craic lot!" he nodded.

"We should leave soon," I told him.

"Are ye not havin' a good time, Jess?"

I gave him my best side-eye. "No?"

"Bahhh!"

I sipped my Greyhound. "You told me they hung you on the courthouse steps."

"Pubs are for spinnin' yarns, Jess! It's all good fun! Y'know *fun*, dontya?" He flagged down the bartender with a wiggle of a pint glass. "This lovely lass would like anudder!"

I held my glass up. "I've still got half a—"

"Ahh, camman. Be *alive*, for the sake of Chroist!"

I had anudder.

———

We hunched on the stairs, a swaying frame of warped lumber tacked onto the back of my landlord's house. 10 a.m. and the day was already sticky and muggy. Morning sunlight glanced off the scrubbed bottles lining the kitchen window above my head. Inside, they threw pretty refractions onto the kitchen ceiling. I leaned into the Bottle Man like a cushion, pressing him against the splintered railing. I sipped ice water from a coffee mug.

"This is nuthin' next to the heatwave what woke me," the Bottle Man yapped. "1911 it was. I goggled it. Oh, that was a devil mess. Killed babies, drove men mad." He pointed to himself. "Raised the dead."

I twisted my neck, trying to stretch stiff muscles. Sleep had not gone well.

"D'ya need a back rub?"

"I need you to get the hell off me," I mumbled into my mug.

"You'd leave me floppin' around on the ground!"

"Damn right."

"You've no respect for your elders is your problem."

"Oh, *that's* my problem," I said with false wonder. My phone vibrated on the step next to me. Third notification in an hour. I was experiencing an unusual amount of friend requests and messages this morning (by 'unusual amount' I'm talking 'more than none'). I didn't recognize any of the names. "What did we do last night?"

"Got roight fluthered!" he beamed.

"Stop making up words."

"Are we goin' out tonight, then?"

I slid my fingertips across my slick forehead. Sweating before breakfast. Cripes. "Why on *earth* would someone go out two nights in a row?"

———

"Lob anudderun inna me, boss!" the Bottle Man slurred at the bartender.

The gathering of college kids gawked at us expectantly. Were they the same ones from last night? I struggled to stay focused and picked up where the Bottle Man left off. "So then the mamma bunny built a little den *right in his ribcage!*" I nodded. "Baby bunnies right. In. His. *Ribs!*" I accented each word with a rap of my empty glass against the bar top. Our audience was enthralled, full of *aww*s and *aaahhh*s and *squeee*s.

"Roight in dar!" the Bottle Man agreed, pouring beer into his face.

I aimed my bar stool at the pretty lumberjack boy sitting next to me. "I want your baby bunnies inside me," I whispered. I thought he smiled. Or did he look terrified? The whole room skewed left so I leaned right to compensate. A Mt. Holyoke girl caught me. "I don't even think he's Irish," I whispered.

The Bottle Man cackled. "What a

———

night," I rasped, balancing my mug on the back stair railing.

"Really somethin'," the Bottle Man agreed with a loosey-goose head nod. "Quite the grand display."

"Jessie," Emily declared from the landing above. "I think

he's evil."

I squinted up at my housemate. "Who?"

"Him!" Emily said, jaw set, arms folded. "I think he's bad for you. I'm sorry, but this is too much."

"Is she talkin' about me?" the Bottle Man asked my ear. "I'm roight *here!*"

"Emily," I sighed. "He's not *evil.*" I put on sunglasses. "Maybe trouble. Definitely annoying. But not evil."

"Oh, yes!" The Bottle Man brightened up. "Trouble! That I am!" He laughed his soup-can-full-of-rocks laugh. It was a pretty good laugh.

"He's changing you," Emily said.

I waved a hand over my head. "It'd be pretty damned odd if he didn't."

"Em, love," the Bottle Man cooed. "Come out with us tonight. We're havin' deadly fun."

"I'm not going out again tonight," I said.

"Ahh, Jess! Don't be all like dat again!" he said with a little squeeze.

I pointed up the stairs. "If you want to hop onto Emily and have a night on the town with her, go for it. This lady taxi is staying in tonight."

"Leave me out of your... *situation.*" Emily huffed. She stomped inside and made sure the screen door slammed behind her.

"I've been trying!" I shouted.

"Lovely girl," the Bottle Man muttered. "She could shame paint off a barn."

My phone vibrated. Lumberjack boy had found my Instagram and liked a selfie from 2017. He was diving deep. Oh, God.

"Noight in," the Bottle Man groused. "Only had two hunnerd yearsa *those.*"

I sipped water from my mug. The ice had melted before we'd even sat down. "Go cry dirt."

———

I lay in bed, the Bottle Man's skull nestled in a valley between the two pillows under me. "Can we look at innernet now?" his muffled voice asked. I told him we were offline for the night. I explained what 'quiet time' meant. When he protested, I told him he smelled like moss and he thanked me for the compliment. I turned on my lamp and opened a John McPhee book. The Bottle Man jabbered about all his old underground friends. His jaw clacked in my ear. It was soothing in it's own weird way. Soon enough he wriggled his head onto a pillow and rested his cheekbone against mine. He contemplated the pages of my book with his thick gaze. Quiet time.

———

Thunder cracked and my eyes were open. The open book hovered above me, held aloft by the Bottle Man. Outside, rain rattled off the vinyl siding, inundating the valley. The heatwave had broken.

"What time is it?" I croaked.

"Midnight sometin'," he said, turning the page.

"I was reading. I fell asleep."

"That you did. And what a book you're missing! I mean, of all the drop dead boring subjects, the man makes fruit interestin'. *Fruit,* Jess!"

"Mmmm," I nodded, dry mouthed. I rolled out of bed and felt my way down the shadowy hallway. I stood in the dark bathroom and drank tap water from a Burger King glass while fat raindrops smacked against the window. I pictured the landfill holes filling with rain, overflowing, sending a cascade of muddy junk down the hillside and into the gulley. What else was buried out there? Who else?

"Oranges, Jess! Of all the things!" the Bottle Man called from the bedroom.

"Mmm." I blerped some hand lotion into my palm and massaged my neck and shoulders. A hundred-year heatwave, over. *Thank Jaysus.* I leaned against the windowsill and wondered what'll happen to him when the leaves change. A flash of lightning lit up rooftops across the neighborhood. I yawned, following the slant of lamplight down the hallway and back to bed.

●

Dead Mall
CIRCUIT CIRCUS
STEREO
VCR • CABLE
DOLLAR-ALL
TEE STOP
Wicker Solutions

DEAD MALL

A week before the cat replaces me, I drive towards the mall, merging onto the on-ramp that connects to the connector that connects to the highway. I ease my Cutlass into the left lane, rocking like a row boat on tired springs, the accelerator pressed to the floor to negligible effect. I cross the Mass./N.H. border and feel I've left something behind, but I don't know what. The new mall emerges from behind the leafless tree line along the highway, a modern multi-level edifice of glass and commerce, so big they gave it its own off-ramp. This is not my destination.

The Granite Mall sinks into its crumbling parking lot just across Route 28, a Bradlees anchoring one end and an Ames dragging down the other. In between, mom-and-pop stores and empty storefronts fill its dim indoor boulevard. The medium-sized corporate chains jumped ship last year, lured by the new mall's shiny promise of customers and functioning restrooms. But my store perseveres here, so I do, too. This place has been my destination since I was a kid, back when there was a Tape World and an arcade and more food choices than pizza and the snack aisle at CVS. This mall courses through my veins (and lungs, too, if you count the asbestos and lead paint dust).

This is my mall.

The dead mall.

———

I don't know how I got talked into catsitting, but I did. Well, I mean, okay, I know how. Rachel asked me and I said yes. She caught me off guard. Kneeling in the dark Dollar-All, I try to replay the scene while cursing the Gods of Security Gates. The store's latch is jammed again. Third time this month.

"Bergeron! Mall opens in eight minutes," Bill Docks calls through the gate, chewing gum like it's his fucking job. His actual job is salesman at the Circuit Circus next door. He loves sales. That says a lot about a person, I think.

"I know, Bill."

"They'll fine ya if ya don't have your gate up on time, Mattyboy," Bill says, smoothing his tie. "Gary'll have your balls on a pike if you guys get fined again."

"Sure." Gary wasn't really a ball-piker type of boss. His management style tended to revolve around sarcastic passive-aggressiveness.

Bill leans against the gate, arms folded, leering at a Bradlee's girl jogging towards her time clock. "God, I'd love to dip my wick in that."

I kick at the latch. "Jesus, Bill. She's like, sixteen."

"If there's grass on the field…" Bill says, miming a golf swing for some goddamned reason. Bill Docks is every asshole I avoided in high school, swear to God. Ten years older and somehow stupider.

Last night's mall-closing conversation with Rachel had been about an audition she'd gone on. We stood in the back parking lot as she described the plot of a TV pilot—a Chicago police drama filming in Toronto. She got a callback, had to leave town for a few days, and needed someone to watch her cat. Course I volunteered. I don't know jack shit about cats. They sleep a lot, right?

"Where's your girlfriend?" Bill gestures towards the shuttered Tee Stop kiosk near the mall fountain: a cart weighed down with Co-Ed Naked Rugby hoodies, generic Class Of '92 sweatshirts, Rawk Dawg Street Wear, bootleg Budweiser frog t-shirts. This is where Rachel works (or at least sits in a director's chair reading magazines).

"Packing for Toronto and she's not my—"

"No shit she's not."

"Fuck off, Bill." I focus on the latch.

"When I said 'grass' before, I meant bush," Bill murmurs. "And when I said 'wick' I meant my cock." He holds up a fist. His voice drops an octave. "The Sledgehammer!" He beholds his forearm from multiple views, adoring it like an idol, a monolith, an awesome tower disappearing into the clouds. "*Whoahhh!*"

"Fuck off, Bill."

"Two minutes," he grins, his teeth whistling on the *S*. He taps his wristwatch. "Tick-tock."

———

"How much is this?" a woman calls down the aisle. She holds a spatula over her head.

"Everything'sadollar," I say, my syllables collapsed from overuse. I slouch behind the counter, my head hanging over a book, only three hours into my shift. Dollar All is a real dollar store—not "99 cents," not "Items Starting At

A Dollar"—perched on the tax-free side of the Mass/NH border. There are seventeen signs in this slatwalled room that clearly communicate that items cost one dollar each, yet I still answer the question six to one thousand times per shift.

The woman arches an eyebrow. "Really?" I picture her walking into Tire Warehouse and asking if they sell tires.

"Yes, ma'am."

She turns on the heel of her flip-flop as if awoken from a trance, truly seeing the wrapping paper and cleaning supplies and Virgin Mary night lights for the first time. The veil of consumer indifference falls from her eyes, and a hidden world of bargains reveals itself. A shopping basket levitates off the stack and into her waiting hand. We live in a time of magic and abundance. Unseen forces propel her towards the back of the store.

Sean shuffles into the store and dumps his backpack behind the counter. "Sup."

"You're late?"

He waves a hand.

"Housewares needs to be restocked."

"Yeah." Sean points his chin towards the back room, the back corridor, the fire exit, the loading zone next to the dumpster in parking lot B. "Gonna grab a smoke first."

"Sure," I nod, as if he's asked permission and I've graciously granted it. Sean is a high school senior, ready to bail on this job in a few months. Hard to shift-manage that. He's already walking away, kicking a stray toy football down the aisle.

"You could pick that up," I call after him.

He punts the ball over the potpourri section, fists raised in triumph. "*Hwaaaahhh!*" he exhales in approximation of a stadium crowd roar. I lean against the cash register and sigh, my upper torso suddenly too much burden to bear. I'm exhausted from doing nothing. I feel half gone, the rest of me dead or asleep or still in Massachusetts.

———

I'm startled by a sing-song voice. *"Heyy Maaatt,"* Lisa DeMoulas emerges from the back room. "Howah sales?" she asks. I shrug. Lisa is our regional manager, a lofty title considering she spends the bulk of her time hauling overstock around in her VW and buying replacement belts for battered store vacuum cleaners. She reaches past me and turns the register key. The old TEC rattles out a two foot sales report with a pink stripe smeared across it. "Lissen," she says, absorbing the dismal numbers. "I got some news."

"What's up."

She absently folds the X-report. "Gary no longer works for the company."

"What?"

"We spoke last night. He's out."

"What? What happened?"

"I'm not at libitty to discuss personnel matters." She gets like this sometimes—all business-y and adult-y. Too business-y and adult-y for a dollar store chain. "I tawked with Richard at corporate. I'm going to take ovah the rest of Gary's shifts fah this week while we sort out what to do."

"Fuck."

"Watchyamouth."

Sean strolls into the store from a twenty minute meander, a pen cap clenched between his teeth. He tucks scratch tickets into his jeans pocket. "Hey, Leese."

"Why ah the Chrissmas boxes still in the back room?" she asks him.

"You want 'em out?"

"It's Novembah. Ya think, genius?"

Sean grins. "How the hell should I know, Leese?"

She spins the boy by his shoulders and points him towards the back room. "Chrissmas. Front end caps. Go!" she says. "Fah chrissake!"

"Sure, Leese."

"And take that thing outta your mouth!"

He holds the mangled pen cap up as he retreats. "I have an oral fixation, ma'am."

"Don't you *dayuh* with the ma'am!" She turns to me. "I'm gonna murdah him."

"But we need him to close Thursday."

"Listen, Matt. Ah you interested in the manager position?"

"Me?" I laugh. I've been a shift manager for a year, but the notion still strikes me as weird. Bosses are adults. I'm… *What am I?*

"Think about it," Lisa says. "It'd be a good oppahtunity for you. And it'd make my life a heck of a lot easier."

I think of my two and a half years at Dollar All. I think of Gary and the two store managers that preceded him, Denise and Ray. Three of the most bitter, depressed people I've ever met. "It seems like managers end up miserable."

"You could use the money," she says, tugging at my flannel sleeve. "This could be good for you. Think about it, kay?"

"Sure, Leese."

"Change the registah tape."

"Sure, Leese."

"And seriously, tell Sean to stop chewing on pen caps in the stoah. It's friggin' gross."

———

Empty store, empty mall. The Cranberries' "Linger" echoes on the mall tape loop (during an eight hour shift I'll hear it three times. It's not a very long loop). I return from CVS with my dinner, a Table Talk apple pie and a chocolate milk. Sean kneels on the floor, cramming VHS copies of *Shazaam* into our entertainment section. "Just missed Rachel," he says.

"What? I was gone three fucking minutes!" I gesture towards the mall with the pie.

"She was in a hurry. Had to catch a bus or something."

My shoulders droop. "The fuck."

"I got a nice hug. She said it was for you." He beckons me with open arms. "C'mere, camper. Come get it."

I flip him off and peer behind the counter. "Where's the cat?"

"Back room."

"Did she leave any instructions?"

"Nah. Didn't she give you instructions?"

"*Fuuuuuuck!*" I shout, stretching the cuss into several syllables, synchronized to the rhythm of my stomping All-Stars.

"He's a big boy," Sean mumbles around the pen cap.

———

The cat sits at the battered back room desk, paws resting on the stained blotter calendar that serves as our shift schedule. Wide-shouldered and man-sized, he stands and assesses me, gaze like a lighthouse.

"Matthew Bergeron," the cat says with a small bow. "I understand you are to be my host for a period of time."

"You're…"

"Yes."

"…a big boy. What's your, uh, name?"

"A terrible thing. An unspeakable thing, Matthew."

My head feels numb, bouncing at the end of a balloon string. "No one calls me Matthew," I whisper.

"I shall call you Host then."

"It'd, uh… It'd be easier if I knew your name."

The cat slides over the desk and moves towards me, walking upright like a human, but most definitely not like a human. "Often things are not easy, and perhaps it is better they are not," the cat says. His large paw envelops my hand. My handshake is indecisive. Yielding. The cat's claws leave dimples along the edge of my palm.

I look around the room, hoping this unreality will disappear if I avert my eyes. Boxes of blank cassettes, a dot matrix printer under a dust cover, a human-sized talking cat. *Guess not.* "You have any stuff?" I ask. "A pet carrier or something?"

"If I did, who in the world would *carry* it?" The cat booms laughter, wide-mouthed and bassy, a tuba player toppling over a cruise ship railing into a black sea.

———

The cat stares out the windshield, his wall-eyed gaze seeming to see nothing and everything. The tape deck died last summer and the silence is excruciating.

"So, uh, how's Rachel as an owner?"

"I dislike the term *owner.*"

I nod. "Sure, well—"

"She purchases poor quality food."

I nod again. "That's your full assessment?"

"She is often gassy."

I keep nodding. Seems like the best course of action. I'll just keep nodding til it makes sense.

"Host." The cat gestures towards the dashboard. "Your Check Oil indicator is aglow."

"It comes on every once in awhile, no big deal." I pat the steering wheel. "She runs fine."

The cat laces his paws together. "Stewardship is a concept many young adults fail to understand."

"What?"

The cat falls silent once again. I struggle to fill the passenger compartment with words. "So, I've got a basement apartment at my parents'," I say. "Lotsa space, a couple of windows. You'll like hanging out there."

"I *adore* hanging out," the cat says, each word punctuated with distaste. "They say hanging out is a deeply fulfilling experience."

"Okay."

"Why, I recall many a passage from a Churchill biography where the British Bulldog himself was quoted as saying as much."

"I—"

"*We shall hang out to the end! We shall hang out in our pajamas! We shall hang out with the Sega and the Nintendo, we shall hang out with growing piles of dirty laundry and growing stench in the air! We shall hang out in our basement apartment, whatever the rent may b—*"

"All *right!*"

The cat laughs, his head split open at the equator, the top of his giant skull bouncing against the head rest. The door panels buzz and rattle at his booming guffaw. "Some friendly ribbing. I have altered the words to dear Winnie's Finest Hour speech." He rotates his head towards me like an anti-aircraft cannon. "Though he was unquestionably a great man, he knew nothing of your home gaming systems."

––––––––

"Good morning, Host. Would you like a cup of coffee?" My guest stands in a weird spot in my family's kitchen, only in the sense that no one has ever stood precisely *there*. The cat has liberated one of my button-up shirts and a pair of corduroys from my closet. How my clothes conform to the creature's wide frame muddles my extra-foggy morning brain. I didn't get much sleep while being observed by the shadowy monster crouched atop my dresser, his hell-eyes seemingly lit from within.

"What," I croak.

The cat offers me a coffee mug. Flowery green ceramic from the cupboard. It unsettles me to see his giant brown paw wrapped around such a familiar object from my home. I can't articulate why, or much else. I shake my head. "I'll stop at Dunkin on the way in."

"You could save upwards of twelve dollars a week if you prepared coffee at home," he says, gesturing towards my parents' Mr. Coffee. "I ran a vinegar solution through it and gave it a rigorous scrubbing. This machine delivers an acceptable 'cup of joe' when properly maintained." I rub my eyes, refusing to acknowledge his clawed air quotes, and accept the mug. "We're going to be late, Host."

"You're not coming to work with me," I say, sipping coffee.

The cat smiles, a couple hundred thousand teeth lining his jaw. "You should get dressed."

I pinch my t-shirt's wrinkled collar. "I *am* dressed."

"You should get dressed."

Mr. Coffee gurgles and hisses. I hate to admit it, but it's a decent cup of joe.

———

I retreat to the aisle furthest from the register and contemplate the steps required to cram a case of spoon racks into the overfilled shelves. The cat stands behind the counter, as unsettling as a display cadaver. On the mall tape loop: "I'll Be There" by Mariah Carey.

I call over the bins. "Could you like, go lay down in the back room or something?"

"I find the retail environment scintillating, Host," the cat says, caressing the counter. "One should seize the opportunity to interact with the public, should one not? Community-building! Networking! Who knows who one might encounter. Every day offers opportunity." I sneak a glance over a row of shampoo bottles. The cat lint-rolls his shirt. Well, my shirt.

"Good morning!" the cat beams at a high school girl. "Welcome to Dollar-All! May I help you find a particular product or products?"

She snaps her gum. "You have hair scrunchies?"

"Of course! Host?" he calls. "Could you please show this young lady to the hair product section?"

I raise my head above the bins and point across the store. "Back wall on the left. Stop calling me that."

"Host," the cat blinks. "Could you please show this young lady to the hair product section."

They both stare at me.

"Yeahsurethisway."

An old dude with a rheumy eye approaches the counter holding two packages of non-alkaline batteries. "How much ah these?" he asks the cat. "Theah's no price tags."

"Well," the cat says brightly. "Each item in this store costs one dollar." Lisa walks in, balancing her travel mug on top of a bundle of plastic bags. She frowns at the cat behind the counter. "Those two packages of batteries will cost you a total of two dollars even," he tells the man.

"Well, I'll be," the man says.

"We'll all be," the cat agrees.

I hurry down the aisle, palms raised. "Lisa! Hey, sorry. This is Rachel's—"

"Host," the cat says. "Could you please ring up this battery purchase? I am not authorized to transact on this cash drawer." I slide behind the register as the cat relieves Lisa of the bags. "Lisa DeMoulas, I presume," the cat says. "I was in the back room earlier admiring your monthly reports."

I stuff the batteries into a bag and mumble dollar amounts at the customer.

"Uh, hello," Lisa says, shaking hands with the towering animal. "And you ah...?"

"My name is Puddin' Paws," he says.

"BAAH!" I bark. "Seriously?"

"A child's offhand comment on my colorful markings memorialized for all time," the cat says, licking his paw. "While a name can be a burden, I find it best to examine feelings of shame and learn from them. Wouldn't you agree, Host?"

I cup my hand to my ear. "What's that, Pudd?"

Lisa whacks me in the arm. "It's very nice to meet you," she says to the cat. "And I think yoah paws are lovely."

The cat takes her hand. "You are gracious to say that, Lisa."

"Is theah a name you'd prefer to be called?"

Puddin' Paws pauses to consider this. "Why, no one has ever proposed that to me before. What a charming notion."

"Shitfoot?" I offer helpfully, handing battery man his receipt.

"I have always been fond," he says over me. "of the name Matthew."

"That's my name!"

"No one calls you Matthew," the cat and Lisa reply in unison. Lisa laughs.

"It's very nice to meet you, Matthew." Lisa says, shaking his paw again.

"I feel insane," I say. Lisa and the cat step away, deep in conversation. The girl returns with a pack of scrunchies.

"How much is this?" she asks.

Matt Bergeron, Discount Retail Professional, answers The Question.

———

Bill drifts into the store whistling "Camptown Races," because who the fuck else would do that. "How's biz?" he asks. I don't care and Bill doesn't care, either. We both know Bill only wants to talk about Bill. I drop my paperback on the counter and wait. "Just sold a stereo system to a senile old hag," he says. He does a little fist pump jab thing. "You gotta get out of this shithole. Commission's where it's at, baby."

"I dunno, I—"

The cat returns from an errand. "Host. Did you know Bradlees has some smart loafers in their shoe department?" He holds up a shoebox. "Your colored canvas sneakers are not appropriate for work. The employee manual states—"

"There's an employee manual?" I ask.

The cat eyes Bill critically. "Who are you?"

Bill slips a business card out of his shirt pocket. "Bill Docks from Circuit Circus—"

"The cash register area needs to be available to our customers." The cat makes wide circular gestures with his paws.

"There aren't any customers, kemosabe," Bill cackles, waving at the empty store.

"Please attend to your retail duties next door." The cat tucks the shoebox under his arm and withdraws to the back room.

"The fuck just happened?" Bill asks.

"That's Rachel's c—"

"Hold on," Bill says, squinting. He laces his fingers into a pistol shape and points it towards the buzzing fluorescents. "The name's Bomb," he says in a bad Sean Connery voice. He aims his pretend Walther PPK at me, lifts his leg, and rips a loud, subtropical fart. "James Bomb."

Gross Dude humor has always eluded me. What am I supposed to do? Laugh? Emote disgust? High five? All the above? I settle for a flat "Nice." Just then a woman steps up to the register with a shopping basket full of peppermint incense. Her face collapses in revulsion. The flowers on her dress wither and die. The Christmas display bursts into flames.

"Oh, *Matt!*" Bill accuses. He strides out of the store, mock-indignant. *"Come on!"* echoes down the mall.

To the woman: "I am so, so sorry."

On the tape loop: Madonna's "This Used To Be My Playground."

———

I kneel on the colorless carpet, condensing a bin of L-shaped metal brackets that have been on clearance longer than I've worked here. I have no idea what they're for. No one has ever bought one.

My old manager calls down the aisle. "Hey-o! Checks come in?"

"Gary!"

He is spiffed up—mustache trimmed, pressed shirt, a too-new Celtics hat balanced precariously over his bald spot. "Did they offer you my old job?" he asks. Gary is a lisper, a word-musher, a speed-unenunciator. The question comes out of his mouth a lot like *Dthofferymoljob?*

"Yeah," I say, sifting through the paycheck envelopes under the cash register's always-empty change tray. "I said no. I don't want to be a manager."

"Well, of *course* you don't!" Gary spit-laughs. "Nobody does! But you've got to take the job!"

"But I—"

My former boss puts a hand on my shoulder and cranks up his Wise Elder voice. "Listen, Matt. We're Americans. We live in America. You move up at your job if they let you. That's how things work. You're not allowed to tread water." He dog-paddles the air. "You move up, hating each level more than the last, until you're used up or you snap, and then you quit." Out of habit, he straightens the display of lighters next to the register. "Or you end up VP of Sales or something."

"What happened with you, man?" I ask, handing him his final paycheck. "Jan at Wicker Solutions said she saw you over at the new mall."

"I got scouted. There are new stores opening left and right over there. They've been poaching management from stores up and down 28. I'm managing Cool Lidz now."

"The hat place?"

Gary points at his hat with both hands. "Yes, Matt. The hat place."

"At the new mall?"

"I know, I know," Gary laughs.

"You *hate* that place. You called them zombies once."

"Sure, sure. But that was when I was in *this* shithole. Jaded underdog, et cetera. But I'm one of *them* now." He bares his teeth and holds his arms out stiffly, *Thriller* video style, and laughs at his own joke. "Seriously, though. The pay's better and the customers are quantifiably less trashy."

"Unbelievable," I mutter. *Gary at the new mall. What the ever-living fuck.*

He leans in. "Umm, and have I mentioned Cool Lidz is across from Frederick's Of Hollywood?" He removes his cool lid and wipes pretend sweat from his brow, as if sexual arousal has caused him to perspire. "Oh, mama!"

I'm dead inside and the world is a garbage heap and the universe is indifferent. "Oh, mama," I nod.

The cat pokes his giant head out of the back room. "Host, I cannot seem to locate the dustpan."

"We don't have a dustpan," I say.

"There are spider webs behind the computer. A workplace should reflect—"

"LEAVE IT ALONE!"

The door shuts. "New guy?" Gary asks.

"He doesn't even work here."

Gary arches an eyebrow. "Listen, I could get you into Cool Lidz if you wanted."

"I wish you'd stop saying 'Cool Lidz.' I can hear you pronouncing the Z."

Gary narrows his eyes and smiles. "You want a job or what?"

"I don't know anything about hats."

Gary frowns. "What does that even *mean?*"

The cat opens the back room door again. "Host! I am going to mop the employee area floor."

I stab the air with my finger. "Dontyoufuckin*dare.*"

"It is apparent it has never been properly cleaned," the cat says, retreating.

"Better watch it or someone'll poach that guy right out from under you," Gary says.

"Fine with me," I say. "SINCE HE DOESN'T EVEN WORK HERE!" The door shuts again.

"So," Gary continues. "Cool Lidz?"

"Ol' shift manager Matt is fine right here."

"No one's fine here, Matt. Believe me. This store is a sinking ship. This *mall* is a sinking ship." He grabs my shoulders. *"You're on a sinking ship inside another sinking ship."*

"I'm fine."

Gary sighs. "I gotta get back." He salutes with the envelope. "Seriously though: if you don't want Cool Lidz, take the manager position here. You're smart enough to hate it and responsible enough to do a decent job. Ride it out and get transferred to Plaistow when Granite Mall gets bulldozed, which it definitely will." He shakes my hand.

"It feels like a trap."

"Oh, it's definitely a trap."

———

Night shift, two hours 'til close. In the freshly-mopped employee area, Sean performs box cutter surgery on a pack of glow sticks.

"You're gonna get cancer or radiation or something," I say, leaning in the doorway. I keep tabs on our lone customer, an elderly woman perusing the ceramic figurine display. Sean giggles and pours yellowy-green liquid into a coffee mug. "Hey! I use that mug!"

"You're *fiiiine*," Sean assures me, another pen cap clacking between his teeth.

"Whaddaya gonna do with that anyway?"

Sean motions across the room. "If we chuck this at the wall and turn off the lights, it'll look like a million stars in here! It'll be awesome!" I give him a noncommittal thumbs up.

The woman sets her walker aside and studies the figurines. Little songbirds, playful puppies, little John The Baptist busts (not a Jesus, Mary, or Joseph in the bunch). She's been standing there too long, killing time, eyes resolutely forward. I sigh, too familiar with the scenario. I fake a cough, an unsubtle reminder that I, an employee of this retail establishment, am present and within visual range. She lifts a bluebird off the shelf and cradles it in her palm. *Don't do it,* I think. *It's only a dollar. A friggin' dollar. Cammannn.* She looks down at the floor. I sigh again, louder.

"Sup?" Sean says, busy with his astronomy project.

The woman slips a used tissue out of her sweater sleeve and wraps it around the bluebird. She drops it into her walker basket and makes a slow-motion break for it.

"Shoplifter," I say, rubbing my eyes.

"Blue sweater lady?"

"Yeah."

Sean nods and decapitates another glow stick. "She pulled a heist on Tuesday, too."

I watch her wrestle the walker's tennis-balled feet over the gate threshold and shuffle into the mall. "I'm not calling security on a goddamned old lady over a hundred goddamned pennies."

"Sure." Sean swishes the mug around and peers inside. "How's catsitting going?" he says into the cup.

"Jesus, I dunno." I push my fingers into my eye sockets and turn away from the empty store. "He's stretching out all my clothes."

Sean silently laughs, his exhales whistling through a hole in the pen cap. "Where's he now?"

"He went to the Ground Round with Lisa."

"What?"

"Karaoke, I think."

This cracks Sean up. "Like a *date?*" He's shaking with laughter, glow in the dark shit spilling all over the desk blotter. It occurs to me that maybe Sean is high a lot.

"I don't want to talk about the goddamned cat," I grumble.

Sean wipes his eyes. "Kill the fuckin' lights, man."

———

I walk through the mall alone this morning—the cat had an errand to run. I'd gladly dropped him off at the Men's Wearhouse a few plazas over. Why, for what, I did not care to know. I drag my Converse through the dim mall, circling around the fountain mall management shut off two days ago. Fifteen minutes before open, I find Dollar-All lit up, security gate half-raised. *Did I fuck up my schedule?* "Hey!" I call, crouching under the gate.

"It's just me," Lisa replies, emerging from the back room carrying a stack of foamcore signs. Her keys dangle from a plastic thing coiled around her forearm. "Lawt to do today."

I ball up my trenchcoat and drop it on the stool. "I thought you were closing tonight."

She releases a melodramatic sigh and puts on her business voice: "The Dollar-All Granite Mall location will be closing next week. We're gonna have a big liquidation sale to move old stock." She holds up a sign. ALL ITEMS 3 FOR $1, bold red on white.

"Whoa, holy shit."

"Then we're packing up the fixtures and moving to a space at the new mall."

"What?"

Lisa nods. "This is coming from Richard at corporate. This stoah is underperforming. He feels it's smarter to break the lease here and move now rather than wait for the wrecking ball to take this place down."

I shake my head. "A *dollar store?* At the *new mall?*"

"Richard also feels that this store's underperformance is due to a void in leadership."

I nod. "Sure. Gary quit."

"Yes." She shifts her weight from one leg to the other.

"And you've been filling in," I add.

"But I'm from corporate," she says. "You're the senior store employee."

I frown. "What are we talking about?"

She does the big sigh thing again. "This will be your last week. You won't be moving with us to the new location."

"Whoa, you're *firing* me? Am I getting *canned?*"

"I'm sorry, Matt. Richard wants a clean slate over at the new location."

"Who's gonna run the new store? You?"

"I've hired Matthew."

"The cat? You gave my job to a *cat?*"

"Well, it wasn't your job. You turned it d—"

"This is unbelievable!" I act indignant, though I don't think I actually *feel* indignant. It just seems like the proper response to this sort of situation. "Un-fucking-*believable!*"

"I really am sorry, Matt. We were hoping you'd step up."

"No one told me I was supposed to step up," I say.

She rubs my forearm. "Sweetie, that's what stepping up is."

———

I lean against the Circuit Circus display case. Microcassette recorders, camcorders, police scanners. I chew on a Table Talk pie while a *Star Wars* laserdisc plays on the big projection TV.

"Whelp," Bill says, whistling low. "Everyone saw *that* coming."

"*I* didn't," I sulk.

"Circuit Circus is probably gonna bail in the next coupla months, too. Granite Mall's done with. Kaput." He points at the TV. "Look at that fucking picture quality. Twice as good as VHS. Whadda you got for an entertainment system?"

"It's not that I *like* this place," I explain. "I mean, it's a shithole, I get that. But at least it's…" I search for the right word. "Real."

"You're better off. I keep telling you retail wage is for chumps. You should get into commission."

"Here?"

Bill paces a slow circle and counts off the pros on his fingers. "Hang out with bros, watch *Star Wars* all day, make money selling people things they actually want…" The subwoofer rumbles as a TIE fighter howls past.

"Yeah?"

Bill squints his eyes and adopts his Ancient Chinese Wisdom voice. "Evvytime a daww cwose, a window aowpen."

"I'll think about it," I mumble.

"Attaboy," Bill chirps, clamping a hand on my shoulder. "If you want to apply, you come talk to me." He waves a finger in my face. "Don't talk to Steve. I get a bonus for application referrals."

"Sure."

"Great." He slaps me on the back and dances towards the Circuit Circus stock room. "Perfecto," he calls. "Perrrrr. Fect. Oooooooo."

"Linger" plays on the tape loop.

———

The rusted emergency exit door shrieks as I shoulder it open. A light snow dances around the dumpsters in the back parking lot. Wrapping my trench coat around me, I hustle towards my car. Matthew stands next to it, wearing a blue suit.

"New duds," I say.

"I believe managers should dress appropriately," the cat says. "It sets an example for employees."

"Congratulations, I guess."

"Thank you. That is kind of you to say."

I circle around the cat and unlock my door, nodding towards the cracked cinderblock building. "You closing tonight?"

"Yes." The cat holds up three gleaming keys on a key ring. Back door, cash register, security gate.

"Gate's sticky."

"I've made a morning appointment with a locksmith."

I nod. "Can Leese give you a lift home?"

"I will not be requiring any further 'lifts' from you." The cat gestures towards the car parked next to my Cutlass, a newish tan Mercury Mystique.

"That's *yours?*" I ask, leaning on my Oldsmobile's snow-dusted roof. "You bought a *car?*"

"I applied for an auto loan. It is what adults do." I pick at the edge of my car's faded vinyl top, fourteen New England winters worse for wear, and say nothing. "We had high hopes for you, Matt Bergeron."

"Oh, no more 'Host' huh?"

"You are no longer a host. You weren't much of one in the first place." I grunt and drop into the cold driver's seat, one foot still on the asphalt. "I won't be staying with you tonight," the cat says, circling around the front of the car. "I will be staying at Lisa's."

"What should I tell Rachel when she gets back?"

The cat leans in close, preventing me from shutting the door. "Tell her what you should have told her months ago. It likely will not matter because it is likely too late, but perhaps it would do you some good to try and fail."

"Wow, okay."

"Wow," he says, stepping back. "Okay."

I yank the door shut and force my numb fingers to sort through my keychain. The cat stares at me, morning light catching flecks of blue and gold and green in his giant orbs. I jam the key into the stubborn ignition. A dry scrape. Matthew is still there in my periphery, the wind tugging at his suit collar. I pump the gas pedal and turn the key. The starter pops like a pistol shot. The Check Oil indicator is aglow.

●

MIND THE GAP   A Tuesday Of Triumph and Discovery
MIND THE GAP   Three Hours Of Tuesdays   COX
MIND THE GAP   A Tues-Dimensional Adventure   Jeffrey Cox   SF
Novel
MIND
THE
GAP
S4482   2   SCIENCE-FICTION   MIND THE GAP: An Infinite Tuesday   JEFF COX   553 02112 125
303 K   MIND THE GAP   NOW A MAJOR MOTION PICTURE   THE NULL
NOVEL   MIND THE GAP   A Tuesday Of Triumphs and Discovery   DANIELS   0-553-13104-5
4266   6   FICTION   MIND THE GAP   TOM PAPPAI   Mythology

MIND THE GAP

PART ONE: TUESDAY

It's the end of an endless Tuesday. Jeff Cox lies curled on his living room floor, deeply regretting the Kung Pao chicken he ordered for lunch. He drags the comforter off the couch and rolls himself into a cocoon. Kicking at the carpet with his beat-up slippers, he burps and mumbles a *'scuse me* to no one.

Jeff gropes blindly across his cluttered coffee table, knocking over a Boba Fett figurine and a stack of unread books before his fingertips find the remote control. He turns on the TV. It's an old episode of *King of Queens* (a show he truly despises, but the noise helps him sleep). He lowers the volume and closes his eyes. Jeff Cox bids Tuesday good riddance. He dreams Kung Pao dreams.

———

Jeff hears a woman laugh. He is upright and alert in an instant. *Was I asleep? Am I awake? Did I dream I heard something?* The memory of it fades.

His apartment is dark, except for the constellation of standby lights from electronics which are turned off, but not really. He listens: Television murmur, refrigerator hum, indistinct city sounds mumbling through the apartment walls. In front of the TV set (which has moved on to *Two And A Half Goddamned Men*), an impossible thing floats, emitting a bit of light. Jeff's mind tiptoes past it and chooses something easier to contemplate, like the time. He cranes his neck and squints at the clock on the kitchen stove. 9 p.m., half past 2019.

The part of his consciousness that isn't studiously ignoring the floating thing gives Jeff a nudge. He faces the rectangle of light floating above him. It has no edge, no depth. He tilts his head, eyeing the flatter-than-flat window. *Was that whispering?* A balloon drifts through the portal and bounces off his dusty ceiling fan. He's almost *positive* it isn't his birthday.

The balloon floats towards his bedroom. He's tempted to follow. Instead, Jeff rolls onto his side to get a better look through the portal-to-another-dimension thing, which is what this thing *must* be, because A) He's consumed plenty of science fiction and this is *extremely* General Zod-y, and B) He's looking into a room with three teenagers in it. They are wearing little paper birthday hats and weird, futuristic glasses.

PART TWO: TUESDAY

It's the end of an endless Tuesday. Theda's birthday party shuffles into decline. Her apartment—a source of jealousy among her less-employed coder friends—is littered with empty cups, computer hardware, and wine bottles. The cake on the kitchen island has been horribly disfigured. Candace, a girl she's been seeing for a few months, leans against the wall of glass overlooking the city, arms folded, cradling a Miller High Life. Tess drunkenly babbles at her about corporate security protocols, forgetting she's an outsider, not part of the crew that cracks databases for fun. In the kitchen, Dot and Huck flirt (well, their version of flirting). The boy attempts a Humphrey Bogart voice, whispering something filthy in his girlfriend's ear. It's a terrible impersonation but she howls in laughter anyway, her dimples stretched to their limits.

Theda sits splayed across her couch, wearing a sequined party dress she'd found at a thrift store, frowning at a column of code on her dev's heads-up display. She balances a wine glass on her knee and edits a subroutine in a window labeled **PORT V1.34**. Her dev projects a floating rectangle of video over the cluttered coffee table.

"—and so ends the eighth inning of the 2069 World Series," the sportscaster announces in her dev's earpiece. Theda ignores the game because sports are stupid. She types a few commands and presses a button on the side of her glasses, a modified Telegony devnet interface. It's a high-end piece of hardware, a present to herself for crashing the BankHub network while their security chief gaped over her shoulder. Sometimes white-hat stuff can be fun like that. It also pays the bills and funds darker headgear projects like PORT. She digs deeper into the firmware.

"More cake, birthday gal?" Candace asks. She pushes aside a tangle of charging cables and a bowl of potato chip remnants and places a piece of cake on the coffee table.

"Mmmm," Theda replies. She scraps a block of code and spends a minute rewriting it. At the command line, she types **PORT -1** and reloads the baseball game broadcast. The same sportscaster appears on the floating screen, his hair style and suit different than in the previous clip. Candace tucks herself between Theda and the armrest. The crawl along the bottom of the screen shows the score from the 2068 World Series.

Theda confirms the clip's time stamp and grins.

"Is this your video hack?" Candace asks. "Did you get it working?"

Theda scrolls through an archive directory and loads a soap opera broadcast from 2033. A blue screen floats above her cake. **Signal Not Found.** "If half-working counts as working, then yes."

"MediaCorp's gonna send their friggin' goon squad through that door," Huck warns from the haze-filled kitchen. He exhales a cloud of smoke, his eyes watering. "*Who's taking our fuckin' teevee shows!*" he bellows, marching in place. Dot sits on the counter, kicking her legs and laughing.

"**Fuck 'em,**" Theda texts to their group chat, biting her thumbnail. "**& fuck their paywall.**" She pulls up the Telegony's schematics on her display, contemplating the mess of overlapping lines. She nods and rewrites another segment of code. She types **PORT -50** and selects a stupid-sounding sitcom from the broadcast archive.

Her dev projects a high-def image of a dark room. Theda pushes her wine glass into Candace's hand and leans forward. The layout of the room in the projection is identical to her apartment. When she shifts her view, the walls and doorways line up perfectly. There are old toys displayed on an end table and a poster that says *Firefly* on it. She tilts her head towards the kitchen, where Dot's yellow dress is redacted by a rectangle of dark shadow. Theda peers into the other living room. In the corner, a vintage TV plays a show she suspects is called *Two And A Half Men*.

Candace puts a hand on Theda's knee. "What is that?" she asks. "Some VR thing?"

Theda holds her fingers up to the projection. The air on the other side of the portal is warm against her hand. She jerks back with an exhilarated laugh.

And that's how Theda invents time travel. Happy birthday!

———

Theda types a string of commands and the portal enlarges to the size of a window. She pokes her head in to peruse the collection of strange old junk and notices the clump of blanket on the floor. Red slippers stick out the end. She sits back, hand over her mouth.

Tess wanders over. "What are we watching? Porn? Is it porn time?" She claps and sits cross legged on the floor. Huck wolf-howls from the kitchen.

Theda shushes everyone with an emphatic hand gesture. "**Sleeping dude!**" she texts the group. "**SLEEPING DUDE FROM—**" She consults the video feed's time stamp. "**—2019!**"

"**Buuuuuullshit,**" Huck texts with a turd emoji. He circles around the kitchen island with the last piece of cake and steps towards the portal. Theda intercepts him.

"**SLEEPING,**" she reiterates, staring him down with her cut-the-shit look. Huck raises a forkful of cake in surrender.

"Okay!" he whispers. "Jesus!" Her friends gather close and peek into the projection. Dark room. Buncha old stuff. Definitely a guy sleeping on the floor. Yup.

"**This is maze,**" Tess texts. Dot repeats the phrase with a big blinking arrow pointed at it.

"Hoshit," Candace whispers. "The fuck is this?" She drops back onto the couch. "What does this *mean?*"

Theda dismisses the question as overly philosophical. More practical questions loom larger in her mind, like *How does it work?* and *Did I just become a kajillionaire?*

"What does it *mean?*" Huck hisses, leaning close to Candace. "What does it MEAN?" He switches to the group text. "**IT MEANS WE ARE ABOUT TO UTTERLY DESTROY SOME SHIT.**" He dances a little jig around the coffee table. Theda eyerolls hard.

"Can we go in there?" Dot asks.

"I think you mean in then," Tess murmurs.

Theda dips her hand into the past again and shrugs. "I guess?" she texts.

"This is crazy," Candace protests. "What did you do?"

Huck kneels in front of Theda and rests his forehead against her dress. "**Theda,**" he texts. "**You are an all-powerful coding bitch-goddess. I bow to your superior dev skills.**"

She snorts, mildly embarrassed and vaguely flattered. She slaps him on the side of his head.

"Thank you for the blessing, goddess!"

"Cut the shit."

He looks up at her, fingers laced together. "**CODE!**" Huck pleads in the group chat. "**Share the fing COOODE!!!!!!!!**" He changes his status update to a looped graphic of a baby crying. "Pleeeeaaaassseee," he whispers.

Theda arches an eyebrow at Tess, who posts the old NIKE logo. Dot is giddy, miming tiny excited clapping. Candace stands. "Am I the only one freaked out about this?" she asks through her clenched jaw. "You don't just start fucking around with... with..."

"Time travel," Theda whispers.

Huck is on his feet again, hopping up and down. "**Time. Fucking. Trav. Ull,**" he texts. "**hoshithoshithoshit.**"

"**DON'T YOU PEOPLE WATCH MOVIES,**" Candace text-shouts. "**DON'T YOU READ BOOKS.**"

Theda stares into the middle distance, scrolling back through her code, trying to unravel what the hell she's done. "Who's ready to beta test?" She compiles PORT into an executable file and shares it to their group folder.

Dot runs the hack on her dev and opens a door-sized portal next to Theda's. Morning sun glints off the chrome legs of a 1950's-era kitchen table. "Vintage overload!" she swoons. She steps through the opening in time, mesmerized.

"Dot!" Theda hisses.

Dot pirouettes on the linoleum floor. A giant pot of meatballs burbles on the stove. "Can you smell it, Theda? It smells goddamned maze."

An old woman calls from down the hall. "Carla, are you back from the grocery?"

Candace stomps her foot. "**DOT GET BACK HERE,**" she texts. Dot's portal blinks shut.

Tess opens a portal and almost steps out into empty sky, circa 1919. She leans against the edge of the opening and peers down at the roofs of long-gone brick buildings. She sees Model Ts and horses navigating wide, muddy boulevards. A trolley car dings in the distance. "Ground floor," she says, turning to her friends. "We've got to get down to the ground floor." She dashes out of Theda's apartment, her thumping footfalls fading down the corridor.

———

Jeff squints at the teenagers in his living room time-window. "Hello?" he says too-loudly, as if they're on a video chat and not human beings standing five feet away from each other. "Excuse me! Hello?" He rakes his hair back. The kids spin around. Maybe they're more like 20-somethings.

"Hi!" Theda says.

"C'mon through!" Huck suggests. "It won't kill you or anything probably." Theda expands the portal to door-size.

Jeff tests the opening with an exploratory wave of his hand and steps across five decades. He looks around Theda's apartment, absently rubbing his stomach. "I'm Jeff Cox? I was in my living room?" he says, pointing at the portal. "Taking a nap?" Theda nods. "And. And what have you done to my apartment?" The girl's version of his apartment is completely remodeled: curved doorways, light panels built into the walls, a giant flat screen dominating the living room. It even appears to have slide-y *Star Trek* doors. The apartment is, for lack of a better word, futuristic. Once he fully wakes up, he's positive he's going to be excited as hell. At the moment he feels only confused. "Why are you wearing party hats?"

Theda pulls at the thin rubber band and tosses her cardboard hat in the chip bowl. "I need a sec." She steps over to the wall monitor and scrolls through her project folder, deep in thought.

"Hey, man," Huck says, shaking Jeff's hand. "Welcome to… uhhh…" He frowns and gestures towards the couch. "Have a seat." Jeff drops onto the foam cushion next to Candace.

"What's going on?" Jeff asks.

She takes a long swig from her beer bottle. "Theda just invented time travel."

"Really?"

Candace massages her temple and shrugs.

"We gotta post this, T," Huck insists. He opens a portal in the floor set to the year zero. Fourteen stories below, he sees the tops of pine trees swaying in the wind. Fresh air rises out of the opening. "Jesus, Theda, we gotta post this to the boards *right now*." He closes the portal. "They're gonna freak the fuck *out*."

"Let me *think*, god damn it!" Theda barks.

Jeff feels compelled to ask the stupid question that stupid characters from stupid science fiction movies always ask. He hates himself for it. He leans towards Candace and whispers "What year is this?" She ignores him.

"I've got a better idea," Theda says.

"Is this Earth?" Jeff asks anyone.

"Sell it to the corporations?" Huck asks. "You're gonna be rich-as-shit-rich!"

"Nah," Theda texts to the group chat. "Thinking bigger than that." She shares a link to a folder called TELBACKDOOR. Huck freezes.

Candace leaps to her feet. "NO!" she shouts. Jeff flinches, oblivious to half the conversation.

"Awww, *genius*!" Huck's eyes are alive with mischief.

"We cracked Telegony's customer service network weeks

ago," Theda says, circling around the portal to Jeff's apartment. "We've been waiting for a big idea. Here it is. We upload PORT as a critical firmware update."

"Everyone," Huck nods. "We give it to everyone."

"I think you've both lost your goddamned minds," Candace says.

Jeff raises a finger. "Sorry, just to be clear here," he says. "Are you in my apartment, or am I in yours? Because I'd really like you all to get out."

"This is double maze," Huck says. He grabs his backpack off the table and opens the front door. "Code Goddess, I leave that genius-level mischief to you. Tess had the right idea. I'm going downstairs to check out some shit up close." He salutes Jeff. "Sir, it was an honor to make first contact with you."

Jeff waves awkwardly. "I. Sure."

"I am off to explore the unimaginable," Huck announces. "Embark on an epic adventure. I. Am going. To ride. A dinosaur." He strides out the door.

"This is the best birthday ever!" Theda squeals, clapping her hands.

"Happy birthday," Jeff says, because that's a good thing to say. She throws her arms around him. As any other red-blooded American would do in this situation, he instinctively pulls his phone out and snaps a selfie. The photo captures Theda, grinning, delirious, teetering on the precipice of greatness. Jeff is hunched over, eyes half-closed as he smells her hair.

Theda grasps him by his shoulders. "This is going to be a beautiful mess," she whispers.

———

PORT spreads across the devnet. Theda assembles a grid on the living room video screen: news, tech reporters, and their friends' personal feeds. Tess's dev cam shows her POV on a Civil War battlefield. At least that's what it looks like to Jeff. Very PBSy, but scarier. She crouches behind a rock wall as something explodes. Huck's feed shows a lush jungle—too lush for the East Coast—his hands closing around a large, scale-covered egg in a nest of reeds. Text messages slide across the bottom of the screen at a rapid clip. Most of them include the word "awesome."

Across the top of the screen, Jeff reads the news chyron: TELEGONY CORP REPORTS MASSIVE SECURITY BREACH. ANONYMOUS HACKER GROUP RESPONSIBLE + UNCONFIRMED SIGHTING OF EXTINCT BUFFALO HERD IN DOWNTOWN NYC + CHICAGO MISSING.

"Are you seeing this?" he asks the girls. Theda concentrates on her dev, overwhelmed with messages from the hacker forums.

Candace leans against the arm of the couch, sipping her beer and staring at the monitor with a mixture of awe and dread. "Fucking mayhem," she mutters. She turns her back on the screen and stares out the window at the sleeping city.

Theda snorts. "You wanna try it?" she asks Jeff. She wrestles a spare dev free from the clump of wires on the coffee table and pushes it into his hands.

"I just got here," he says, but he puts them on anyway. A start up screen blocks his vision. TELEGONY SYSTEMS. WELCOME! FIRMWARE UPDATED. SEARCHING FOR NETWORKS. The screen clears. Headlines crawl along the bottom of his peripheral vision. In the upper corner: time, temperature, search icon. Wherever he looks, the dev responds to his gaze with a floating menu of options. He thinks it's pretty cool so he says "Pretty cool."

Across the room, a thing that has no business catching his attention catches his attention. Jeff scowls at the light switch near Theda's front door. It's about as interesting as any other light switch. Plastic, beige, two screws. *Wasn't there a cool sci-fi control panel thing there when I came in?*

The control panel reappears. Just like that.

"Are you seeing this?" he asks again. Candace doesn't turn around. Theda cracks up as Dot photobombs Martin Luther King's "I Have A Dream" speech on the big monitor. Her feed is a split view, her dev's live color footage synced to the historic black and white television broadcast. Her POV shows King's back and the immense audience surrounding the Lincoln Memorial reflecting pool. In the 95-year-old film, they watch her make faces over King's shoulder. Jeff glances back at the control panel. It's a light switch again.

"Come on!" he shouts.

"The fuck, Twenty-Nineteen?" Theda asks, distracted.

"What's going on with your—" The beige switch is gone, replaced by two brown plastic buttons. He remembers switches like this from his grandparents' farmhouse.

"Seriously!" he exclaims.

"Theda," Candace says flatly. She's still at the window, her bottle frozen halfway to her lips.

Theda clears her heads-up display. "What's up?"

Theda and Jeff join Candace by the window. A biplane careens between buildings, the low whine of the engine burbling through the glass. The antique war machine is about to smash into the side of the office building across the street when the building ceases to exist. The pilot banks hard as the building re-appears.

"Whoa," Jeff whispers.

"Not that." Candace gestures towards the horizon. "There."

Jeff squints at the city skyline, trying to figure out what could be more interesting than a vintage prop plane and a building winking in and out of existence. Then he sees it. "Is that the freakin' World Trade Center?" As if the sight of the twin towers isn't baffling enough, the greater part of the mystery is that they're not in New York.

"Hoshit," Theda whispers.

"Hoshit," Candace agrees.

"Hole-eee-shit," Jeff nods. They turn their backs to the window. The minimalist foam slab that was Theda's couch has become a loud and obnoxious lime green leather sofa, straight from a '70s porno. The video screen on the wall is gone, replaced by a squat wood veneer television console. On the curved screen, Dot whispers into King's ear as he leaves the podium. Headlines crawl over their heads: SALINGER REFERENCES FOUND IN ANCIENT SUMERIAN TEXTS + BOUDICA ATTACKS LONDON + COBAIN ANNOUNCES NEW ALBUM + NUCLEAR STRIKE THREATENED BY DAUGHTERS OF THE REVOLUTION.

"What did you do?" Jeff asks.

The three of them have identical platinum blonde flattop haircuts. They wear silver jumpsuits, the national uniform of Eastroes, The Holy Kingdom, founded in 12204.9. A blink later, they're back to normal.

Candace takes a sip of beer, her hand unsteady. "Am I the only one who just—?"

"No," Jeff says. "Yes. That."

"Hoshit." Theda opens Huck's feed. "Huck. Trouble. We need you back here." On the TV set, his POV is sideways, a bloody hand in the foreground. A gigantic lizard-tiger-thing passes through dense vegetation. Jeff takes a step towards the portal to his apartment.

"Might go lay down back at my place," he murmurs. Tomorrow, when this dream/hallucination/food poisoning/whatever is over, he'll be sitting in the bank's break room eating lunch and one of his co-workers—maybe Dawn—will ask him what he did last night. His typical reply of *Ordered some Chinese and stayed in* might not fully convey his evening thus far.

A portal opens in the kitchen and an old woman floats into the apartment on a hover scooter. "Theda!" she cries. "I've found my way back to you!"

"Who—?"

"It's Dorothy!" the woman grins. "Your old friend Dot!" She holds her trembling hands to her lips. "Candace! Why, look at you! So young and beautiful!"

"Theda," Candace says, stepping back from her elderly friend. "I think we—" and then she isn't there anymore. Her beer bottle drops to the floor.

"Oh, my goodness," Dot says. "She's been unborn."

"I think I'd better go lie down," Jeff says quietly, retreating to the open portal. His slippers scrape across the rough plywood floor, which was wall-to-wall carpet a moment ago. Headlines crawl across his peripheral vision. SENTIENT TREES TERRORIZE CANADIAN SUPERCITIES + PRESIDENT GALLAGHER TO ADDRESS NATION + MIDDLE EAST RENUKED. The headlines switch to a language Jeff doesn't understand. But he does understand it and has always understood it.

"Candace?" Theda frowns at the pool of beer soaking into the shag carpet. On the television, the grid of dev feeds switch to USERS NOT FOUND screens. Her body goes numb. Not USERS OFFLINE. *USERS NOT FOUND*. She laughs a crazy little laugh and picks at a sequin on her dress. "What did I do?" she asks Dot.

The woman tilts her head forward. "What, dear?"

Theda turns to Jeff, biting her fingernail. "What did I do?" she asks again.

Stepping back into his apartment, Jeff pauses on the threshold of the portal. Which, it turns out, is a very bad thing to do when history is collapsing. His foot slips into the middle space between his old-now and his now-now. He falls. *What did she do?* he asks himself.

———

What she did was collapse time and history into a 4.6 billion year mess. Think of it this way: the moment she opened her portal to my 2019, a minor ripple in time occurred—a single raindrop falling on a placid pool. No big whoop, really. Nothing the universe couldn't correct. Theda's gravely innovative misstep was altering a popular consumer product and granting god-like, mess-making powers to nearly everyone in the world. And nearly everyone in the world is, generally speaking, very stupid.

On that particular Tuesday evening in 2069, the placid pool of Time endured a million raindrops, a billion pebbles, a quadrillion skipping stones. Changes to history rippled out, concentric waves overlapping other concentric waves. So much change occurred, Time itself could barely keep up. People, places, and things flickered in and out of existence, changing shapes and shifting styles. Families switched ancestors. Timelines fractured and collapsed. Histories were overwritten, refashioned, and undone.

Before I step away from my Pool Of Time metaphor, let's pause for a moment and acknowledge that this talented young lady may have performed The Mightiest Cannonball Of All Time.

— EXCERPT FROM *MIND THE GAP: MADMAN OF THE MULTIVERSE* BY JEFF "THE NULL" COX

PART THREE: TUESDAY

It's the middle of an endless Tuesday. Theda waits on the floor of her apartment, legs splayed. She squeaks her boot heels against the hardwood floor and spins a blade in a slow circle. It changes from a cheap paring knife to a battery-powered laser wand and back. She scrolls through her news feed. Another goddamned update about Hitler, the latest on the satellite wars, dinosaurs somewhere they're not supposed to be. Same old shit. Theda sighs and looks at her stuff on the kitchen island: a backpack, a cupcake with a candle stuck in it, and an old paperback book.

"Fuck you," she tells the book.

She fidgets, impatient for things to begin so everything can end. She spins the knife, which is a sharpened femur with a knotted leather strap for a handle. It is a hyper-evolved bladefish capable of telepathic communication. It is a boxcutter.

She digs her heels into the floor. Black streaks mar the wood. Fuck the deposit. She waits.

———

WICK > PORT > ACCELERATED EVOLUTION — Say you take a few chipmunks and send them back in time a few millennia. The edit rolls out across history and you notice that chipmunks are smarter than you remember, and always have been. Now imagine taking a few of *those* chipmunks and sending them back in time. Suddenly these adorable small rodents are capable of simple speech and tool manipulation. You can repeat this until their species is superior to humans, and your ancestors are enslaved and slaughtered for food, and you cease to exist, and the timeline of the accelerated evolution of chipmunks collapses into mootspace. This is happening all the time.

AT THE TIME OF RECORD RETRIEVAL, THE ASCENDING KINGDOM OF SCIURIDAE IS MOSTLY (97.7%) EXPANDING ITS PROSPEROUS REIGN AS ITS FOES ARE NIBBLED LIKE SO MUCH BLACK OIL SUNFLOWER SEED IN A BIRD FEEDER.

———

Jeff half-opens his eyes. Across the center of his vision are words he can't read because everything is too bright, too ter-rible. TELEGONY SYSTEMS. REBOOTING. SEARCHING FOR NETWORKS his display reads. He tries licking his lips, but his tongue feels like a baseball glove. CONNECTED TO DEVNET. UNKNOWN HARDWARE CONFIGURATION

DETECTED. PLEASE CONSIDER PURCHASING A REGISTERED ODYSSEY CORP. PRODUCT!" He dismisses the screen without really trying to.

"Ngghg," he grunts, his head pounding. Jeff curls himself into a ball on the floor. He gropes for his comforter. It's not there.

"You had quite a tumble," Theda says. "Appeared mid-air, landed on your face, threw up. I expected a grand entrance, but that was... something."

"Theda?" he squints at her.

"You know my name. Great, perfect." She says, her tone implying neither greatness or perfection. "Are you okay?"

He wipes his mouth with his shirt. "I'm fine, I'm totally fine," he says. This is his standard response to the question *Are you okay?*, his automatic reply since childhood. He does not in any way, shape, or form feel totally fine. He sits up. "Totally fine."

"Your nose is bleeding."

He looks at his shirt. Blood and puke. "Cripes."

"You look really bad," she says. "And weird. You're too constant."

"Thank you?"

"I mean it's hard to look at you."

"Same for you. Same for everything," he says. Every surface of the apartment shifts before his eyes. He focuses on his hands: Still. "You look..." He squints. "...different." She *does* look different, he's pretty sure. Her sequined dress and party hat have been replaced with jeans, a leather jacket, and a knit cap. Her bangs hide her eyes, but Jeff swears he sees a few more wrinkles than he saw before. "What year is it now?"

"2069."

"2069," he considers, looking around the room. Everything is covered in denim. "Feels different than the other one."

"You're the Null, aren't you."

"Hmm?" He waves off her question. "I've got a headache."

The floor shifts under him, from oak to tile to oak again. The letter K ceases to exist. No one notices because it's a pretty useless letter.

She points down the hall. "Bathroom's there. There's a sinc in it. You should use it." The letter K returns with different rules, kausing an infinite number of ruined Sckrabble games before sorting itself out.

He rises unsteadily and gestures at the knife. "Are you going to stab me?"

"If I need to. Haven't committed yet."

He nods. "I guess I'll use the bathroom then."

"Mind the tap," she deadpans.

"What?"

"Joke."

He frowns. "What?"

———

LEFT BAD. LEFT BAD.

LEFT BAD.

LEFT BAD.

LEFT BAD?

LEFT BAD. LEFT BAD.

LEFT BAD? LEFT BAD?
<<<the infinity of timespace>>>
NOT RIGHT NOT GOOD.

– EXCERPT FROM *LEFT BAD AND OTHER POEMS*
BY JEFFREY COX

———

Jeff takes off the dev glasses and stares in the mirror. He looks trampled to death. Feels about the same. He gingerly pulls his gross shirt over his head and drops it in the waste basket. He isn't feeling particularly laundry-ish.

The new Theda stands outside the bathroom door. "Why did you come here?" she asks.

He has no *why*, so he attempts to trace back the *how*. "I was taking a nap, then I was here, and now I'm here again," he says. He splashes warm water on his face. "But now here is different. And you're different." Jeff drinks from the faucet while the fixture shifts from sleek chrome to old brass. He swishes and spits, wondering if he's still asleep on his living room floor. *How bad was that Kung Pao?*

He puts the glasses back on. In the corner of the display, a notification blinks. The dev acknowledges his glance and opens a pop-up. "Welcome, [null_user]. This is your first time logging onto the Wick. The last user edit to your public profile was .42 seconds ago. You have 212.3 billion unread emails. You have 178 billion pending friend requests. You have zero friends. Click here to begin the setup wizard!"

"Christ," he mutters. He trashes his entire inbox. "What's the Wick?" he asks Theda. She rolls her eyes so hard he hears it through the door. Her boots clomp down the hall. A second pop-up answers his question.

WICK > THE WICK — The Wick is the largest user-curated encyclo-social network database on devnet, collecting all history, original and revised. The reliability of user-generated data is malleable. All entries should be refreshed for latest probability. Upload your edits to history using the sidebar.

AT THE TIME OF RECORD RETRIEVAL, THIS ENTRY IS 99.1% CORRECT.

Jeff searches her medicine cabinet for a spare toothbrush. He finds a box of gel pods called "MouthBlast Minty." He misses his brands. He needs to get back to his *brands*. Jeff sighs and lets a soft chemical pod dissolve on his tongue. Apparently, in this world mint tastes like licorice.

"I don't like it here!" he shouts at the door.

"No one does!" the girl shouts back.

———

Jeff steps out of the bathroom, too queasy to feel self-conscious about being shirtless in front of a stranger. A pop-up appears. "**Update your status now!**" it prompts. He can't figure out how to dismiss it, so he walks back to the living room with his head tilted, peering around its edge. The apartment is different yet again, an unfurnished space with cardboard boxes stacked along primer-white walls. Out the window, buildings flicker in and out of existence, the city skyline pulsating like a graphic equalizer. A steampunk flying machine soars over aerodynamic blobs of fiberglass. A jetpack dude buzzes their building.

He rests his forehead against the glass. "Hello, world," he mutters. The pop-up disappears and his dev posts his status update. A digital billboard across the street flashes the phrase "**HELLO WORLD**" in twenty-foot tall letters. He opens his mouth.

"Don't," Theda says, his status update centered on her dev's heads-up display. She swipes it aside. "Please don't." She turns and rummages through a cardboard box of clothes. "I've got something for you to wear. My mom bought it for me when I was in high school." She extracts a fistful of cotton. "Clearly, Fate picked it out just for you." He puts it on, his hair wild with static electricity. Across his chest, the phrase "I'M NOT AN IDIOT!" cries out in neon orange letters.

"Do you maybe have another—?"

"You're welcome." She strides into the kitchen and shoves the paperback into her backpack. Jeff notices the cupcake with the candle.

"Is it still your birthday?"

She tosses aside the candle and licks the frosting. "How'd you guess?"

"I was at your party."

"I haven't had a birthday party since I was a little kid," she says. He shrugs. *What else can you do but shrug sometimes?* "My idea of a party this year was to sit here and wait for you." She bites the top of the cupcake off. "Habby birfday toome," she monotones.

"You knew I was coming?"

She licks the cupcake wrapper. "Everyone knows you're coming. You're the Null."

"What's a Null?" His dev auto-searches the Wick.

"The Null is bad news," she sighs.

———

WICK > NULL — The Null (redirect from [null_user]) is an unknown devnet user who appears online for three hours in May of 2069. He posts mysterious messages [see WICK > NULL> <u>NULL MESSAGES</u>] to every networked device, via unknown master admin access to the system. The Null is viewed by conspiracy theorists [flagged for bias] as a malevolent threat—a parallel universe timeline-jumping superuser bent on dismantling the devnet. Certain religious cults view him as a savior/deity [see WICK > NULL >

NULLISTS]. The government and the Odyssey corporation consider him to be a terrorist threat [see WICK > SIGNAL INTRUSION]. The majority of people view the Null as a pop culture meme of little significance, other than an excuse to get the day off from work and drink. [see also: WICK > NULL > NULL DAY]

AT THE TIME OF RECORD RETRIEVAL, THE IDENTITY OF THE NULL IS 100% UNKNOWN.

———

"You think I'm *him?*" he laughs, dismissing the pop-up. "I'm no mastermind god or whatever. I mean, it sounds cool, but—"

"The Wick says the Null appears today. You appeared today. I heard you mumble 'Hello world' and the Null's first message was transmitted to every goddamned person on the planet."

"That's a common phrase," he says, unconvinced.

"And," she continues. "The only recording of the Null sounds just like you." She sends him an audio clip. "This paradox crap has *got* to stop!" he hears himself say in his dev speakers. There is muffled cheering in the background. He hears Theda say "Hang up" and a different woman say "Thank you for replying to my message." The clip ends. He points at her, eyebrow arched.

"Yup," she says. "That's you and that's me. It's from an interview, recorded an hour or so from now. I recognized my own voice about five years ago."

"How did you hear it five years ag—"

She squeezes the bridge of her nose in irritation, unsure if his ignorance is genuine or some sort of trick. "Someone in the future went to the past and posted it on your Wick page. Happens all the time."

"That's crazy."

"The world's crazy, Mister Null."

"I," he begins. He pauses and looks out the window again. "My name's Jeff."

"Well, *Jeff*," she says, somehow turning his name into an insult. "You're going to post random crap all over devnet today. I don't want any conspiracy theorist nutjobs figuring out where you're transmitting from. So far, they haven't found you today, but history's malleable. I'm going to try and bend things in our favor and keep you here." She deadbolts the front door.

"That's nice of you," he says. "Thank you."

"It's not nice. It's self-preservation. I'm stuck with you for awhile."

He sits on a kitchen stool. "Couldn't you leave?"

"I could try, but it probably wouldn't stick."

"But you said history is malleable."

"But sticky."

Jeff ponders this, trying to make some sense of the situation. "Can someone send me back to my normal 2019? I need to get back to my—" He almost says 'stuff' "—time."

"There's no such thing as your normal 2019," she responds. "It's been overwritten. Collapsed timeline. You shouldn't be here. You shouldn't exist."

"That's the meanest thing anyone's ever said to me."

"Sorry you're so special, Jeff," Theda deadpans. "I guess you're just different than everyone else." He winces. If Jeff Cox could live his life in the background of someone else's story, he definitely definitely gladly would. He's no Luke Skywalker. Hell, he's no Uncle Owen. He's more of an Uncle Owen's neighbor type.

"This is a really aggravating conversation," Jeff says.

"I expected nothing less," Theda agrees.

His stomach growls. "Is there another cupcake? I'm sort of—"The apartment building ceases to exist. He falls through a dense canopy of pine, his body bouncing from tree bough to tree bough. The giant trees dump his body onto the forest floor, a blanket of orange needles providing precious little cushion to his landing.

WICK > RMS TITANIC > EDIT HISTORY — The first wave of history editors are tourists, renting boats to watch the grand old ship go down. In subsequent iterations of the timeline, editors pull survivors out of the water, while others board the ship pre-iceberg and steal souvenirs. Soon, the area is so crowded with interlopers, the Titanic strikes barges of onlookers instead of the iceberg, killing tourists a hundred years before their births. As the historic event is increasingly corrupted the doomed ship avoids the area altogether, suspicious of the waiting fleet of tourist ships. This causes some angry spectators to chase the Titanic and sink her out of spite.

AT TIME OF RECORD RETRIEVAL, THE RMS TITANIC IS MOSTLY (94.3%) A FLOATING CASINO ANCHORED IN ATLANTIC CITY.

In the shade of the forest, Theda crouches over him. It's definitely not Theda. It's her eyes and maybe her mouth, but things are all out of whack. But it's totally Theda. "Wha happened?" he groans. He shifts position, his movement startling the... well, he doesn't want to say it. *Ah, shit... Cave woman.* Theda leaps back, eyes wide and alert under one hell of a unibrow. She's wearing a bear hide. It smells fucking terrible. "Theda?" he asks, raising himself up on an elbow.

"They-da," she repeats back in stiff, underdeveloped speech.

"You remember me? Jeff. The Null?"

"Nuh."

"Yeah. You got it." He sits up slowly, sore as hell, the girl circling from a safe distance. He looks up at the towering pines, glad their apartment wasn't on a higher floor. Thunder rumbles in the distance. Jeff touches his palm to his forehead. More blood. "Ahh, jeez."

"Jeez," Theda says, moving closer. She sniffs the air. Cautious, cautious. The girl pushes a fingertip against his forehead. He allows it, wincing. She draws a red line beneath each one of his eyes, painting him up like a psychopath football player.

"Stop that, okay?" he says.

She leans in close. "They-da nuh jeez." She reaches into the bear hide and withdraws a crude blade carved from a bone.

"Aww, c'mon," he pleads, sliding back on his elbows. The cave woman straddles him and holds the knife high. She prays to the tree gods, thanking them for their gift. "We don't need to do that," Jeff says.

A terrific noise rises in the distance, a million marble-filled subway cars smashing through a million panes of glass. Sweeping in from the east, a wave of commotion engulfs the horizon. Buildings and roads warp, twist, collapse, and relapse in a storm of dust and torn roots. Bodies and telephone poles and cars and mailboxes plow across the plains. Jeff curls into a ball and screams into the furious sound of human advancement. He is swallowed by death and resurrection, consumed by sound.

A deafening silence follows, an absence that somehow blots out his own screaming, and then Jeff recognizes the ooga-ooga toot of an old-fashioned car horn. He opens one eye and sees high heels and sneakers and stroller wheels giving him a wide berth. A woman stands over him as he trembles on a sidewalk, her black trench coat swept dramatically back. Jeff squints at her. Her hair is longer, tied in a neat braid, and she seems marginally less interested in gutting him.

"Th-Theda?"

"You're not very good at keeping a low profile, you know that?"

WICK > SEPTEMBER 11 ATTACKS > EDIT HISTORY — The towers fall. The towers are saved. The hijacked planes are repopulated with vengeful would-be heroes. The towers are built in a different part of Manhattan. The towers are designed with comical jet-shaped holes built into their upper floors. The terrorists are murdered as babies. The towers are built underground. President George Bush and Vice-President Dick Cheney are kidnapped and placed on the 95th floor of the North Tower. New York ceases to exist. Islam and Christianity and box cutters cease to exist. Everyone stays home that day. In the distant future, indestructible buildings are designed and constructed and sent back to the beginning of time, creating eternal, unchanging super-cities, making New York moot. "9/11" becomes known as "9996834/2995.8/blue" (reassessed calendar system).

AT TIME OF RECORD RETRIEVAL, THE WORLD TRADE CENTER IS MOSTLY (77.7%) INTACT, EXISTING IN A LIFESIZE 9/11 MUSEUM EXHIBIT IN WINNIPEG, MANITOBA, THE CURRENT CAPITAL OF THE NORTH AMERICANADIAN TERRITORIES.

Hover cars sigh down the boulevard twenty meters above compact electric one-seaters, city transports, retro rat rods, and antigravity glass spheres. Buildings and roads flicker in and out of existence, but they've been mostly almost always built, so they're mostly almost always there. Jeff watches as a hover car (the design stolen from *Blade Runner*) becomes a 1989 Dodge Diplomat and drops from the sky like a... well, like a 1989 Dodge Diplomat. At the last moment, the film designer Syd Mead is un-not-born in 1933, allowing the spinner to re-exist and accelerate away.

Theda navigates the crowded sidewalk, back straight, a purposeful stride. The crowd defers to the woman in the trenchcoat, sensing her determination, moving their bodies out of her path. A man takes a photo of her with an old Polaroid camera. She smiles politely and puts on sunglasses. Passing pedestrians murmur as Jeff hustles to match her pace. *Theda Daniels. Theda Daniels.*

"Wow, you're..." he says. "Why's everyone acting weird?"

"People get funny about celebrities. It's not their fault."

"What?" he snorts.

She spins on a boot heel and stares him down. "Do we have a *problem*, Jeffrey?" She pokes him in the stomach. "I know I'm *only* a billionaire who invented the most popular app of all time. An app that, by the way, redefined physics and the fabric of our society. I'm so *sorry* if that doesn't impress you."

"What? No! I—"

"We don't have time to reenact this petty conversation, Jeffrey," she says. "You're drawing attention to yourself. You're too constant. We need to get you to safety." A black Lincoln Continental idles at the curb. She slides into the backseat and holds the door for him. "Get in and shut up," she commands. "No status updates. No interviews. Got it?"

"I'm not an idiot," he says as his dev screen flickers. The phrase flashes across her dev. She grabs him by the collar and drags him into the car.

"Quit reading your fucking t-shirt," she says, using every ounce of her willpower to not punch him. "Just sit there. I've got a safe house in the country. We're going there now."

He stares dumbly at his shirt front. "You just tried to kill m—"

"Different me, different timeline, Jeffrey. Try to keep up.

I'm trying to keep you *alive*. Keep us *both* alive." She hands him a handkerchief. "Your forehead's bleeding."

He dabs and grimaces.

"There are corporate saboteurs looking to undo my achievements," she mutters, checking the Null's Wick entry for any edits to the near future. "They think they can use your unique gifts to erase my legacy. I won't allow it."

"Unique?"

She reaches into a door pocket and tosses a paperback book onto his lap. *Mind The Gap: A Tuesday Of Triumph and Discovery* by Theda Daniels.

"Wow, you wrote a book."

She lights a cigarette and sighs smoke out her nostrils. "Actually, you did. But we put my name on it. Better for sales."

He flips the book open to a chapter heading. "LEFT BAD," he reads. "What's that mean?"

She rolls her eyes. "It means don't go left." The limo stops abruptly. "**Trouble?**" she texts the driver.

"Traffic," he replies through the tinted divider.

Jeff stares out the window. His dev alerts him that the traffic jam is due to a Protoceratops that decided to lay down for a nap in the middle of a major intersection. Along the sidewalk, pedestrians open ports and step through. To Jeff, they don't seem sufficiently *awed* by what they're doing. But then again, he figures people have been time-traveling since, well, the beginning of time. On a nearby building that is most always concrete (but occasionally brick), he reads fat-lettered graffiti: *WWTND?*

————

WICK > HISTORICAL GRAFFITI — The historical record is under constant attack from pranksters and malcontents who alter the past with sophomoric jokes and nonsensical references. PORT users who dedicate themselves to the theoretical notion of a "real history" [see WICK > PRESERVATIONISTS] fight against this tide, righting wrongs when they discover them. Their efforts to undo the graffiti are outpaced by constant editing of history. At time of record retrieval, the following historical events are flagged for correction: Someone wrote "Stacey is a whore" on the moon with a giant laser in 1602. Tibet is known as Dalaiwood. The novel *To Kill A Mockingbird* was written by a woman named Latoya Primavera [see WICK > GREATEST AMERICAN AUTHORS]. There is a small town along the Gulf coast named Bag Of Dicks, Louisiana. The Y2K disaster was revealed to be a planet-wide rickroll [see WICK > CLICK HERE FOR FREE NUDES].

THIS ARTICLE IS A STUB. YOU CAN HELP THE WICK BY EXPANDING IT.

———

The bus rocks as it turns towards Downtown Crossing, its anti-grav lifters poorly maintained. Video screens mounted above the windows broadcast a sitcom called *I'm Not An Idiot!!!* The episode ends with a man driving a car into a candlelight vigil. He moans the catchphrase the audience is waiting for. The bus fills with laughter.

Jeff steals a glance at Theda. She's back to her leather jacket and knit hat, hunched against the bus window, hugging her backpack close to her chest. It's a different backpack. "Hi," Jeff says.

"What?"

"Do you remember the big black car?"

She closes her eyes and rubs her temple. "What?"

"You were a badass billionaire," he says, half-laughing at his own story. "Like some kind of badass *Matrix* cosplay billionaire. Like a minute ago."

She holds up a hand. "Our building's two stops away. Shut up for two stops. Just two stops." Theda turns her attention to her dev, scanning news streams for any Null sightings.

A pop-up blocks his vision again, prompting him for a status update. "I hate the future," he grumbles. The phrase **"I HATE THE FUTURE"** flashes across the bus video screens. The passengers *woo* and *hyyeaah*. Theda punches him in the arm wicked hard. "I didn't mean to—"

"*Chhht!*" she scolds.

He massages his arm and looks out the scratched plexiglass. The sky fills with Japanese Zeroes. The sky is obscured by an enormous steel dome. The sky is blue and cloudless. He looks away, his head hurting. The paperback is still on his lap. Sort of. *Mind The Gap: Three Hours Of Tuesdays* by Jeff Cox. He rubs his thumbs along the book's dogeared cover, as if this gesture might verify the thing's realness. He opens the book to the dedication: "Never check your inbox on a Tuesday."

He glances at the notification icons in the corner of his display. His dev opens his overflowing inbox: Media outlets, fan mail, death threats, prayers, cease and desist orders. Several subject lines refer to his famous "I hate the future" quote. A new message arrives, titled **"Thank You For Replying To My Message."** He clicks on it like a goddamned idiot. His dev connects to Diane Westerdale, the only reporter to ever speak directly to The Null.

"A News495 exclusive! I've got the Null on chat, right on schedule!" she announces on the bus's video screens. The passengers fall into thrilled silence. Theda, lips pressed tight, gives him the death glare. "I realize our conversation will be brief, but the world has so many questions," Diane says, sharing a split screen with a default avatar. A timer counts down below, as The Wick entry on this conversation has always stated that the Null will disconnect in eighteen seconds. Diane recites her part of the conversation, taught to her in second grade history class. "We already know your answer, but perhaps in this iteration of time you might elaborate:

How have you managed to gain ungoverned access to the entire devnet? Can you elaborate on your "I hate the future" post from a few moments ago? Can you explain the phrase 'Time is broken and you broke it'? Why are you here and what is your plan?"

He texts Theda. **"What should I say?"** She puts her hand on his cheek and pushes his face towards the aisle. A big guy looms over Jeff, holding the overhead bar. He wears a bright yellow t-shirt that says "WHY ARE YOU HERE AND WHAT IS YOUR PLAN?" in pink block letters. The man is ecstatic, gaping at the nearest screen.

Jeff taps him on the arm, mouthing the words "Excuse me." He points at the man's shirt and makes a spinning hand motion. The grinning man turns, happy to show off his sweet tee. Printed on the back: "THIS PARADOX CRAP HAS GOT TO STOP!!"

Jeff reads the shirt, recalling his voice in Theda's audio clip. He doesn't want to say it, but he agrees with himself so emphatically he can't help himself. "This paradox crap has *got* to stop!" he blurts out. The passengers sing along, erupting in cheers and laughter. T-shirt guy thumbs-ups everyone around him. This is a huge moment in pop culture history.

"Hang up," Theda groans, sounding exactly like the archived footage of the interview.

The onscreen timer nears zero. "Thank you for replying to my message!" Diane Westerdale says, balanced upon the pinnacle of her career. Jeff hangs up.

"This paradox crap *has* got to stop!" he insists earnestly.

"Just… Please shut up."

Behind Theda's head, a chrome grille fills the window. A trailer truck full of frozen fish patties barrels out of an alley and rams the bus, bulldozing it across the intersection.

———

WICK > KENNEDY, JOHN FITZGERALD > CORRUPTION OF ORIGINAL EVENT — Over the course of corrupted time, the 35th American president is shot, unshot, re-shot, saved, and sacrificed a nigh-infinite number of times. Tourists flock to Dealey Plaza, opening millions of ports to witness the moment. Meddlers appear out of thin air to stop Oswald, or to prove him innocent, or to take a shot at JFK themselves. Brazen souvenir seekers snatch Jackie's pillbox hat off her head again and again, flooding the collector's market with so many duplicates they become worthless. As interlopers reshape history, books cease to exist, causing book repositories to cease to exist. Texas ceases to exist, and then the democratic form of government ceases to exist. It all comes back and disappears again. All the while, Preservationists work to undo these things, to reassemble a shattered historical record that can never be reassembled.

AT THE TIME OF RECORD RETRIEVAL, ON NOVEMBER 22, 1963, KENNEDY, JOHN FITZGERALD IS MOSTLY (88.6%) SHOT IN THE HEAD BY CIA PATSY ALDUS HUXLEY.

———

Jeff flails, unable to find the ground, unable to inhale. Tiny bubbles float past him and he chases them to the surface. It takes him a little over four hundred years to find air, and then he treads water and retches. He shouts guttural, confused sounds at the sky. He scans the horizon. Nothing but ocean.

"Where am I?" he gasps at his dev.

"Downtown Crossing Station," a pop-up answers. "Altitude plus thirty meters."

"I don't think that's correct," he shouts, spitting water.

"Global positioning unable to update map," the pop-up says. "Please log on to devnet."

Jeff flops through a wave. "Open a time thing!" he demands. "Open it! Port!"

He can't breathe. He can't move. Is he sinking? Has he already sunk? Jeff spasms in blackness. He can't tell if his eyes are open or not.

———

I can't quite describe what a fall feels like. It is perhaps most alarming because it doesn't feel like <u>anything</u>. You're in a Now, then you're in a Now on a parallel timeline. Your eyes tell your brain something major just happened. A shift. But the rest of your body reports business as usual. The opposing signals can be quite jarring. Over time, it can chip away at your sanity.

The only times you really feel stuff (physically, I mean) is when the solid ground of one timeline becomes a basement or a crater in another. Or if you're in a building that ceases to exist. Or if the new timeline's ocean levels are radically different. Then you're bound to feel <u>something</u>.

— EXCERPT FROM *MIND THE GAP: WORLDS OUTSIDE TIME* BY DR. JEFFREY COX

———

A cultist rolls the yellow t-shirt guy's body off Jeff. "I found him!" he cries. "The Null! Target acquired!" Two robed men extract Jeff from the mess of mangled seats and broken glass and drag him away from the bus wreckage. He's dazed and soaking wet, staring dumbly at Theda's knit cap in the gutter next to a burning anti-grav core. He can't seem to connect that bit of information to anything else. *Hat*, he thinks. Just *hat*. His dev suggests alternate routes around a possible terrorist attack. Car alarms whoop and bleat in the smoke-filled intersection. Everything smells like seafood. Jeff coughs up salt water and blacks out.

———

Infinite Hills / Waste And Harm

We Wait In The Valley,
As The Valley Grows Around Us,
Ever Deepening, Ever Compressing.
The Pile Grows Dense,
Until We Cannot Fathom The Base.
Consumers Are Consumed,
And Denied A Receipt.
No One To Crush The Cans,
Or Shred The Plastic,
Or Pulp The Paper.
No One To Shatter The Glass,
To Melt And Recycle,
Into Glass Blades,
To Slit Our Own Throats.
— EXCERPT FROM *GAPMINDER: POEMS & FRAGMENTS* BY NULLJEFF

Cutface drags the unconscious soft-skin by his ankle. He pulls him across the Deadpile, a miles-wide landscape of empty yogurt containers and reusable shopping bags. The soft-skin gradually comes around, first squirming like a bait worm, then twisting weakly as his head dips below the surface of the knee-deep single-serving yogurt cups.

"Hey! Leggo!" the soft-skin cries. Cutface glances over his scuffed shoulder pad with his one good eye. "You're me!" the soft-skin cries. "Your name's Jeff!"

Cutface grunts. There is a similarity that is plain to see. The soft-skin does not have his sunburnt shaved head, his chin tattoo, his meandering facial scar from a long ago honor battle. His captive twin is unscathed, like a harem girl. The man he is dragging is stick-armed and weak, dressed like a jester. Where did he come from? It doesn't matter. He is one hundred and seventy pounds of meat for the traders.

"WHAT'D YOU DO LAST NIGHT, JEFF?" Jeff shouts

in a hoarse falsetto. "WELL, DAWN!" He writhes and kicks at Cutface with impotent fury. "I ORDERED SOME CHINESE!" He twists among the snack debris. "AND! STAYED! IN!"

Cutface drops Jeff's leg. "We were a real pain in the ass." He squats over his prize and punches him in the gut. Right in the ol' Kung Pao. The soft-skin passes out again.

———

WICK > PORT > FREQUENTLY ASKED QUESTIONS > PARALLEL EXISTENCE — A common question: Can you port back in time and meet your younger yourself? Yes. But it's annoying. Imagine walking down a sidewalk as someone approaches. You move to your left as they move to their right. You both try to compensate and end up in each other's way again. You mutter simultaneous apologies and try to move past each other. Meeting yourself is a lot like that, except a thousand times more annoying and harder to get past.

AT THE TIME OF RECORD RETRIEVAL, YOU ARE MOSTLY (93.5%) BUYING YOURSELF A COKE.

———

Jeff wakes up duct taped to a large steel shelf, upright, his arms spread like Jesus. Rows of fiberglass trash barrels shaped like cartoon fish stand at attention near shelves of boxes marked "PLACEMATS" and "LOBSTER BIBS." In the center of the warehouse, a semicircle of silent figures watch him, their faces hidden in hooded burlap robes.

"Where am I?" he whispers. His dev tells him he's in the Cap'n Grampy's Haddock Shack corporate headquarters. A pop-up presents him with a $5 off coupon. Jeff struggles against his restraints.

At an unheard cue, the cultists withdraw candles from the folds of their robes. The cult member closest to Jeff lights his candle and places it at his feet.

"Hello, world," he says.

"HELLO WORLD," the cult repeats.

The next cultist lights their candle and says "I'm not an idiot."

"I'M NOT AN IDIOT," the cult repeats.

"Oh, man," Jeff moans. "Guys..." He licks his lips and tastes ocean.

The ritual continues as each Null cult member recites the Statuses Of The Null, holy words sent back from the futurepast: I HATE THE FUTURE. THIS PARADOX CRAP HAS GOT TO STOP. LET ME GO. TIME IS BROKEN AND YOU BROKE IT. WHY CAN'T I FALL UP.

"Guys," Jeff pleads. "Guys, really."

In the distance, a forklift rumbles towards a loading dock. The first cultist steps forward holding a knife.

"Guys," Jeff says. He really needs to stop saying guys. "Guys?"

The cultist steps in close to Jeff and raises the blade between their eyes. Jeff is afraid to open his mouth, petrified he might say "guys" again. The cultist stands motionless, a hint of goatee protruding from the shadows of his hood. Twenty seconds pass. Forty. Finally, the cultist whispers to Jeff. "Tell us what to do."

"What?" Jeff whispers back, eyes wide.

"Tell us what to *do*," the man prompts. He sounds impatient.

"L— Let me go?" Jeff stutters. "Let me go!" His dev posts his status update to the Wick.

"Thank you," the cultist exhales, reading the message on his dev through tear-filled eyes. He pushes the tip of the blade into his robe. Jeff watches in horror as the man hunches forward and crumples to the floor. Jeff screams. The next cultist approaches with knife drawn.

"No," Jeff begs. "Nononono."

Each cultist steps forward and commits suicide at their savior's feet. The pool of blood spreads across the concrete floor, creeping towards the regiment of fiberglass haddocks. The ritual continues, even after Jeff faints.

————

WICK > CHRIST, JESUS TIBERIUS — Born in Bethlehem in the year 9994844/ 2911.3/ orange (re-assessed calendar system), Jesus Christ spends his early life in the desert, until things get "blown all out of proportion" by cultists who believe he is the Messiah [see also: WICK > <u>FRED ROGERS</u> > <u>THEORIES</u>]. At age 33, Jesus escapes to southern France with his wife to raise their son, Judah. Jesus works as a carpenter of middling skill (he could be better, but tourists are always bothering him at his workshop [citation needed]).

AT THE TIME OF RECORD RETRIEVAL, JESUS CHRIST IS MOSTLY (76.4%) ANNOYED BECAUSE HIS PREPUCE IS UP FOR AUCTION ON EBAY. HE POLITELY REQUESTS IT BE RETURNED.

————

Jeff lies flat on his back in a field, arms spread wide, bits of duct tape stuck to each wrist. The sky is clear and uncorrupted, the air crisp. Roughly cut back cornstalks jab into his back, but he refuses to move. He's afraid that if he moves, this moment of peace will be taken from him. He closes his eyes and listens to the wind. *I can stay here forever*, he decides. *I will eat old corn.* This, he thinks, is a fantastic plan.

A starling lands on his stomach. Jeff raises his head and

scowls at it. "Tsssttt!" he spits. The bird is unimpressed. *Leave me alone. Leave me alone. Leave. Me. A. Lone.* "Tsssttt!" he says again, trying to wiggle his belly without moving his body. No go. The bird hops onto his chest. "You son of a bitch," Jeff whispers. "I hate you," he whispers. "Die," he whispers.

"You are very rude," the starling says. It pecks the impolite man on the nose. Jeff hollers and swats at the bird. His mouth is full of snow.

———

Candiss stops in her tracks and listens. Though the wind batters the heavy insulation of her survival suit, she still hears the scream. It comes from below her boots.

In her two tours of duty patrolling the High Road to Bostinium, she has never encountered another human. There shouldn't be anything or anyone out here except winter wolves and jötnar. She grabs the avalanche shovel from her pack and digs. Two feet down she hits something soft. It is a man buried in the snow. She cannot fathom how he got there, nor does she understand how he's out this far wearing only a single cotton layer.

"Are ye tryin' to get dead? Where's ye kit?" she shouts above the howling wind. The man is semi-conscious and wet. She slaps his face and drags him out of the hole. "Ye gear!" He doesn't respond. She pulls an emergency thermal layer out of her pack and wraps the insulated foil jacket around him. Candiss lies down next to him, opens the front of her survival suit, and pulls him inside. The suit expands to accommodate the second body. She zips it up and pulls the hood down over the back of his head.

"Ey! Ey traveler!" she shouts. Now that she's close, she realizes his body doesn't feel very cold. "The hell goes on?"

The man opens his eyes. "Candace?" he whispers. "The bird ruined everything."

"Who are ye? Where'd ye get my name? Did Coulton put ye up to this? Campbell?" She gives him a shove, which is hard to do to someone you're sharing a survival suit with. "It's god-damned Campbell, rite? What's this hazing bullshit ye boys keep playing at?" Three months of harassment from those bootlickers back at base. She's had just about enough.

The traveler struggles to explain the situation. "They blew up the bus. They thought I was god," he whispers.

Candiss scowls at him and unzips the suit. "Fock this. Fock Campbell. Fock ye!" She pushes him out onto the High Road. She catches a glimpse of his confused expression in the swirling snow, his mouth an O, as he rolls back into his icy hole.

———

WICK > PORT > EARTH RELATIVE/ABSOLUTE LOCATION — The PORT app defaults to an Earth Relative location (for example, if a user opens a port in their backyard, they are able to see what that area looked like at any previous point in time). Hackers discover the ability to switch PORT to Absolute Location: Open a port in a backyard, and that port will match the exact coordinates of the user's location in the universe, regardless of where planet Earth is currently rotating in her orbit. This discovery leads to an unknown number of deaths [citation needed]. The Absolute Location toggle for PORT is available for free in our Download Store [Firmware patch v2.0023b - Not Recommended/Advanced Users Only].

———

In 2069, Stephanie Crawley, a British coder, opens an Absolute Location port to the beginning of time. She is sucked from her bedroom in Surrey Heath, launching her body into the earliest moments of our galaxy's inception. Her frozen space corpse becomes the core around which a new planet is formed: Steff (4th planet from the sun, named in her honor). The existence of Steff alters the formation of the solar system, which affects Earth's orbit and weather patterns. Steff causes the Cretaceous-Paleogene extinction event to unoccur, leaving dinosaurs alive to dominate the planet, thus drastically altering the development of the human species, which causes her birth to unhappen, creating a paradox which collapses the timeline. Things like this happen a lot. Time is a mess.

There is a nigh-moment somewhere in there where I appear, spiraling through outer space between Earth and Steff's second moon, DickButt (don't ask). A satellite captured nine video frames of it. Look it up on the Wick. I am mid-exhale, half conscious, floating and wet. Before my brain is starved of oxygen, I disappear.

— EXCERPT FROM *MIND THE GAP: LEFT BAD AND OTHER WISDOMS* BY JEFF COX
(16TH EDITION)

His foil jacket snags on a ladder rung, slamming Jeff into a concrete wall. He hangs there, damp and exhausted. Something smells rotten.

"Hey!" a familiar voice calls from above.

"I'm in a well!" he groans, struggling to focus his eyes in the dim chamber. "A gross well!" He looks up at Theda, a silhouette against a circle of sky. Her hair is poofy and stiff. She presses thick plastic glasses against her nose and leans into the open manhole.

"Are you okay?!" she asks in that voice people make when they're hanging upside down.

"I'm fine," he nods, shivering.

"*Fine* stands for Frightened, Insecure, Neurotic, and

Error-prone,'" she recites.

"What?"

"It's like, in your book."

"What?" he repeats. He tugs at his jacket collar, unsure where the shiny foil thing came from or how it's caught on the ladder. The rung seems to pass through the fabric. No rip, no snag. Just *through*. Theda taps a stainless steel blade against the lip of the manhole.

"I remembered to bring the knife!"

———

Crouched in the alley, Theda embraces her quivering destiny. "You're okay," she soothes. Jeff looks into the manhole, then up at the sky. She knows he has questions he thinks she can't answer. He also has questions about her white turtleneck and baggy pink Garfield sweatshirt. She knows these things because of a book she read in high school.

"You…" he says, teeth chattering. "You look, uh…"

"I know," she says, rubbing his shoulder. "Shhh."

Theda wraps the foil jacket tightly around him and guides him into a pub across the street. The hostess greets them with a gum-chewing "Happy Null Day. Hail Satan. Tyable for teow?" Her wrists are wrapped with Swatches and neon jelly bracelets. Her earrings are pentagrams.

"Hail Satan," Theda responds. "Yes, two."

They follow the pseudo-valley girl hostess into the main room, passing men in pastel Izod shirts, women with massive '80s hair, and, you know, obviously, large tapestries depicting various hellscapes hanging over the booths. They are seated under an explicitly graphic ritual goat sacrifice.

Jeff averts his eyes, focusing his attention on the cocktail list. The first one is called The Eviscerated Nun.

"Everything seems…" He slides the list under the menus. "Is it Halloween or something?"

"You don't like it?" Theda says with mock indignation, putting her hand over her claddagh pendant. She cackles, a loose, free laugh. "Just kidding. It's just a fashion thing," she explains. "Moot-timeline '80s stuff is totally in right now. To the max!"

"And Satan."

"Oh, sure! That, too," she nods enthusiastically. Her hair moves as a single unyielding mass. "Prince of Darkness and whatever, yeah. It's rilly rad."

———

Jeff buries his face in his palms, careful to avoid the tip of his bird-pecked nose. His stomach stings from where somebody (*was that Candace?*) jabbed him with a shovel or something? He needs a towel and twelve hours of sleep. It's generally been a shit day slash half-century slash time loop thing.

He peeks between his fingers and reads a banner taped over the bar. "*I hate the future,*' he mumbles. He's pretty sure he's said that before, but now everything coming out of his mouth feels like a slogan or a meme.

"The future hates you, too." She somehow makes it sound kind.

"Hail Satan," The waitress chirps as she coasts to their booth on roller skates, pulling an order pad out of her apron. "Ho mah gahd! Wow! Jeff Cox! I *love* your writing!" He nods dumbly, thinking of the unfinished *Starblazers* fanfic on his Mac, back at the apartment in the time/world that doesn't exist anymore.

"Thanks. I wanted Wildstar to have a—"

"Could we have a minute?" Theda smiles.

"Sure! Of course!" the waitress grins. "Drink specials are on that card. Gag Me With A Scythe. Unholy Thirstification. Pigfuc—"

"Thanks."

"Back in a few!" the waitress says. She skates away.

Jeff leans back against the booth. "I'm really tired," he whispers.

"I know!" she says. "I'm *so* sorry! Your day has *totally* sucked!"

"It *has* sucked," he nods. "You're the first Theda who's given me a damned bit of sympathy today, you know that?"

She bobs her head like she's listening to her favorite song. "Sorry, I'm being a total groupie dweeb right now."

"I don't understand," Jeff says. This is the current top contender to be his epitaph.

Theda puts her hand on his. "Sorry, sorry. I keep forgetting when you are. You totally wrote about how confused you were right now."

"I'm just having a little trouble," he says. "Keeping up."

"You slipped out of time," Theda explains. "Remember when you stood in the open port between your apartment and the other Theda's?" She holds her palms a few inches apart. "You fell *between* times. It's like when they warn people about getting caught between the subway train and the platform. 'Mind the gap.'" Theda folds her hands. "You didn't mind the gap."

She slips a creased paperback out of her Care Bear backpack and slides it across the table. "*Mind The Gap*," Jeff reads aloud. "*An Infinite Tuesday*, by Jeff "The Null" Cox."

His dev searches the Wick:

WICK > MIND THE GAP: AN INFINITE TUESDAY — A bestseller by Jeff Cox (aka the Null [see WICK > NULL]), published in 2072 (and preretroactively published across all time) chronicling a bank teller's adventures across concurrent "timeworlds." Cox claims to travel ("fall") across multiple instances of time while using a malfunctioning piece of moot timeline tech [see WICK > NULL > TELEGONY

<u>DEV</u>] to post to all of devnet anonymously. A widely beloved classic, the tale is unverifiable by current technology and generally categorized as a work of fiction.

AT THE TIME OF RECORD RETRIEVAL, THE KING JAMES VERSION OF MIND THE GAP HAS BEEN ADAPTED INTO TWO HUNDRED AND ELEVEN TELEVISION SERIES, NINETY-FOUR COMIC BOOK SERIES, AND ONE HUNDRED AND THIRTEEN FEATURE LENGTH FILMS [SEE WICK > NULL > MERCHANDISING & LICENSING].

Jeff doesn't know how to process this information, so he makes a sound sort of like "hoo."

"You write that over the next two years. It's a bestseller in the future. People take copies back to the past. It's a bestseller there, too. It's a bestseller across all time. I read it in my freshman English class."

He flips the book over. In his author photo he looks a bit older, a few more wrinkles around the eyes. There's a peaceful quality to his expression though, a relaxed something he's never glimpsed in his bathroom mirror. The photo is captioned *I'm totally fine.*

"How and why do books still exist?" he asks.

"They do in some timelines. Not others, I suppose," she shrugs. "But we're in this one, and they exist, and that one's yours. Your whole story's in there: The ocean, the talking bird, me breaking time."

He remembers a line from the cult ritual. "Time is broken and you broke it," he says. A pop-up flickers on his dev. His post is broadcast to the world. The phrase disrupts the football game on the video screen over the bar. Satan-worshipping preppies erupt in a drunken roar and chug. Null status updates are apparently a drinking game.

She taps a glittery fingernail on the book cover. "You explain it all in here. We're going to live together in a cabin. You'll write every day. I'll take care of you. It's in the afterword."

"We will?" he says. "A cabin?"

She nods. "Vermont."

"You mean I'm done? No more falling? This is where I land?"

"Right here," she smiles. "With me." She touches his hand again. He flips the book open to the first page, where he has dedicated the book to her: *To Theda: You are the perfect you, stable and permanent. Everything is exactly how it turns out.* He arches an eyebrow. Cryptic yet mushy.

He flips to the back. "What else is in here?" he asks. There are charts and diagrams and timelines, science he can make little sense of.

"Everything," she says. "The cult, the field with the talking bird, the battle with the knights—"

Jeff looks up from the book. "Knights? I haven't battled any knights."

"Maybe you like, forgot. You'll remember later when you write it. You've been through some mega crazy stuff, right?"

"I have, but I wouldn't forget *knights*. I *love* knights," he says. "I've *always* loved knights. When I was a kid, me and my friends used to have BMX jousting matches."

She squeezes his hand. "I *know*."

He scowls at the book. *Did* he battle knights? The ketch-up bottle changes into a catsup bottle. The napkin holder becomes an electronic sterilization dispenser. "I mean, I'm pretty sure…"

"Well," she says, waving a hand. "You said you met some knights. They captured you and dragged you through a bunch of empty pudding cups."

"Yogurt," he says. He can still smell it on his clothes. Jeff pushes the book towards her with a fingertip. "What if it's a different me who writes that?"

"Don't be paranoid," Theda laughs. "You and I, meeting right now, it's in the book. You appear in the manhole in the alley. You need a knife to cut yourself free and I bring you one. It's all in chapter—"

"I'm not saying it doesn't happen to *you*, to you and Jeff," he says, trying to wrap his head around what he's saying. "But if I'm falling between different timelines, maybe I'm falling in and out of different *mes*, too." His voice quivers. "I might not be the same Jeff you end up with."

"I don't know the science," Theda admits. "I sort of only like, *skimmed* that part of the book?"

Jeff tries to contemplate the nature of consciousness, which is an overwhelming task when you're sleep-deprived and damp in a Satanic pub. Tears and snot run down his face. "What if I keep falling?" he says. "What if it never stops?"

"It's over, Jeff," she says. "You're home now. I'm going to take care of you. You're safe, I promise. You'll be rich. You'll be famous."

He rubs his face. "I want to be unfamous. I want to disappear."

"Aww, don't say that," Theda smiles. "You're special, Jeff. You're different than everyone else."

"That sounds terrible."

She laughs.

"I'm really tired," he says. "Truly."

"I know."

"I need to pee."

She points past the bar. "Down that hall." He stumbles away without a word, giving a rowdy group of frat boys a wide berth. The men's room door is locked. Occupied. He leans against a payphone and waits. Jeff slides his finger into the coin return slot, a childhood habit. *Paper books and payphones*, he thinks. *Hell of a future.*

"Cawx," a frat boy calls. Three wide-shouldered drunks clog the narrow hallway. "Jeff Cawx, right?"

Jeff looks at the wall of muscle blocking his exit. Ocean Pacific t-shirts, Champion sweatshirts, upside down crosses on gold chains. The leader has *666* branded on his forehead.

"Youah super-rich, huh?" 666 slurs. "Big Null money,

right?" The other two grunt.

Jeff takes a weary step back. "I'm not rich yet," he says, arms out. "I think maybe in a couple of years?" His back is against the restroom door. The Satan worshipping jocks press forward. "But I'm not sure how that even works? With time, I mean?"

666 holds out a meaty hand. "Give it."

The restroom door opens and a businessman steps between them. "Say! Jeff Cox!" The man raises a hand to shake. Jeff seizes him by the lapels and shoves him towards the frat bros. He launches himself into the restroom and deadbolts the door behind him. Fists pound against the door as Jeff collapses against the sink, out of breath and panicked. He doesn't look in the mirror, which is probably for the best.

WICK > LINCOLN, ABRAHAM (no middle name) > CURRENT STATUS — Abraham Lincoln, the 16th and 73rd President of the United States sits in a karaoke bar in sector Twelve-Red-Thirteen-RosePetal, San Tokyo (Roppongi, Minato, Tokyo) with Fumiko Hooper, a history buff who removed him from Ford's Theatre moments before a severe historical edit in Shakespearean-era England caused his assassination timeline to collapse.

AT TIME OF RECORD RETRIEVAL, LINCOLN, ABRAHAM (NO MIDDLE NAME) IS SLIGHTLY (13.7 CENTS) FLAT ON THE CHORUS OF POISON'S "TALK DIRTY TO ME."

"What in tarnation!" the prospector hollers, covering his privates with a tattered copy of *Mind The Gap: A Tues-Dimensional Adventure* by Jeffrey Cox. "Portin' intuh a man's terlet! Come on, now!"

Jeff spins around, his slippers digging into the outhouse's

dirt floor. There is a piece of paper next to the old man, the wrinkled receipt from his Kung Pao chicken, with "LEFT BAD" scrawled across it. He snatches it up and squints at it. It's his writing.

"I was gonna use that as a bookmark, y' weasel!" the prospector says.

Jeff shoves it into his pants pocket. "I think it's important."

"Could you git, please?"

Jeff does not git. He leans against the outhouse's rough-hewn door. "I keep falling. I don't know how to stop falling," he mutters. "Fall into the ocean, fall into a hole, fall into a toilet. Keep falling. Can't stop."

"Whyn't you try climbing then?" the old man suggests. "Climb right the hellfire outta here!"

Jeff looks at the man, dumbfounded. "Up," he repeats. "Why can't," he begins. His status update window pops up with the words *Why can't* transcribed, followed by a blinking cursor. He pauses. "I," he says. The dev transcribes it. He recalls the Null cult reciting this thing he might say, should say, will probably say. Jeff can't tell if he's repeating the memory or creating it. He tries to cancel the screen with his eyes. No dice. *Trapped*, he thinks. *Trapped with broken things in a broken world.* The cursor waits patiently. "Fall up," he whispers, defeated. His dev posts the Null's final status update to the world. The prospector stares. "Why *can't* I?" Jeff asks him.

"I was bein' sarcastic, son," the old man says as the Null's post flashes across his retina display. His eyes grow wide. "Waita— Y-Yer Jeffrey Cox! Yer the gorshderng Null!"

Jeff isn't listening. He checks his dev's clock, astonished that only three hours earlier, he was asleep on his living room floor. He asks his dev how far he's gone, and despite criss-crossing multiple timelines, it tells him he's only traveled a mile and a half. He thinks hard for a minute. *Three hours. One and a half miles.*

Jeff fumbles through the PORT app on his dev and

manages to open a portal to three hours earlier. A port opens between the two men, showing Jeff an unoccupied outhouse seat. He examines the floating rectangle, the edges only perceptible by comparing the differing angle of sunlight peeking through the plank walls. "Could y'sign my book?" the old man asks from behind the port.

"Mind the gap," Jeff mumbles. He hooks his arm around the edge of the port and inches forward and to the right. He slips his head into the gap between the two times, into the backstage area of Time itself. He gapes at a vast space populated by an infinite number of dead Jeffs floating in an endless expanse of nothing. The bodies drift and bump softly against each other. Jeff grips the edge tighter, sure these are Jeffs who didn't grip the edge tightly enough. He pulls himself back to the outhouse. The prospector is yelling at him.

"Are ya goin' through the dangblasted port or not?"

Jeff finds the left edge of the port and leans into the gap. He sees himself looking through the gap, and beyond that he sees himself looking through the gap, again and again, off in an infinite ribbon of Jeffs. He shrieks as one might when confronted with boundless recursion. His brain boiling, Jeff is thrown backwards, collapsing against the outhouse door. His hair has turned white.

"Jesus Phineas Ke-Rist," the prospector murmurs, peering around the port. "You okay, kid?"

Jeff pushes his trembling palms into his eye sockets. "Don't ever do that," he advises the old man. "Don't ever do that."

"I do wish you'd get the hell outta here, boy. All I want t'do is shit and read."

Jeff clambers to his feet, leaning against the creaking structure for support. "Yeah, yeah, yeah, yeah." He blinks and rubs his eyes again. "Mind the gap. Mind the gap. I need to warn me." He reaches into his pocket and pulls out a crumpled receipt and a pen. He scrawls "LEFT BAD" and tosses the receipt next to the unoccupied shithole in the open port.

"Yer bughouse, kid," the old man says.

Jeff reaches over his head, searching for the port's gap. He hoists himself up into a dark and cramped space that smells like shit. Sharp things scrape his forearms as he crawls forward. As his eyes adjust to the darkness, he sees ductwork beside him. Ahead, a taut wire blocks his path, running from floor to ceiling. A buzzy hum fills the claustrophobic space. Then the floor, which is a ceiling, collapses.

———

WICK > GREAT SPHINX OF HANES ULTIMATE™ MEN'S COMFORT FLEX FIT® ULTRA LIGHTWEIGHT BREATHABLE MESH BOXER BRIEFS — The Great Sphinx of Hanes Ultimate™ Men's Comfort Flex Fit® Ultra Lightweight Breathable Mesh Boxer Briefs (redirected from Great Sphinx of Giza) is a limestone statue on the Giza Plateau, representing a mythical creature with the body of a lion and the head of a human. Its construction is attributed to ancient Egyptians from the reign of the Pharaoh Bezos [see WICK > AMAZON.COM > OLD KINGDOM > GIZA DISTRIBUTION AND ORDER FULFILLMENT CENTER].

Through nigh-infinite edits of history, the Sphinx has been restored, destroyed, moved, returned, defaced, and re-faced. Notable face reassignments include U.S. President Ronald Reagan, Indian playback singer Asha Bhosle, an anonymous user's deceased basset hound Rosco (whose image was so widely beloved it remained in place for seven centuries), a butthole (nicknamed, naturally, "The Sphinxter"), and a neverending back-and-forth between American actors Nicolas Cage and John Travolta. The monument is considered to be one of the 263 WONDERS OF THE WORLD. Despite having the ability to travel back in time and witness the monument being built, conspiracy theorists insist it was constructed by Ancient Astronauts, often going to great lengths to fabricate evidence of Ancient Astronauts, including dressing up as Ancient Astronauts and posing for photos in front of the statue.

AT THE TIME OF RECORD RETRIEVAL THE GREAT SPHINX OF HANES ULTIMATE™ MEN'S COMFORT FLEX FIT® ULTRA LIGHTWEIGHT BREATHABLE MESH BOXER BRIEFS IS MOSTLY (98.5%) LOCATED IN LAS VEGAS, NEVADA, NEXT TO THE STATUE OF LIBERTY AND THE EIFFEL TOWER AS PART OF A THEME PARK DISPLAY. ANCIENT ASTRONAUTS ARE MOSTLY (97.5%) A POWER POP TRIO FROM NASHUA, NEW HAMPSHIRE.

PART FOUR: TUESDAY

It's the end of an endless Tuesday. Jeff lies sprawled on the floor, surrounded by broken ceiling tiles, electrical conduit, and insulation. He rolls onto his back and stares at the jagged hole in the restroom's drop ceiling. Jeff laughs as he gets to his feet, a crazy laugh that sounds crazier bouncing off the tile walls. A motion sensor flushes the toilet as he stumbles away.

He limps into a TikiFrüz, a popular chain of Hawaiian-themed frozen yogurt shops. The floorplan is exactly like the Satanic '80s pub, but this place is plasticy and bright, harshly lit by greenish fluorescent lights. A worker wiping down the counter scowls at him. "The bathrooms are for customers only," she says. Jeff gapes at the topping buffet through the cough shield. The strawberries do not turn into not-strawberries. Everything appears permanent. Very coherent. Reality is so hellishly stable it makes him dizzy.

The worker moves closer to the phone on the wall. "Can I help you?"

He mumbles an apology, circling around the buffet. An old man studies him from a nearby booth. There is a paperback book on his lime-green table. Jeff averts his eyes—refusing to even glance at the cover—and backs through the glass doors to the street. He makes a wobbly circle on the sidewalk, examining the surrounding buildings, recognizing a couple of buildings and the general layout of the area. He lived in this neighborhood fifty years earlier. It's not so different. Next to the TikiFrüz entrance, a plastic sign decorated with balloons advertises their new Maui Madness promotion. "Right." Jeff yanks the balloons free and turns towards Theda's apartment. "Right."

———

"**Fuck 'em,**" Theda texts to her friends' group chat, biting her thumbnail. "**And fuck their paywall.**" Her dev projects a high-def image of a dark room. There are old toys displayed on an end table and a poster that says *Firefly* on it. In the corner, a vintage TV plays a show she suspects is called *Two And A Half Men*. Theda holds her fingers up to the projection. The air on the other side of the portal is warm against her hand. She jerks back with an exhilarated laugh.

And that's how Theda invents time travel. Remember?

———

Theda types a string of commands and the portal enlarges to the size of a window. She pokes her head in to peruse the collection of strange old junk when she notices the clump of blanket on the floor. Red slippers stick out the end. She sits back, hand over her mouth.

"**Sleeping dude!**" she texts the group. "**SLEEPING DUDE FROM—**"

A white haired man bursts into her apartment holding a fistful of balloons. He is both damp and dusty, his frostbitten cheeks smeared with dried blood. He wears a ripped foil jacket, slippers, and a t-shirt that proclaims I'M NOT AN IDIOT! Jeff Cox sways in the center of Theda's living room, frayed and damaged, about five minutes before he's about to come in. He smells like spoiled yogurt. Jeff raises his arms.

"Don't open the port!" he hisses desperately.

"Uh…" she says, stealing a glance at the open portal.

"Close it!" he begs. "Close it!"

"**The fuck?**" Candace texts the group. The man's dev is identical to the spare glasses charging on her coffee table.

Huck steps forward, palms up. "Listen, man. Eeeeaasy."

Jeff looks at the boy in the party hat. *Kids in party hats. Birthday party.* He releases the balloons and fumbles in his pocket.

"Ex*cuse* me, sir?" Dot over-enunciates. "This is a private *residence?* You need to *leave?*"

Jeff holds his phone out to Theda with an unsteady hand. "Birthday." She squints at a photo of a man—*this man?*—embracing her. She's wearing the dress she's wearing right now, the dress she bought at the thrift store this afternoon.

"Birthday. It's your birthday. I brought you, b-balloons." He looks around and can't find them. Jeff squeezes his eyes shut and tries to remember what he wrote, what he might write if time would stop tossing him around long enough for him to remember what to write. "You are the perfect you, stable and permanent," the trembling man recites. "Everything is exactly how it turns out," he adds, giggling. A tear wets the dried blood on his cheek.

She laughs nervously, the kind of laugh you might make after narrowly escaping disaster. Without taking her eyes off his red slippers, Theda closes the portal.

———

Jeff hears a woman laugh. He is upright and alert in an instant. *Was I asleep? Am I awake? Did I dream I heard something?* The memory of it fades.

His apartment is dark. He lies back down on the floor,

pulling his comforter cocoon tightly around his chin. He burps and mumbles. Above him, a balloon bumps softly against the ceiling.

●

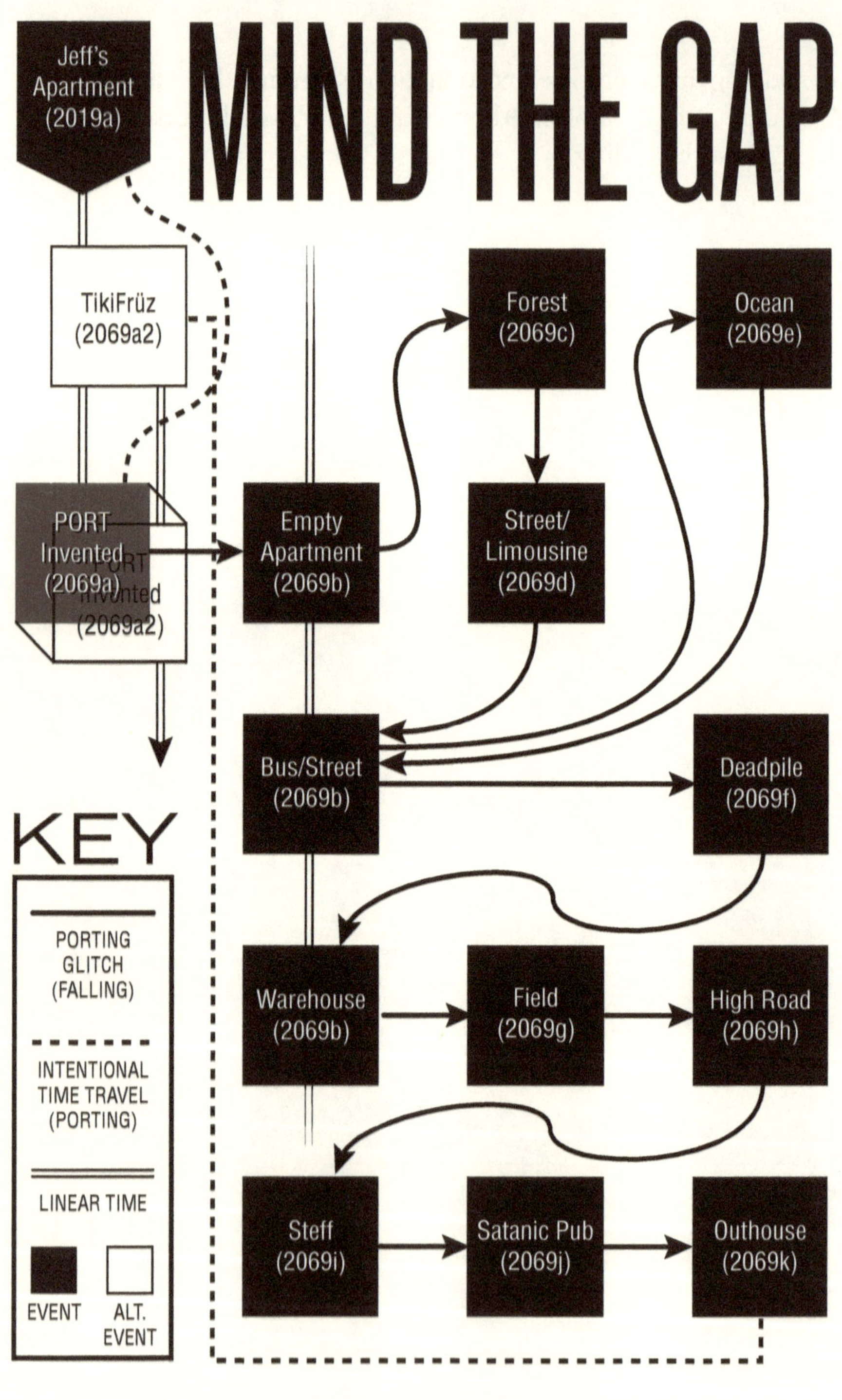
MIND THE GAP
Jeff's Apartment (2019a)
TikiFrüz (2069a2)
PORT Invented (2069a)
PORT Invented (2069a2)
Empty Apartment (2069b)
Forest (2069c)
Ocean (2069e)
Street/ Limousine (2069d)
Bus/Street (2069b)
Deadpile (2069f)
Warehouse (2069b)
Field (2069g)
High Road (2069h)
Steff (2069i)
Satanic Pub (2069j)
Outhouse (2069k)
KEY
PORTING GLITCH (FALLING)
INTENTIONAL TIME TRAVEL (PORTING)
LINEAR TIME
EVENT
ALT. EVENT

GIGANTIC

GIGANTIC

"There's a big dog downtown," she said.

"Uh-huh," I said. I was having trouble figuring out what made this observation phone-worthy. We rarely called each other; texting usually covered most of it. I'd pulled over to the side of the road to take her call and was feeling a little impatient.

"No, a *big* dog," Beth said.

"Okaaayyy…"

"It's taking up all of Main Street, and the sidewalks, too." I laughed, not getting the joke. Her tone was serious. "It just appeared. People are trapped under it. It's on Facebook and Twitter and—" I could hear her tapping at her laptop's keyboard. "Jesus, Ian. The photos."

I'd just crossed the bridge from Hadley to Northampton. I decided to drive downtown.

———

Yellow DO NOT CROSS tape fluttered across the four

lane width of Main Street, from the cell phone store on the east side, looped around a cruiser's side view mirror, to the candy store on the west side. The cops stood gaping, ostensibly there for crowd control, but the crowd was apprehensive. The roads leading into downtown were choked with cars and people. I abandoned my car by the railroad bridge and pushed my way forward, trying to comprehend the unreality obstructing our little shopping district. The dog. The big dog.

It looked like a basset hound, but the distorted scale twisted it into something grotesque, almost unrecognizable if you were too close. The creature (later determined to be female) pushed against crumbling buildings on both sides of the street. She lay there, her house-sized head flopped across the northbound lane, eyes closed, apparently fast asleep. Under a flap of lip there was a bulge, which would later be identified as a flattened 2010 Chevy Cobalt. In the following days, eighteen people would be declared missing and presumed dead. Two would later be revealed to be insurance scams, one an attempt to escape child support.

Witnesses claimed the animal just *appeared*. First, she wasn't there, then she was. And then there was screaming and muffled car alarms and the grinding sounds of buildings twisting and buckling. She didn't fall from the sky, she didn't lumber out of the mountains and lie down for a quick nap, she didn't rise up from the ground. She didn't slowly materialize like on *Star Trek*, nor did she suddenly grow from a normal-sized dog to a Hindenberg-sized one. The dog just suddenly *was*.

———

You'd expect black helicopters. Hazmat suits and quarantine plastic bubbles. Swift, bloodless government response. Movies and books have led us to believe that this would be the case. And why not? We all waited for it. Twenty-four, seventy-two hours of anticipation.

Don't get me wrong. There were helicopters. Plenty of helicopters, mostly media. And sure, there were a fair number of conspicuously inconspicuous sedans with out-of-state plates parked on side streets those first few days. Men appeared in town wearing sunglasses and suits and earpieces. They drank our coffee and crossed our crosswalks. They assessed, reported, and left. It was three days before the White House issued a short statement classifying the basset hound as a non-terrorist threat. Federal authorities didn't want to touch the problem. Neither did the state. The dog was deemed a municipal problem. No National Guard, no Red Cross, no disaster relief. The city council pleaded their case to state and federal officials as if the basset hound was a tornado. The officials insisted it was more like a beached whale.

Ted's Boot Shop, a bank, and Birdhouse Music were destroyed. Across the street, a hair salon, a clothing store, and another bank were badly damaged. Thornes, an indoor market, had to seal off its Main Street entrance, which was now completely blocked by a wall of hair and fat. Eventually three buildings would be razed after being found structurally unsafe, displacing thirty-one upper-floor residents and eleven businesses. Traffic was diverted a block over, down State Street, to the dismay of remaining Main Street businesses and State Street residents alike.

The dog required 24-hour protection. People were approaching her, touching her, climbing on her, pulling her two-foot long hairs out and selling them on Ebay. The Northampton police department put officers on overtime until the budget was stretched too far. Before long, the city council couldn't allocate any more money for the detail—they'd already dipped into the snow emergency fund. The city was in crisis. A non-profit organization was formed. The board of directors raised funds through concerts, house parties, a spring fun-run. Over time, they embraced merchandise, seeking to balance respect for the sleeping creature with the reality of the situation. There were T-shirts, stickers, movie licensing. The income allowed the foundation to construct a viewing platform along the head and belly of the beast. A ramp was constructed over the dog's hindquarters, allowing foot traffic to flow relatively unimpeded. The dog hair continued to be sold off through officially sanctioned auctions (humanely harvested, naturally shed hairs, of course).

The shallow breathing was a concern at first. The Five Colleges assembled a team of scientists and researchers to study the basset. Breathing, heart beat, hair growth—the data pointed to some sort of fracture in time. The dog appeared to exist on its own plane of existence, swaddled in a temporal bubble of unknown origin. The team published a formula that tied the animal's unreal scale to the way she experienced time. That fall, while the citizens of Northampton regrouped, coped, and adjusted their lives, the scientists estimated that the dog slept for about an hour in giant-dog-time. She snoozed undisturbed through winter and into summer, except for one bad dream that lasted most of July (she slowly twitched her back leg, systematically demolishing the Haymarket Cafe as she chased what was popularly believed to be a giant-dream-squirrel).

The town was divided into factions: Wake Her Up versus Let Her Sleep (the city's official position was Let Her Sleep). The topic crept into every city council meeting, local forum, and letter to the editor. There was always talk of trying to move her, though no one knew quite how. Even if they did, there was no other town interested in taking her. A multimillionaire from Nevada expressed interest in airlifting the creature to the desert, to put her on display in one of his casinos. The foundation said no. That gave Northamptonites something else to argue about.

———

Time passed and the sleeping behemoth became a part of everyday life. The town adapted and learned to function around her and in spite of her. Visitors couldn't help but express disbelief when they'd see townies strolling past the beast with their morning coffees or smartphones, not even glancing up. The dog was given a thousand nicknames: some cute, some clever, some disparaging. In a somehow deeply New England way, the one that stuck was "The Dog."

As the one year anniversary approached, the foundation decided to celebrate. Plans were laid for The Dog Day Festival: a dog parade, dog show, food carts, music, activities for children, speeches, a memorial for the victims. The community pulled together to celebrate and mourn. People and pets came from all over the country, and the media returned in full force. It was a beautiful New England day. Hundreds of basset hounds sniffed hundreds of other basset hounds' butts. Kids wore officially-licensed floppy-ear hats. As the mayor approached a podium placed on the platform for the plaque dedication, there was a rumble.

———

By the time the four-day fart tapered off to safe levels, seven people and thirteen dogs had died, and an entire neighborhood had been evacuated. The asphalt beneath The Dog's rear end had melted, and City Hall was deemed uninhabitable. The historic building was razed, and the debris was burned and buried in an old rock quarry up on the mountain.

The federal government maintained that this was not a terrorist attack, either.

I was awake at 5 a.m. on a Sunday morning, restless and roaming downtown, killing time until the coffee shops opened. I ended up in front of The Dog, because there was really no way to stroll around downtown without eventually ending up there. The on-duty security guard, subcontracted by the foundation, snoozed in his Hyundai.

It was unusually warm for February, and the piles of snow turned to an impenetrable fog as I climbed the ramp to the viewing platform. Like many a New Yorker and the Statue Of Liberty, I'd never actually stepped foot on the thing before. I looked up, the curve of the beast looming in the whiteness. I sat on a bench for awhile, picking at the already-peeling paint and staring at her wrinkly face. Folds of brow and ear and jowl drooped menacingly overhead.

Over the course of the last year, The Dog had come to fill many roles for the town: part confessional, part wishing well, part memorial. Visitors often spoke to her, bowed their heads in silent meditation, or left flowers, little notes, candles. It had never occurred to me to talk to her before, but that sleepless Sunday morning seemed to be the morning to start.

I'd had a rough year. I told The Dog about my heartache, and my workache, and my acute dissatisfaction with most everything in my life. I talked about Beth moving out. I talked about my grandfather, six years dead, and my perpetually broken car. I promised The Dog I would exercise more and eat less meat. I vowed to make more art and curb my Netflix binging. I told her I'd always wanted to see what Austin was like, SXSW and brisket. I would make a meat exception for Texas brisket. I told her that I was sad and lonesome. I told The Dog that I desperately needed coffee and sleep. I don't remember how long we talked. When the police interviewed me that night, I guessed around twenty minutes, but I don't really know how long it was. I just remember the fog pig-piling on us, and the relentless silence of a sleeping town. I leaned over the railing and ran my palm across part of her mist-covered brow. It felt and smelled like a damp mop. The whole morning did.

The Dog made Northampton too small. I had lived here long enough to watch the college girls grow up and have children. I'd watched as sushi bars and cafes nudged out repair shops and thrift stores. The street punks and anarchists of a decade ago had graduated into full-fledged panhandlers and addicts. I was surrounded by stores full of bullshit for out-of-towners and condos locals couldn't afford. I had no friends and two hundred nodding acquaintances. There wasn't any air left in this town.

I wiped my hands on my jeans and closed my eyes and asked The Dog a question, a question hundreds of people had asked her over the past eighteen months. Joking, cajoling tourists speaking in stupid baby-talk voices, trying to wake the beast, trying to make their companions laugh. "Would you like to go for a walk?" I whispered. Just my luck. Just my goddamned luck.

I stood transfixed for the next half hour as she opened her terrible, boogery eye.

●

ILLUSTRATION & PHOTO CREDITS
*above: Rick Guidice (NASA), grass: Ochir-Erdene Oyunmedeg, skull: Ahmed Adly, roots: Valeriia
Miller, mall sign: Dj1997/Wikimedia, dog fur: xandert. All other illustration, design, and layout by
Standard Design.*

BROKEN LINES

An Illustrated Novel

When demons burn her life to the ground, a waitress squeezes
into a stranger's stolen rental van and embarks on a journey
of evil-fighting and bad road coffee. Vigilantes, bureaucracy,
and pure evil pursue our heroes to the bottom of a bottomless
pit in the lower intestines of Hell. Will Maggie find her way
back home again? Does she even want to?

> "A Douglas Adams-inspired roadtrip…"
> — *Tulsa Book Review*

ONE MORE CUP OF COFFEE

In Which The Author Barely Talks About The Coffee

Follow author Tom Pappalardo on a black coffee tour of cafes, diners, and convenience stores, traveling the potholed side streets and witch-cursed back roads of Western Massachusetts. Grab a table and sit. Nod and smile at whatever the waitress brings you. Does it taste like a 9-volt battery dipped in old, hot Coke? Good. You're in the right place.

> "These hilarious shorts are a perfect snarkfest."
> — *Publishers Weekly*

EVERYTHING YOU DIDN'T ASK FOR
Comics and Stories

A best-of comic collection covering a decade of writing and comic-tooning, featuring favorites from Pappalardo's two comic strips. This mighty tome also includes poster designs, illustrations, and odd bits of writing. What more could you ask for?

> "I never sent this book to reviewers."
> — *The Author*

Tom Pappalardo is a graphic designer, writer, cartoonist, and musician. He lives in a manky old house in Western Massachusetts.

———

TOMPAPPALARDO.COM